EXCLUSION:

THE FIGHT FOR CHINATOWN

Gino Ranno's Ultimate Battle

LOUIS ROMANO

Also by Louis Romano

Detective Vic Gonnella Series (True Crime)

INTERCESSION

YOU THINK I'M DEAD

JUSTIFIED

Gino Ranno Series (Organized Crime)

FISH FARM

BESA

GAME OF PAWNS

The ZipCode Kids Series (Teens & Up)

ZIP CODE

Poetry Series

Anxiety's Nest

Anxiety's Cure

Anxiety Unleashed (2018)

Historical Fiction

Carusi:The Shame of Sicily (2019)

Dedication

To all the legal immigrants entering this country,

may you be welcomed into the United States better than

in days past,

and may all global child traffickers attempting to bring

innocent children here, and those already here

who abuse them,

go to hell

Acknowledgments

I'm grateful... to my content readers, Linda Longo for being honest on the early first draft, and to the late Jennifer Moore, esq. for her intelligent guidance and dispassionate early review. I'm thankful for my dear friend, Frank Cali, who always seems to break me apart and build me up at the same time.

...to two of NYPD's finest, Detective 1st Grade Ming Li (Ret.) who gave me an inside look at New York City's Chinatown and the quiet people who generally don't talk to anyone outside their community, and Detective 3rd Grade Matt Baker who is a fictitious character, modeled after my great friend in the NYPD. He knows who he is and I am grateful for his opening the door for me on this book.

...to my pre-pub date reader, Eugene Duffy who is always there for me.

Special thanks to Deb Craig and Monica Schuley.

My friend Diana Chu has given me great insight into the minds of the Chinese people.

Ben Roth, my cigar and brainstorming buddy, helped with a few chapter ideas.

Thanks to my friend Colin Lively for his introduction to the great photographer Michael Cavotta in Cleveland, Ohio who captured the real me on the back cover.

Thanks to Kathleen Collins who spent countless hours making revisions, changes, and tolerating my, "I want it done yesterday" New York attitude. There is no book without her dedication.

And to my entire family for letting me do my thing…even Rocco my Jack Russel.

CHAPTER 1

Mafia Throwback to April, 1984 - NEW YORK CITY

"Julio, no charge for this lovely and gorgeous signorina. Her lunch is on me today. She is too beautiful for me to take her money," Carlo calls over the counter. This flirty move has actually gotten him laid a few times. The young woman smiles, mouthing a thank you, then hauls the two-slice lunch in a white take-out bag back to her office, only to be hit on by three construction workers, a UPS driver, a cop, the lobby security guard, and finally...her boss.

It's eleven o'clock in the morning at Famous Original Ray's Pizza Shop on East Forty-Third Street, near Third Avenue in Manhattan. The full lunch crowd will begin trickling into the long store in about twenty minutes. There is a sense of anticipation on the first, warm, spring-like day. This is the day the young women take off their winter coats and walk around the city in their lighter, more revealing wardrobes. Soon, they will be wearing next to nothing when summer will bake the city streets. Today, construction workers line up along the sidewalks to watch the spring fashions and to kick-start their testosterone.

At Ray's, most customers, unaware of who Carlo really is, will gobble their lunch at the long, green, Formica counters. They stand like horses eating their half-folded pizza slices and sloshing down their choice of sugar or aspartame-laced, liquid poison. The stream of customers builds to a maddening crowd serviced by five rapid fire counter men until two o'clock in the afternoon when the place becomes more quiet than a graveyard.

"Let's go! I need twelve pies up top. Gimmie two with pepperoni, one mushroom, and two, like me, à la Siciliano. And keep them coming," Carlo Ricca bellows. Carlo acts like the pizza shop and the street are his stage. He barks out instructions all afternoon to the four, pizza pie men who are all branded like cattle with oven burns on their arms. The darkened, brown spots are in different stages of healing - a reminder to the

1

short, dark, hard-working Mexicans to respect the heat of the oven. The pie men wear uniform white pants and shirts and barely look up from the ovens and the marble slabs where they make lunch for a thousand. They seem to have a signal or perhaps an innate male radar which senses when an attractive woman is ordering her slice. The quick glances or flirty smiles from behind the counter are like a human interest side show.

Carlo makes sure the pie men are cranking out pizzas as fast as their Popeye-like arms can make them. Unlike the pie men, Carlo is dressed in an Armani shirt, with his ample chest hair bursting through the two, open, top buttons like a sexy billboard. His one size too tight slacks print his cock and balls down the left side of his pant leg. The slick back, dark brown hair and pointy European loafers, no socks, finish that certain look which is like honeysuckle to bees.

Carlo is a 'zip'. A broken English-Sicilian on an extended work Visa from Palermo, Italy. Along with his two brothers, Nunzio and Filippo, they own six Famous Ray's pizzerias on the island of Manhattan. Not so bad for three sons of Filippo and Nunziata Ricca who raised their sons to be full-fledged mafioso, and none of whom exited the sixth grade.

But, pizza wasn't their only business. The Ricca's sold wholesale heroin and cocaine, not in dime bags, but by the Kilo. Illegal drugs which originated in Afghanistan, Turkey, and Colombia respectfully. The Ricca brothers brought the swag, the heroin, into New York and New Jersey, hidden in bundles of cut flowers from Naples, in boxes of socks and golf shirts made in China, and loaded into heavy crates of colorful and often gaudy pieces of ceramic vases made in Caltagirone and Taormina, Sicily sent from the port of Messina.

The cocaine came in from Colombia while the Turkish and Afghan connection processed poppy into a morphine base which was finished into heroin in hidden processing plants in the hills of Sicily. The distribution was then made through pizza shops throughout New York and New Jersey, independent of the five New York Mafia families.

One thousand, six hundred, fifty pounds of illegal drugs enter through the ports in Italy and Sicily with a street value of 1.6 billion American dollars annually. The Ricca brothers took their small piece of it which amounted to fifty million dollars- far more than three pizza shops could ever make in ten lifetimes.

Lunch was now over, and the pie men either cleaned up or took a break and smoked cigarettes outside when their turn for a break came. Famous Ray's was empty and the three Ricca brothers met at the Forty-Third Street store for their daily meeting.

They did a 'walk-talk' down to the East River so as not to be recorded or overheard by any law enforcement agency that could have been snooping. The conversation was in their dialect which often turned into a coded Sicilian pig-Latin the brothers devised when they were kids on the streets of Palermo. The brothers knew their conversation could be pulled from electronic monitors two block away. They took no chances.

"I heard from our friend near the water," Carlo began. He was referring to their main distribution man, Salvatore De Franco in Messina.

"How is the weather there?" Nunzio Ricca asked.

"Over eighty, but it feels like two hundred he said," Carlo replied, referring to two hundred kilos of heroin which were shipped that day.

"How is his mama?" Filippo inquired.

"Not bad. She is in Catergirone with her sister," Carlo answered, referring to a shipment of artistic ceramics.

"Does she still have her brother in New York?" Filippo followed.

"No…no, he is in New Jersey now, near our friends," Carlo replied quickly. The shipment was going to Port Newark where one of the main customs agents was on the Ricca payroll.

"Hmmm… I hope our cousin visits soon. I miss her so much," Nunzio blurted. Inventory was low and demand high.

"In two weeks, maybe sooner," Carlo replied.

"Perfect. I will meet her at the airport," Nunzio laughed.

"How many pies did you sell today, Nunzio?" Carlo inquired.

"Oh, I'm not sure, maybe sixty-seventy," Nunzio answered. Seventy kilos of H was the correct answer.

"And our friend in New Jersey? How many pies did he do?" Carlo asked.

"Probably eight to ten. No more than that I'm sure, not bad for Jersey," Nunzio replied. Ten kilos sold in Asbury Park, New Jersey by their partner and cousin, Gaetano Mazzara.

But in that same April of 1984, no one could ever guess that the infamous "Pizza Connection" fiasco, code named by the Feds, was about to take place and further, no one could ever imagine it would still be, in 2018, costing the Sicilian mafia in New York City millions of dollars, a fact Don Gino Ranno was really pissed about.

Six hundred arrests had been made around the world. A case which took twenty-seven months, agents of the FBI, officers of the Drug Enforcement Agency, undercover narcotics detectives of NYPD, New Jersey State Police detectives, operatives at INTERPOL along with the federal police in Sicily, Italy, and Switzerland toiled day and night to put the largest Sicilian mafia drug distribution operation in the history of planet earth out of business.

Any possibility of a snitch or rat had to be dealt with swiftly to help avoid prosecution.

CHAPTER 2

One Month Later, May, 1984 - PALERMO, ITALY

Since 1834, L'Antica Focacceria S. Francesco Ristorante has been serving Sicilian comfort food in the same spot in Palermo, Italy.

It recently added a mahogany wood storefront surrounding the original marble sign which honors Saint Francis of Assisi. Small cars and Vespas zoom past the restaurant on the tiny street which separates the famed, local eatery from the church square at Via Alessandro Paternostro. There is a patio across the street from the restaurant where diners can enjoy the food and relax in the square. A floodlight casts its beam onto the old, stone church at the opposite end of the small square giving it a melodramatic, almost eerie look. Apartments surround the square in this working-class neighborhood where everyone minds their business after their day of labor. Residents know who is who, as known mafia frequent the L'Antica Focacceria, so they leave the restaurant mostly to tourists in the evening.

This evening is no exception. A couple from London sit trying to make sense of the menu as two Italian-American couples, friends from Brooklyn, New York discussed what macaroni dishes their Sicilian grandparents prepared when money was short. And it always was.

At one table furthest from the street and whispering of the recent arrests of hundreds of their mafia associates, sat Giancarlo Cali and Pino Muti. In their mid-twenties, Cali and Muti were not on the federal police's radar screen, thereby eluding being arrested in the huge bust. They were both low-level mafia 'runners' who did what they were told to do without question. That was the only reason they had both survived since teenagers in the life, since they had begun delivering drugs and other contraband for their bosses.

"What now, Pino? What if we get picked up?" Cali asked with a bit of panic in his voice.

"Johnny, if they missed us by now, chances are we will not be fingered unless someone points their finger at us," Muti answered.

A waiter brought out platters of food on an enormous serving tray, without even taking an order. There would be no menu, and more importantly, no check given at the table with the two, slick-backed hair, five-day unshaven, handsome young men. Arancina alla Norma, fried eggplant, and salted ricotta cheese inside fried rice balls the size of baseballs, Pani e Panelle, fried chickpea fritters, pasta ch'i sardi, homemade boccatini pasta with sardines with capers and pine nuts with a drizzle of toasted bread crumbs on top. Finally, four milza sandwiches, sautéed cow spleen on small fresh rolls with shredded mozzarella cheese. A comfort-food feast.

Cali and Muti ignored the piping hot food, leaned in closer to each other, cigarettes smoking in their hands, espresso coffee cups on the table beneath them, wondering what fate had in store for them.

"I can tell you one thing, my friend. I'm not going inside for twenty because I delivered a few packages. Yeah, we whacked a few guys along the way, but that I will never admit. The drugs?…I dunno, they were packages I was told to deliver…and I got a few lousy euro, that's it. Come see the dump of an apartment I live in Mr. Prosecutor, then tell me I'm la mafia. Fuck that shit!" Cali said, letting Muti know how he was going to handle any cops snooping around.

"And if we are made to talk, you know, give names of our bosses and…?" Muti began to ask.

"Make up some names. Listen, between me and you, and I will kill you in the street if you breathe a fucking word of this... I was already called in," Cali said.

"Police called you in? Holy Madonna, fuck me," Muti stammered, leaning way back in his chair in disbelief.

"Yes, and I said I was on pensione, welfare, no job, no schooling, a Palermo street kid, the whole bullshit I just told you," Cali confessed.

There was something in Cali's eyes that told Muti his friend was not exactly telling the truth. Maybe it was the way his eyes darted away and stared at the illuminated church.

"I guess I'm next. I may take off for Malta or Sardinia or Naples," Muti declared.

"Fuck Naples, it's a sewer."

"Yeah Malta, I have an old girlfriend there. She can cook and loves to fuck, perfect until this shit blows over." Muti kept his eyes on Cali's face looking for more tells, more hints he was lying.

The waiter came out of the restaurant carrying the same serving platter to serve the Americans their dinner. A Vespa blew past him nearly knocking him down, food and all, to the ground. A Fiat pulled up in front of the L'Antica Focaceria screeching to a stop. The motorbike, with a black-helmeted driver and a rear passenger flew into the square, stopping abruptly in front of the dining patio.

The passenger of the bike took a pistol machine gun from the inside of his jacket. In an instant, before they could take cover, Cali and Muti where both shot in their chests at close range.

The couple from London were in a daze and didn't move, looking at each other as if to ask, *did you just see that?* The American women screamed, their husbands pulling them onto the slate floor beneath their table for cover.

Two men, who very much resembled Cali and Muti, quickly walked around the corner, ski masks covering their faces as the Vespa sped away.

Cali was stone dead. Muti was on the patio floor gasping for air. One of the two men went over to Cali's body pumping four shots from a .38 mm caliber handgun into his head. His head exploded like a pumpkin thrown from atop a nine-story building.

The second assassin approached the air-sucking Muti, whose eyes were popping from his head like a fish on a hook.

"Looks like wrong place, wrong time for you. You hang with a rat, you get what he gets," the killer seethed.

A long switchblade was produced from the assassin's back belt. He ran the blade along Muti's throat like he was slaughtering a pig. Most of the blood sprayed under the table, with some shooting twenty feet onto the English couple.

The two hit men walked calmly over to the waiting Fiat. The driver drove calmly down the small road into the ancient and mysterious streets of Palermo.

§§§§

MEANWHILE, IN DOWNTOWN PALERMO, THAT SAME DAY...

Thousands of citizens had taken to the streets of Palermo in protest. They came in waves, a sea of brown-haired, young people carrying posters, some the length of the streets they walked. Others, holding small placards with photographs of missing family members and bloody bodies in the streets of Palermo, screaming out to the elected officials their distaste of a life controlled by criminals.

One sign said what the people of Sicily had been saying forever. "La Mafia E Merda...Ma Politici sono le mosche." The mafia is shit and the politicians are flies. Another homemade poster simply said, "NO MAFIA."

One woman in her late twenties spoke through an electronic bull-horn, "My husband has been missing for months! There is no sign of him after two mafiosi came for him. The carabinieri answer me, 'What do you want from us?' Useless! There is no justice in Sicily because the mafia controls the entire Island. These sons of whores poison our children's blood with their drugs while the politicians eat at the mafia's table."

The octopus like, suffocating, stranglehold the mafia drug lords enjoyed for decades was coming to an end. The Sicilan mafia around the world was weak; an opportunity the Chinese mafia in Chinatown, New York was more than glad to step in on.

CHAPTER 3

Back Across the Ocean, May, 1984 - NEW YORK CITY

Up in Manhattan, the head of the Bonanno crime family, Freddy 'Short Fred' Tamburrino, met with Carmine Miceli, Sr., Don of the Miceli crime family at his office on East Seventy-Ninth Street. Mikey Roach sat in on the meeting.

Carmine, Sr. played the big hit song of 1984. "Last month this freakin' song made it all the way to number one on Billboard Magazine. Of course with a little help from our friends on the West Coast who sprinkled some scarolla around. We bankrolled this broad. I can't even remember her name, but she's Italian that's all I know. We're doing okay in this legitimate business.

"Carmine, listen to me! I came to talk with you about this headache I have. I'm happy about your boons and the music, but I have bigger things to discuss. These drug busts have flipped me upside down and sent my head spinning like a fucking top. Unless you are willing to jump in and take over distribution for us, we are out of the drug business. Otherwise, who knows who will pick it up? The demand is always gonna be there. The profits are enormous, better than anything else that you have. I can set things up with the producers in Europe and South America. Twenty-million a month is easy my friend," Tamburrino blurted.

Carmine studied "Short Fred" for a long moment before he spoke.

"Freddy, I have stayed away from that stuff my whole entire life. I guess I'm like Don Corleone. I think drugs are bad business and not as easy as you say. Twenty million a month, then after a while I'm like you, facing God knows how long in jail. Bad enough the feds watch every move we make as it is. I am not going to leave this kind of business to my son. I'm just not interested."

"So, what do I do? Put a for sale sign on the business? C'mon Carmine.

Don't tell me you were never in the drug business. Like Don Carlo and the old timers back in the day you put out a death sentence for drug dealing but you, like all of them, took envelopes and looked the other way. It's just a money-making business, Carmine."

"At the moment, there is no business, Freddy. Your family needs to go back to what you know best. This drug business is going to put you all under. Not me," Carmine Miceli said emphatically. He ignored Tamburrino's envelope remark and insult.

"So, the Chinks will move in and take this over for sure. They've been asking for a piece since I was a kid. They will make this money and grow balls, Carmine. These Chinese, what do they call them? These Tongs, they will move into your other businesses over time and crush us all, mark my words," Tamburrino declared.

"Freddy, we will watch them closely. Right now, you have no option. The feds have closed you down and your people can never get back in. Never! Do you hear me? You had a long run, now cut your losses and move on. Go back into the area you grew up on."

"And no piece for us?"

"In my opinion, you can't be a little pregnant. Either you're in or you're out. It's time to get out, my friend."

"Chinks controlling the drug trade in our city and our country? How could we let this happen, Carmine?"

"Carelessness, stupidity, bravado…a lot of mistakes along the way. Right now, you need to hold it together and walk away. If I'm right, and the demand for drugs is as it always has been, the Chinese are already making their plans to bring the product in. Fuck it; let them have it. And as for our other "territories", don't worry... if they get out of line we will for sure send them a crystal clear, fucking message."

CHAPTER 4

AT THE SAME TIME IN CHINA...

There was an innocent and sweet, little girl by the name of Schuchan Ping who lived in the northern part of Fujian, a Province in mainland China. Her pigtails bounced in the wind as she skipped along on her way to and from school. Although they were poor, her mother always tried to make Schuchan feel special; she saved money so Schuchan could wear pretty, red ribbons, tied in bows around the rubberbands which tightly held her jet black hair.

Shengnei Fuzhou, the town Schuchan's family lived in, was part of the thirty-seven million inhabitants of Fujian Province, on the southeastern coast, only one hundred ten miles across the Strait into Taiwan.

As the years passed, young Schuchan could barely remember she had an older sister, the one who was in the United States, in New York City, places she could only imagine from pictures her parents showed her which were sent by her big sister.

"This is your big sister, Cheng Chui. She is not as beautiful as you, but she is very, very smart. She has her own store in New York City. Very respected. Maybe one day you will visit her and have your own store," her mother repeatedly said.

Schuchan's dream was far removed from owning a store anywhere. She thought of having an education. Maybe I'll be an engineer, someone who will help build large glass and steel buildings like I see rising into the sky all along the waterfront here. Or perhaps I'll be a medical doctor to help with our rural population who does not have much access to good care. The idea of selling things in a store ran her blood cold.

Schuchan's parents were on the lower economic level of Shengnei Fuzhou where there seemed to be two classes. Educated and uneducated. The more school a person had, the better jobs were available to them. In a society which was designed not to have distinct classes of people, being poor saw no way out. The thoughts and dreams of higher education in Schuchan's world were like the odds of winning a lottery.

Her father worked hard just to put some food on the table, and times were often rough, especially when typhoons came at the end of the scorching, hot summers in the sub-tropical province. He worked in a tea factory, in rice fields, garment manufacturing, sugar cane fields, any job which was available to keep a roof over his family's heads and a daily bowl of rice to keep their hungry stomachs from growling.

Her mother also did her part by working in the fields and taking in wash from those who where more fortunate than the Pings. Their income was never enough.

"Look at your father; he is growing old quickly. His back is bent from hard labor and his face shows signs of more pain each day," Schuchan's mother stated sadly.

"Mother, may we ask your daughter for help? Surely she can find a way to send some money to us."

"We do not ask our children for money! We are not beggars. You will soon be able to work and carry your own weight. Look at you, tall, beautiful. Don't you see how men look at you when we walk in the market? I myself was once looked at in that way. And I did what I needed to do to put food on the table when I was your age."

Schuchan was indeed a sight to behold. At fourteen her legs were long and athletically shaped from her participation on the track team at school. Schuchan was good at running long distances but nowhere near good enough to be selected for the university. Her grades were also competitive but also not at all outstanding. Schuchan's breasts were already full and pushing against the blouse in her school uniform, and the same for the clothes she wore when she joined her mother in their trips to the fish and vegetable markets.

"You are missing my point, daughter. Search yourself for what is most important. Your family, here and now, or your big dreams that you may never see? It is time for you to grow up and help your father and me feed all of us."

"You can ask me for help but not Cheng Chiu who is living well in another country and..."

A slap across her face was her mother's only reply to Schuchan's insolence.

Schuchan began to help her mother as much as she could after school with household chores. She also took whatever jobs were available in the rice fields and in the tea factory where her father's boss, Mr. Ying, a twenty-eight year old father of two and the son of the owner of the factory had a keen eye for beauty. Her father was moved to a different part of the tea manufacturing process- boxing and labeling the product for shipment. This move enabled Mr. Ying to approach Schuchan while she worked sorting the Chinese Jasmine tea leaves with the other silent workers. The fifteen-year-old did her best to sit upright so her shoulders did not droop like the older worker's shoulders did, bent over from near exhaustion. Mr. Ying, at his wit's end from desire would give Schuchan hard candies and rub her back and shoulders, occasionally rubbing his erect penis into the teen's back. None of the workers, for fear of losing their jobs, acknowledged what was happening. Schuchan said nothing in fear she and her father would both be booted from the sweltering factory.

The teen's part-time work helped to supplement the family income until Schuchan turned sixteen. It was then, her generous boss, instead of candies, gave Schuchan three day's pay as a birthday gift. He placed an envelope with the money down the teen's blouse, pausing long enough to touch her breast. Schuchan was both repulsed and aroused, keeping her head down, separating the long tea leaves from the bitter stems.

Some days passed after her birthday when Schuchan's father came home from work on a school day when his daughter was not working at the factory.

"Daughter, I have some very good news for you. Mr. Ying thinks very highly of you and your hard work. He has asked you accompany him to the tea farms in another province. He has promised to teach you about buying tea and will introduce you to the right people so one day you can become a buyer on your own. You will have to leave school for this important opportunity."

"This is wonderful news. To learn a real trade, in a good business. You can climb the ladder quickly," Schuchan's mother added.

"But I would like to finish my schooling father," Schuchan announced.

"Nonsense. You will take the position and do what is right for the family and for your future," her father insisted.

"I think Mr. Ying wants to teach me more than knowing about teas."

"How dare you say a thing like that, daughter? You will march down to the factory tomorrow morning and accept this position, or you can leave here tonight and fend for yourself," her mother announced.

Schuchan did as her parents demanded and within a week, she had lost her virginity to Mr. Ying who treated her as his concubine. The boss paid her well for her time and her sexual favors, teaching her nothing about tea.

Soon, friends of Mr. Ying were pouring their generosity upon Schuchan.

At sixteen years old, all of her dreams of further education and a professional career were distant memories. She was a now a full-fledged prostitute.

CHAPTER 5

2018, 34 Years Later, NEW YORK CITY

"Mickey? Is this place scrubbed?" Gino whispered. He needed to know if there were any pain-in-the ass surveillance bugs or cameras at work. So many men in the life had succumbed to the loose words they let out of their mouths.

"Naturally. Clean as a baby's ass," Mickey responded. The old man was taken aback by the question from his boss. He knows better than that, Mickey thought.

Gino could feel the anger welling up inside him as he thought of how conditions had changed for the Miceli family and the rest of the organized crime world over the years. Even with the closest members of his crew, Gino knew he should try to hide his feelings, but he just couldn't.

"I tell ya, ever since the Pizza Connection fiasco in the eighties these Chinese bastards have grown a new set of balls," Gino Ranno, the Don of the Miceli Crime family in New York City declared.

Carmine Miceli, Sr. had died of natural causes seven years ago and his son Carmine, Jr. had abdicated his position as Don of the Miceli family to Ranno when he was arrested for racketeering. Carmine, Jr. retired from the life rather than face a lengthy sentence in a federal prison.

The new crime boss was sitting with five of his closest associates at the large, round, corner table at Forlini's Italian Restaurant on Baxter Street in New York City's Chinatown.

"No, shit! We lost the heroin trade to them even though our old boss, Carmine, Sr., rest in peace, would have whacked anyone of us who traded in drugs. He had looked the other way, though, when I took those fat envelopes to him every week. It was all drug money. No disrespect intended," Mickey Roach said, making the sign of the cross in remembrance of his late boss. Mickey's loyalty and cold-killer history with the family now made him Gino's consigliere, his number one adviser on the street side of the business.

"And this Danny Chu, this Cabbagehead fuck and his Flying dragons gang, or Tong, or Triad or whatever the fuck you want to call them, are so flush with cash now, they can't even count it all," Joey Santoro, a capo in the family in charge of the construction end of the family business chimed in.

Joey Clams, as he was called, has been with Gino since they were kids in the James Monroe Projects in the Bronx. They both lived in the legitimate world until the reluctant Gino ascended to the top of the Miceli mob family when they were both in their mid-sixties. Gino did not hesitate one bit when he made Joey his capo.

"Okay, this is the reason I wanted to meet with youse all tonight. Why is our business suffering during the best construction boom in the last twenty-five years? What the fuck? How did the Chinese muscle their way into the construction of that new, high-rise hotel at 50 Bowery? I think we took our eyes off the ball, Joey," Gino admonished his life-long friend. "I promised Carmine, Jr. I would not let these fucks take any more of our business assets away! Don't you remember what those fucking, Chink bastards did? Don't you remember?" Gino's veins in his neck were starting to pop, and his face was turning various shades of red. "Our boys, Carlo and his fine brothers, and their cousin Gaetano Mazarra, they were stuck between a rock and a fucking, hard place! Gaetano was among those arrested and charged with drug trafficking and a slew of other charges. After he posted a four-hundred thousand dollar bail, he had to scramble for his next move. He couldn't get at the tens of millions he had stashed in off-shore accounts, and his lawyer, Jay Atkins, informed him preliminary information indicated the FBI had enough information on his pizza parlor drug fronts to put him away for at least twenty years. Escaping to Sicily was not even an option as the Italian government had cracked down on the Mafia on the island and was preparing for a maxi-trial, the maxiprosesso l in Palermo. Nearly four hundred of Mazzara's drug partners had been locked up tighter than a crab's ass in the Ucciardone, the massive, octagonal prison in Palermo, awaiting the fucking trial of the century. That poor fucker, Mazzara, was caught in a fucking vise-like grip by two, fearless governments which were bound and determined to stop the flow of heroin and cocaine onto the streets of their..THEIR... cities. Ha! And the Chinks? They just stood in the shadows waiting to take millions of dollars away from us. Fuck that, these low-life, wanna-be-mafia Chink-asses," Gino preached.

"Gino, come back to earth. They went non-union on the Bowry job and that took a lot of our muscle away. We tried to get in the door all the way from the demolition of the old building and the excavation, but they beat our people on price every time. And for big money. Look, it's in Chinatown, and they have the cheap labor with their own people," Joey Clams stated.

"And what about the window installation? This is no small, fuckin' job. Twenty-one stories and two hundred plus rooms! Are you telling me we couldn't compete there, either? Even with the windows from Italy we control?" Gino was demanding answers.

"We had no shot. This Safire Windows Company in Queens is owned by a friggin' Chink, and we only win against him when we have a union lock and we can make up requirements no one can meet. We were three million high on the hotel job," Joey Clams replied.

"So what the hell did we get out of this, then? Only the concrete?" Gino queried.

"That's it. And now the slopes are dragging their feet paying our guy! It's always, 'next week...next week' with these fucks," Joey Clams said.

"They really played us on this one. And they spit right in our faces, those miserable bastards," Mickey Roach declared.

"Look, it's time we sat down with this Cabbagehead and let him understand we did not roll over and die after Gotti. Maybe this Hip Sing Tong gang he runs needs to be reminded about our little to do with the Russians in Brighton Beach a few years back? I understand Chinatown is theirs, but we need our tribute. They can have the gambling, loan sharking, firecrackers, the shakedowns, and the prostitution...within their own community only, but once they start in construction without giving us our taste, they have a problem. This end of our business, plus the ancillary services we control is in the many, fucking, hundreds of millions of dollars a year for us. I tell ya, allowing these guys to get into our affairs will spread like cancer. We can't have it. So, after this fancy, boutique hotel is up and running, we want our piece of the pie. Laundry service, food delivery, produce, bread, booze, the works," Gino said. He paused and looked around the table.

Gino continued, pointing his finger in the direction of two of the men at the table.

"Vinnie, Sal, after we have dinner go over to their joint on Doyers Street and see that our friends over there get the message. I want our concrete guy paid…in full…tomorrow, with a vig for waiting. Tell them in no uncertain terms. Come to the club after you meet with these hardons and let me know what happened. Now, enough about business. Let's get into this fabulous food before it's cold and mushy."

§§§§

Doyers Street in the heart of Chinatown is a few blocks walk from Forlini's Italian restaurant. Vinnie Dolce and Sal Palusso needed the walk in the cool, fresh air after eating the heavy, old school, Neapolitan fare, which they finished off nicely with homemade cannoli and demi-tasse, corrected with a shot of Marie Brizzard anisette.

As they strolled the streets of Chinatown, the two lifelong friends made the conversation light.

"I'm looking forward to Salvatore, Jr.'s First Holy Communion this Sunday. I can't believe that kid is already in the second grade. My Godson! What a great kid," Vinnie Dolce exclaimed.

"He is something special, isn't he? He's starting little league this month, too," Sal declared.

"Madonna mio, I remember when you and Cathy used to make out in the park on Hughes Avenue. Now, look at youse, big house, two kids. We both did okay with the Micelis, Sal," Vinnie beamed.

"Could be better, could be worse. I worry about the kids and my wife and the future a lot. What happens if we get clipped or we go away to college for a while? This life is not always good for our family."

"No way I would let anything happen to your kids, Sally boy. Cathy is like a sister to me."

"I feel the same about Lorraine and your kids, you know that," Sal uttered.

"Let's just make sure we are smart and keep control of things around us. Keep our mouths shut and do what we gotta do."

The two-hundred foot, one block, Doyers Street has a sharp bend right in the middle of it giving it a strange, almost foreign feel. Doyers street was called 'The Bloody Angle' due to the sheer number of murders that occurred on that block in the early part of the last century. Back in the day, the Chinese bad guys used hatchets to carve up their enemies, soaking Doyers Street in blood all the way from Pell Street to Bowery.

§§§§

In a tunnel under Doyers Street there is an assortment of small stores: a hair salon, a rub and tug massage store, and a small office in which Danny Chu, AKA Cabbagehead often holds the Tong meetings. Danny's grandmother gave him his nickname, Cabbagehead, because he was a slow learner as a baby. He wouldn't speak, took too long to toilet train, and just stared at people when he was spoken to- hence the name, Cabbagehead.

Cabbagehead was born Deming Chu in the province of Guizhou in The Peoples Republic of China, in the southwestern part of the country where people were starving, others perished due to dehydration from lack of clean water, and early death came to many due to lack of proper medical care. Deming was his parents' only child- a wish of the govern ment to keep the population in check. The Chus now lived in the province's capital city of Guiyang, an overcrowded, industrial, smelly, and bleak place. His family moved to Hong Kong where his father, through underground contacts, scratched and saved to pay for him to have a job. Chu's mother took in laundry, and his father somehow squeezed out a living as a bus boy. His dad also picked up odds and ends work, most days hard at it for sixteen hours.

Fate, as it sometimes does though, shone down upon the Chu family, and Deming was selected to go to the Unites States of America on a temporary Visa at the age of fifteen, on a cultural exchange program.

Deming's eyes, however, were opened in New York's Chinatown with its cramped and teeming streets. It was a new world of plenty, so long as you worked until you dropped. Deming soon became Danny and later became Cabbagehead when he told the story of his grandmother's nickname for him. That was after a tough guy, Flying Dragon recruited Danny to be a green lantern, a trial member of the street gang.

Rather than work long, hard hours in a restaurant as his father did, Danny learned the fine art of extorting cash from Chinese storekeepers throughout New York City. He enjoyed hitting people, smashing faces with his fists or anything within his reach to get the protection money which was due to the Hip Sing Association. He was quickly initiated as a full-fledged Flying Dragon, tattoos and all.

Danny rose quickly because of his size- a five-foot, nine-inch stocky build- along with his terrifying eyes and incendiary temper. Not even a senior Dragon would stand up to the two-fisted Danny Chu, and his reputation as an earner within the Dragons moved him up the ladder quickly.

By his eighteenth birthday, the name Cabbagehead threw fear into the bellies of anyone who lived in Chinatown.

On his nineteenth birthday, defiantly ignoring the advice of his superiors, Cabbagehead went alone to settle a territorial dispute with the Ghost Shadows, the largest rivals of the Flying Dragons.

Down ten steps into the basement of 126 Mott Street, the Ghost Shadows had been making some noise about taking over a Flying Dragon's Mah Jong parlor.

Cabbagehead moved into the room like a whirling dervish using his arms and legs as if they were independent maiming appendages. In his right hand, a twelve-inch, sharpened, serrated blade opened flesh like it was butter. In his left hand, Cabbagehead wielded an ivory and oak club crashing in on the heads of anyone who dared confront him. Some witnesses, devout Mah Jon players, had said Cabbagehead's eyes were actually bleeding and a flow of steam was coming from the top of his head when he entered the smoky gambling den.

Cabbagehead came away with a cracked skull and a deep puncture knife wound in his side. Three Ghost Shadows lost their lives, and four were permanently maimed at Cabbagehead's hands. This fight gave all the street cred Cabbagehead needed to make him both respected and feared in every Chinatown from New York to San Francisco.

Before long, Cabbagehead's vicious temper and calculating mind brought him all the way to the top of the organization which had made him a stone-cold killer and professional criminal. The only thing bigger than Cabbagehead's ego, was his greed.

§§§§

Vinnie and Sal headed for the Nom Wah Tea Parlor at 13 Doyers Street to meet with a few of Cabbagehead's boys. No one knows how many corpses the Nom Wah Tea Parlor's storefront has witnessed in the ninety years of its existence.

Sal opened the door to the Tea Parlor allowing Vinnie to lead the way. Once inside the place, it was as if the two, portly, swarthy Italians had stepped back in time. Nothing had changed since 1927. The restaurant had a brown, tin ceiling darkened by age, surrounded by walls which had seen a lick of paint only once since opening day. The bar to the right was now used like a counter in a cafeteria, with a few Chinese factory workers noisily slurping up the special, hot soup which had the famous, long noodles. The walls were dotted with shelves which held antique tea boxes from before World War II. The patrons, all Asian at this hour of the night, were taught as children not to converse while eating. Unlike the world where Vinnie and Sal are from, where Italians are almost shouting to make their opinions known to each other and the healthy volume of the music of Frank Sinatra and Dean Martin piped into the room, at Nom Wah, the clanging and clamoring from the kitchen were the only sounds in the place.

Toward the rear of the restaurant were four, young, shaggy-haired members of the Hip Sing Tong sitting at a round table which could easily seat eight. All four men had the same look of contempt and danger on their faces. Vinnie recognized the men as members of Cabbagehead's crew and slowly made his way to the table. Sal followed, looking around the room for signs of danger from any other Tong members. Both Italians wore gray business suits with open, button down collars and no ties, each of them strapped with nine millimeter pistols concealed in holsters on their ample hips.

One of the four Hip Sing members pointed to two empty chairs which Vinnie accepted and Sal ignored, instead standing to the side of his partner. No one was smiling.

"We need to see Danny," Vinnie blurted.

"He's not here. Maybe he's in Hong Kong," Peter Fong, the spokesman replied. A tattoo of a dragon's head peeked above his tight, black, tee-shirt onto his neck.

"Fuck that shit. We have important business to discuss and a message from our boss," Vinnie said looking past Peter, trying to see if there was anyone behind a worn, green drapery which hung from a faded, gold valance which led to the rear of the restaurant.

"I'm Peter Fong and I speak for Mr. Chu. I can relay your boss' message," Fong said in perfect, unaccented English. Peter is an ABC. American Born Chinese, with a degree in finance from Hunter College in New York City.

"I'll play your game, Fong. We're here to collect a debt for the concrete our guys poured for that piece of shit hotel you guys threw together on Bowery. It's way past due and we need the cash, plus a vig for waiting. And this ain't Hong Kong, pally. We want payment tomorrow morning the latest," Vinnie said as he leaned into Fong's personal space.

"Or, what? Are you threatening me?" Peter asked.

"Fuckin' A," Vinnie seethed.

"We don't respond well to threats from anyone, especially goombas. So, take your fat, little sidekick, and your garlic breath and leave here in one piece," Fong replied in a low monotone.

Sal opened his jacket and fingered his sidearm.

"Maybe you don't understand English all that good, you Chink fuck. We don't leave here without a commitment," Sal blurted. Some of the patrons, seeing there was tension at the table, made a quick exit from their seats and bar area and headed for the front door.

"And maybe we shove your gun up your guinea ass before we throw you out!" Fong said with an ominous smile, his head cocking from side to side.

"I can see you people have short memories. So now I go back and tell my boss we just can't reason with the asshole, Cabbagehead's people, and we need to come back tomorrow with a larger staff and a different attitude," Vinnie stated.

"That would be fun," Fong said.

"Suit yourself, scumbag," Vinnie replied.

As Vinnie stood from the table to leave, he went for the gun on his hip. He envisioned smacking Fong on the side of his face with the pistol. Sal drew his piece knowing what Vinnie was about to do.

One of the Dragons quickly raised an AR-15 assault rifle from his lap and sprayed Vinnie and Sal with bullets. Another Dragon, who was standing behind the green curtain, came out shooting with his own AR-15. Chairs crashed down loud and hard onto the tiled floor. Blood and guts sprayed everywhere from the backs of the two Miceli soldiers. At eight rounds per second, Vinnie and Sal were dead before they fired a shot. They both hit the ground with a thud. The brown, tin ceiling and the faded walls were peppered with bullet holes as the remaining patrons of the Tea House fled for their lives. Two bystanders were hit with the erratic gunfire and fell to the black and white tiled floor, bleeding profusely.

Fong gave his crew rapid fire orders in a Mandarin dialect.

Cabbagehead sat in his office in the tunnel beneath Doyers Street watching the action from a closed-circuit security camera. He was laughing so hard the veins in his round, bald head looked as though they were about to burst.

Fong then gave an order in English to his band of Flying Dragons.

He was almost salivating when he blurted, "Drag them both onto the street. I will send the Micelis a message they will never forget."

CHAPTER 6

It had only been a mere three years since Cheng Chui Ping, Schuchan's older sister died a miserable death from cancer in a federal prison camp at Bryan, Texas. In Chinatown, in New York City, she had been known to the locals, tourists, and her regular male customers as Sister Ping.

"Where is Sister Ping? Where is Sister Ping?" was heard daily on the streets still. A very well-known business woman, Sister Ping had been a tiny woman with a mouth full of large, pearly white teeth which were always displayed by a constant, almost painted on smile. She had owned a small, variety store on Mott Street in New York's Chinatown packed with cheap toys, hand fans, Chinese papier-maché umbrellas, cheap, colorful dresses which hung from the ceiling, an assortment of 'I love New York' t-shirts, and plastic Statue of Liberty replicas tourists would bring back home. Ping openly bragged hers were the lowest prices on the street.

Sister Ping had also run a money exchange business, mostly for Chinese and Vietnamese nationals, from her cramped store. Both the variety store and her money wiring business were strictly legal except for the paying of taxes part. Sister Ping had worked strictly by cash and therefore flew under the taxman's radar as all Chinatown store owners do.

But what had gotten the attention of the federal government of the United States of America was another entity Sister Ping had much experience in and what she brought with her from Shengmei Fuzhou, that small village in which she grew up. She was a child-sex trafficker for those sick, perverted souls who, in exchange, gave her cash...and lots of it. The business model was not very complex, yet it was a most efficient cash-cow and didn't need a single business office anywhere in China, Taiwan, Viet Nam, Cambodia, and Thailand from where her human inventory came.

Chung Leung, her first cousin, was Sister Ping's biggest supplier of young flesh. Leung, a thirty-five year old with a good-sized, pot belly, and the smile of his dear cousin, lived in a lavish high-rise in Hong Kong Island's Happy Valley section. He also owned two of the seven-hundred, sixty-two apartments at Confucius Plaza, a forty-four-story, brown brick building, the tallest edifice in New York's Chinatown.

Leung's demeanor was as smooth as Chinese, pure silk chiffon. He would enter the poorest villages, towns, and hamlets in the latest model car he could muster and begin his not so subtle sales pitch to groom his intended victims.

Leung would always announce his opening salvo to the small crowd which would inevitably gather around him, as he smiled wearing a western-cut, wool suit, woven silk tie, and French-cuffed shirt and gleaming gold cufflinks. The arm tags that were stitched to the jacket of his right sleeve by the manufacturer, showing the suit size and fabric type, had purposely not been removed to declare the newness of the garment. Not very different from people in the states who drive around for a month with the new car sticker on the back side of their window. Lueng's shoes were black, patent leather which shone like his polished and buffed, black car. His driver was also dressed in a western suit and tie along with a black driver's cap.

"I once lived just like this. My god, what a nightmare that was! Like you, Leung was working the land from meal-to-meal, saving my money as best as I could to make a better life for myself. I soon will pick a wife, but why should I rush now, with the life I have built for myself?"

"Leung, tell us how you did it! You look like a rich man," a well-positioned shill would ask.

"I am indeed a wealthy man. A millionaire many times over, now. From a poor, rice farmer to a...well...see for yourself. Look at me now! I have homes in China, Hong Kong, New York, Paris, and soon Geneva. It was hard work but actually very easy! I followed a man walking around in my hometown, dressed as I am now, who had a fancy, black car and a Rolex watch like this!" Leung would say, pausing dramatically, displaying a chunky, gold timepiece on his wrist for the crowd's pleasure. There were several 'oohs' and squeals of excitement from the mob of young people looking on. Leung smiled knowing his grooming methods were working. He would soon have some new 'product' to be sold.

Leung continued. "That was only two years ago and look at me now!" Lueng would say.

The shill was no longer needed.

"Tell us how! I have daughter I want to see successful. How can it be done? I do not want her to have to live the life I've lived," a stooped over, weather-worn woman, dressed like a farmer in her long, gray dress and wide-brimmed, white, sun hat, asked.

"Well, it's not for everyone, Madame. Naturally, there is a cost to enter a new opportunity. My friends in New York have the right contacts to get her an American Visa and a good paying job in a restaurant, in a factory, or in an office, and certainly also safe housing for the youngster. It's up to the child, though, to work hard, get recognized, and climb the ladder. There are many openings for good jobs in America for both girls and boys," Leung would say. At this point he would feign walking away without interest of continuing the conversation.

"Leung wait! Tell us more!" someone would shout.

"I must be running to an appointment. Time is money! I will tell you very quickly. The fee is forty-five thousand dollars, American, of course. For a new life. A life like mine. That is the bargain of a lifetime, don't you agree?" Lueng would say matter-of-factly.

"Who here has that kind of money? That is an enormous sum," the woman said with sorrow in her voice. The look of hope had vanished from her face.

"And how do you think I did it, lady? My contacts in New York know how difficult that fee is for you, so all they ask is ten percent down payment. The rest is paid by your daughter or son from their weekly paycheck. They pay the balance in no time. My father and I scrimped and borrowed for the ten percent to send me. I paid my debt back to him after I paid off my meager debt to my sponsor. But if you can't get the down payment, well that is too bad for your child; they will have no real future to look forward to."

Within a week's time, Leung would generally collect the down payment from five families. Twenty-two thousand, five hundred dollars in cold, hard cash. Passage plans and documents were then made via ship from the nearest convenient port, and then the young people were off to a life of horror they never imagined could even exist on this earth.

But since Sister Ping had gone away to prison and subsequently died, Leung had decided to work for his other cousin- the former prostitute, still pretty but now bitter and nasty, and even more fierce and nefarious than Sister Ping-Ping's sister, Schuchan.

Schuchan is known on the streets of Chinatown as Miss Suzie Ping. She, too, like her sister before her, is a favorite among the tourists in NYC, especially those families with small children. Because of the brutal rapes and attacks on her as a child, she no longer was able to conceive any children of her own, diagnosed with hydrosalpinx, a painful condition where an infection causes the fallopian tubes to be blocked and filled with fluid... and besides, as she often thought to herself, I don't want to have to marry some fucking guy who would probably treat me just as badly as my old boss in China, that rapist fuck. But as sweet and charming as she was on the outside, to the treacherous Cabbagehead and his Flying Dragons, the infamous street gang enforcers of the Hip Sing Association, she is known as Baby Sister, a ruthless and money hungry bitch.

Sadly the life from which she escaped was now what she was doing to others. Sometimes at night, though, when she was alone, she would muffle her sobs into her pillow. I feel badly for what I do to these poor children, but I have no choice. I must also survive. In the morning, no one would know she had any heart at all with the commands she would bark out.

CHAPTER 7

Gino spoke from the back seat as Mickey Roach drove his boss and Joey Clams up to the 'club' on East Sixty-First Street. "When Gotti held court at the Ravenite Social Club, everyone on Mulberry Street knew the boss was there. Every old, Italian lady, every waiter, every wise guy, and every FBI agent in Manhattan was on high alert. 'Gotti's here' could be heard all over the street. We are not making that mistake again."

Club Macanudo is a swank public restaurant and cigar lounge. Gino liked his smokes and didn't talk much business while there, preferring to people watch and enjoy a Knick, Ranger, Yankee game, or anything on television except Fox News and CNN.

"I can't tell you how many times we warned him, but John was John. His bella figura brought him down in the end," Mickey said.

"That and giving the finger to the federal government. I will stay as low-key as possible. I don't need Brioni suits and a fancy Mercedes to shine a light on us. This Range Rover is even too much," Gino declared.

"It could disappear if you want," Joey Clams blurted, looking back toward Gino..

Gino gave Joey a stern look of disapproval.

"Let's just have a couple of drinks and a smoke and wait for Vinnie and Sal to show up," Gino said.

Instead of throwing the doorman at the Post House next door to Club Macanudo a twenty to watch the car, Gino insisted Mickey find street parking so as not to make a grand entrance.

Once inside Macanudo, the trio found a nice table in the rear of the bar area. Eva, their regular waitress knew what drinks to bring, and Joey Clams followed her ass as she walked back to the bar with her empty serving tray over her exposed shoulder.

"She is amazing," Joey proclaimed.

"You always liked the young blondes, pally," Gino laughed.

They all lit a Cuban Monte Cristo number three which Gino had taken from his personal humidor box along the wall.

Gino was watching a Knick play-back of that earlier evening's loss to the Pistons while Joey Clams and Mickey watched the female action at the bar. The place was always crowded with young lawyers and executives who bought drinks for the hot, young women who could stand the cigar smoke, looking hard to meet mister right. These types of 'sophisticated' ladies didn't go to bowling alleys to meet cops, bus drivers, or mechanics.

About an hour and two drinks after they arrived, one of Joey's crew members walked into the Macanudo with an ashen look. Joey walked over to his man and they both walked outside.

Joey Clams returned to the table in a hurry, looking harried and disheveled, as if he had just gotten punched in the stomach.

"We gotta go," Joey whispered.

"What's wrong? Sit down," Gino ordered.

"Vinnie and Sal got it. The Hip Sing shot them up. We better get out of here."

"Areyoukiddinmeorwhat?" Mickey said in a hushed voice, but with eyes wide open.

"It's worse. Those bastards dragged their bodies out onto Doyers Street and buried hatchets into their skulls," Joey declared.

Gino was speechless. He felt his face go flush with anger at the same time that sick feeling he had knowing his decisions always had other people's lives- or deaths- in his hands.

"He's right, Gino, let's get you where it's safe. Those Chinamen have sent a message," Mickey warned.

"Four of my guys are outside. Wait here; sit tight and I'll go get the car," Joey muttered. He left the club after throwing two, hundred dollar bills onto the table.

Gino looked at Mickey and finally spoke. "What message?"

"Gino, years ago, way before my time, these Chinese fucks would kill each other in the streets. Doyers Street was not what it is today. Back then they settled things with hatchets and left their victims right there on the street. That's where the word 'hatchet man' got the name. These pricks are letting us know Chinatown in theirs, the old-fashioned way. We need to talk about what our next move will be…but not here."

Gino glared at Mickey like he was a mental patient.

Joey Clams returned with one of his crew.

"The fucking car is gone…gone! I called for backup," Joey announced.

CHAPTER 8

"Sun Tsu said, "If you know the enemy and know yourself you need not fear the results of a hundred battles," Cabbagehead quoted. He was in his office in the tunnel below Doyers street speaking to Peter Fong and a small group of his Hip Sing Tong. His foot was propped up on the seat of his chair, and he rested his elbow on his knee while he sucked on the toothpick in his mouth.

"These Italians are so predictable and so stupidly arrogant. They fell right into our trap. I watched the action right from this screen here on my desk, he said as he patted his surveillance video machine. I have to say you did a masterful job, Peter. Gino Ranno and his gang still think Chinatown belongs to them somehow, those stupid jerks," Cabbagehead proclaimed.

"So what do you think their next move will be?" Fong asked.

"There will be a black or white response. The Italians don't know how to see gray. They'll try to come after me to kill me or seek a sit-down, one or the other. Either way our message tells them who the boss will be from now on, and it's just too fuckin' bad that it's right in their old backyard of Little Italy. The boss will be me. Just like Shrimp Boy in San Francisco, nothing will happen in this city without my fingerprints on things. For too many years we respected and feared these Italian fucks. Their boss, Gino-the-amateur-Ranno has muscles weak like a woman. His wit is like a bowl of soup." Danny spit his toothpick across the room for effect.

"You're right. This hotel is our line in the sand," Peter Fong declared. "Fuck them."

"And their stronghold on the construction business? With their control of the unions? Will soon come to an end. We took the heroin business when they thought that business was theirs alone, didn't we? My god, what our people forgot about moving smack, theirs will never know. Now the Micelis will understand our power and determination, my friends. And their beloved construction business will come to us over time," Cabbagehead announced.

"Danny, the truth is these wops will not go away without a fight. Are we prepared for a long battle? Willie Huang asked. Huang was Cabbagehead's right-hand man and his first cousin from Hong Kong. In the organization, Huang is a 438, a Vanguard, the operations master of the Tong. Cabbagehead is the 489, the Mountain Master, or boss. The numbers and their symbolism are used to identify rank in the Chinese mob.

"Our people have a much longer history of fighting than these watered-down, American dagos. We use our experience and our cunning rather than our emotions. This mafia plans poorly for war; they always act from emotion. Compared to us in battle? They are unarmed," Cabbagehead said as he laughed and paced the dusty floor with his eyes starting to flash wildly in a way his comports have seen before.

"They will prepare for us to hit Ranno," Huang said.

"Precisely, and that, for the time being, is exactly what we want them to think. But... my plan will be far different than what they expect from us." Cabbagehead was almost giddy now. "The Miceli's fear will keep them off balance while we chip away at their soft underbelly," Cabbage-head hinted.

"So our next step?" Peter Fong queried.

"Pretend to kiss their ass. Pay them in full, plus a healthy vig, for their concrete work on the hotel. The Italians will take that as our typical sign of fear, of weakness, 'idiota' as they say in Italian! Ahhh, yes, they will soon only view our hit against them as a cost of doing business," Cabbagehead reasoned. He rubbed his hands together and smiled at the thought of the war which was to come. Unlike Gino, Cabbagehead enjoyed murder.

"But they will never forget," Huang declared.

"Forget? Forget??? Do you know what the Chinese Exclusion Act was cousin?" Cabbagehead asked.

"No idea," Huang said. Peter Fang on the other hand, smiled broadly.

"Educate my dear cousin will you, Peter?" Cabbagehead directed. He slapped Peter on the back and patted his young, uninformed cousin on the cheeks, just this side of being a real smack across the face. He then grabbed Chuang's cheeks with both his hands and said, "Listen up!"

"From 1882, our great-great-grandfather's time, no Chinese could immigrate to the United States. Why? Because we were being fucking discriminated against when the Americans were building their precious railroads across this goddamn continent. What they called their manifest destiny- to grow their country from one ocean to the other. This act of the US congress was supposed to end in ten years in 1892, but guess-the-fuckin'-what? They did another bigoted act against our people which lasted until 1943! That affected our grandfathers and fathers! And even then, no large amount of our people immigrated to this country until 1962," Fong exclaimed.

Cabbagehead interrupted. "Somehow our people have forgotten this sting of prejudice, so these guineas will just have to learn to forget the killing of these two, low-ranking gangsters who got a nice, Chinese crease in their skulls. They were only 'small potatoes' anyhow, as they say in their language. It is now our time, the Chinese, to emerge as the powerhouse mafia family in the world and the one to be reckoned with!" Cabbagehead, in this one instant, was declaring his desire to rule the unnderground by any means necessary, and by showing his grandmother he was anything but a 'cabbagehead,' a name he loathed and carried a chip on his shoulder about. This combination of the put down by his own family member and the put down because of his heritage, colliding with his psychopathic personality could scare even Hillary Clinton. He got up walked over to the Chinese flag he had proudly displayed on his wall and pounded his fist next to it. "Our duty to our ancestors is to remember their sacrifices and make more money than any other group of people to enter this country."

There was another sting Cabbagehead was dealing with, but he never even flinched as he was speaking; his tattoo artist with his needle whirring, giving Cabbagehead some new ink.

There was a pregnant silence in the room. Cabbagehead held onto a thousand-yard stare before he spoke again.

"Peter, tomorrow you reach out to Ranno's crew. Pay them in cash for the concrete. Admit nothing and do not apologize for what happened here tonight. It is simply a payment for services rendered," Cabbagehead ordered.

"Done," Fong said.

"Let's see if these mafiosi are made of more than their soft, ricotta cheese."

CHAPTER 9

The day after the Hip Sing Tong's killing of the two Miceli family soldiers, Doyers Street looked, sounded, and smelled much like any other day in Chinatown. Early in the morning the streets teemed with locals, looking to buy their fruits, vegetables, medicinal herbs, and lotto tickets. The sound of firecrackers exploding on Mulberry Street could be heard coming from the Chinese Wah Lai Funeral Parlor and its next-door neighbor, Ng Fook Funeral home as coffins were brought to their hearses. The fireworks were in honor of the soon-to-be buried. Life went on as always.

On the blacktop of the public park just across from the tandem funeral homes, under the shadow of the federal court house, the Metropolitan Criminal Court and the New York City Central Booking building, better known as The Tombs, a group of Chinese senior citizens do their daily Tai Chi exercises, in a somewhat strange silence by western standards.

The aroma of fried dumplings, roast pork, Peking duck, and fresh fish permeated the streets which awaited the throngs of tourists looking for a good, inexpensive lunch and hot bargains.

Things were seemingly normal in Chinatown except yellow, police, crime scene tape had blocked the two entrances to Doyers Street and two, uniformed officers from the Fifth Precinct guarded the entrance to the Nom Wah Tea Parlor. The uniformed division of the Fifth submitted the appropriate '61' Complaint Report. Detectives from the fifth squad interviewed waiters, kitchen workers, patrons, and anyone else who was around during the homicides the night before. They scribbled notes onto small, note pads to be used later for the 'Fives', the complaint follow-up, their internal NYPD reports. So far, not one person interviewed heard or saw anything.

Unlike most other ethnic groups, the Chinese do not take time to gossip about murders. Some people shot some other people, not our business, life goes on. Not even the shoemakers in their makeshift stands on the streets are willing to discuss the prior night's events, as they, like so many others in Chinatown, are content to only eek out their meager existence... in silence.

Only one person was showing concern, sitting in her plush office on the second floor of her corner office on Elizabeth and Mott Streets. That person was Suzie Ping. Unlike what her twenty-three-year older big sister did, Baby Ping lived a much more lavish lifestyle.

"Any minute now that cute detective will be knocking at our door seeing if we know anything about that ridiculous violence last night. This testosterone driven nonsense is never good for business. First the media, then the cops, then the politicians come calling, in rapid fire succession. They are like piranhas, looking to feed on the flesh of those of us who are actually working and making money," Suzie Ping stated. She was talking to her two female assistants, Diana Lung and Alison Chin, both FOBs. Fresh-off-the-boat Chinese girls Suzie took away from the life of massage parlors and happy endings, giving them both real office jobs as opposed to working on their backs.

On occasion, Suzie would ask the two, twenty-year old beauties to do her a favor and service a business contact, but those occasions were rare, and the girls could refuse without penalty. The girls rarely turned down the date as the money from Suzie's business associates were generally enormous.

"Oh, you mean Matt Baker? Cute is not the word. Hunk is more like it," Alison said.

"Let's focus on business for the moment. If the police come, and they will, let me do the talking and you two go about your daily routine. Remember we have sixty new visas coming in this week and we need to place them into jobs quickly. The money doesn't flow until these bodies are all working. Remember, I have a few dinner appointments this week so you ladies need to work long hours.

"Whatever you need, Suzie. We are here for you, always," Diana Lung stated with Alison nodding her head in agreement.

A soft knock on Suzie's closed, office door interrupted their meeting. It was the temporary office receptionist. Temporary until the flood of new recruits were put through Baby Ping's system.

"Miss Suzie, there is a Detective Baker here to see you."

Suzie smiled at the receptionist and looked at the two girls sitting in front of her custom-made, mahogany desk.

"I wish I could predict tomorrow's winning lottery numbers as well as I can the police around here," Suzie stated.

Alison and Diana moved quickly to their offices as Suzie checked her look in a full-length mirror behind a closet door in her office. Suzie was nothing less than drop-dead gorgeous.

Unlike Sister Ping, Baby Sister had perfect teeth from years of ortho-dontics, paid for by her wealthy and generous older sister. Suzie's skin was like porcelain, and her body was absolute killer. Perfectly sized and placed implants in her butt and breasts gave her the stunning, Asian look with a hot, western body. Suzie was dressed in a white, revealing blouse, a short maroon, pleated skirt with black leggings underneath, finished off by Jimmy Choo, maroon-spiked heels.

The receptionist escorted the young detective to Suzie's office, with a put-on wiggle she must have practiced for years.

Matt Baker was one of the youngest members of NYPD to rise to third grade detective after a stint in O.C.C.B., the Organized Crime Control Bureau, and under-cover narcotics up in the Bronx. At twenty-eight-years old, Matt was tall and well built, just under six feet two inches, with Italian good looks he inherited from his mother's side of the family.

"Must be nice! Look at this office. Italian marble, Asian carpets, fancy furniture. Real nice," Matt blurted.

"It doesn't come easy, Detective. Long hours, almost seven days a week. Working with banks and insurance companies here and in Asia is not a picnic, I shit you not," Suzie replied.

"And the girls you hire get better and better looking."

"Thank you, Detective. If you are ever in the need of a date for the patrolman's ball I'm sure I can introduce you to a lovely lady. I hear tell that our Alison has eyes for you."

"Thank you, Miss Ping but I'm seeing a Puerto Rican girl from the Bronx and she has kitchen knives," Matt laughed. Suzie chuckled.

"So, to what do I owe this pleasure, Detective?"

"I'm sure by now you've heard about the homicides on Doyers Street. I'm polling the neighborhood for leads. Knowing that you have your pulse on the area I thought I would stop by and see if you can at least point me in the right direction," Matt queried.

"Homicides on Doyers Street? How awful, this is the first I've heard," Suzie lied. Matt tried hard to keep his no-tell poker face. He paused, looking directly into Suzie's large, slanted eyes. "It seems two members of the Miceli crime family were gunned down in the tea parlor."

"Terrible! Do you know by whom?" Suzie asked. When she said 'terrible', she shockingly put her hand to her chest, but it was only a ploy to open her blouse just a bit more.

"We have our suspicions. I'll let you know as we progress. It may be Dragon involved. Would you like to take a guess?"

Suzie spoke softly and sweetly, "Detective, as you already know, our business is money transferring to Asia." She moved from behind her desk and sat on the front edge of it with her legs crossed, her spiked 4" heels calling Matt's name like the Songs of Siren. "We have two-hundred eighteen locations in New York City, Flushing, Brooklyn, New Jersey, San Francisco, Chicago, and so on. We also represent various youth groups in the Chinese communities in various cities. We have no, and I will repeat myself, no affiliation to any Tong. As far as we know, a Tong is exactly what it means. A meeting place. That's how the name Tong came about and that's all we care to know."

"So this is the business you took over for your sister, is that it?" Matt asked. He also unbuttoned his official shirt now as he felt it getting warm in her office.

"On the contrary, I started this business myself a year after my sister was incarcerated. My contacts in Asia and my grasp of the English, Italian, and Spanish languages were a perfect fit for this lucrative business. We will soon be expanding into the Caribbean as well as Central and South America. I had nothing to do with my sister's business dealings other than to be the recipient of her generosity when I was a young girl in China. As a matter of fact, Detective, I hardly even knew my older sibling. Now that she is dead, I wish to respect her memory and not discuss her any further."

"My apologies, Miss Ping. I fully understand and respect your wishes," Matt pronounced. After a brief pause, he spoke again.

"And the Miceli family? Gino Ranno? Do you have contacts with them at all? I hear they have a big presence in Chinatown. Is that true?" Matt asked, looking at Suzie's face for a tell...and looking at Suzie's open blouse for a show.

"I know nothing about the mafia. I have only met Mr. Ranno twice. Both times at charity functions. We both raise funds for inner-city scholarships. I have also met and worked closely with his eminence Cardinal Dolan and the last two mayors at these events. As a matter of fact, I have a black-tie function tonight at the Waldorf Astoria. Would you care to be my escort? I have an extra ticket," Suzie invited.

"I'm working the turnaround tonight so I have to pass. Thank you. Maybe some other time, Miss Ping."

CHAPTER 10

Because of the tea parlor hit, Gino was ensconced in his penthouse apartment on Johnson Avenue in the Riverdale section of the Bronx. Although Riverdale was not chic and was a bit far from the 'in' crowd which defined Manhattan, Gino saw no need to move from this place as he spent little time at home. Besides, it was his first bachelor pad since his divorce and Gino had a strange, sentimental attachment to the panoramic view of the Bronx where his family had lived for decades.

Mickey Roach had the Riverdale building surrounded like the federal reserve bank. Six, hard-bodied soldiers in the lobby, four men in the hallway leading to Gino's apartment, and two Cadillac Escalade SUV's, with four, heavily armed men perched right outside the building's main door, had one goal. No one was getting close enough to Gino Ranno to harm one hair on his full scalp.

Gino's neighbors knew who he was and what he did for a living, so no one bothered to call the management company of the building to complain about any inconvenience.

Gino, Mickey Roach, Joey Clams, and Charlie 'C.C.' Constantino sat around the kitchen table overlooking the Bronx from twenty stories atop a natural, high hill, sipping their morning espresso and munching on Thomas' English muffins with butter and grape jelly.

"I got a call from one of Cabbagehead's crew already. This sfaccime Peter Fong has an envelope for us. It seems they want to pay the concrete tab all-of-a-sudden, with the vig, no less," C.C. said.

Gino absorbed C.C.'s words, paused and turned to his consigliere.

"What do you make of this, Mickey?" Gino asked.

"First we take the money. Business is business. I'll go with a few of my crew and make sure it's not some sort of sneak attack like they did in Pearl Harbor," Mickey warned.

"Ah…Mickey…that was the Japanese. Pearl Harbor was attacked by the Japs. We are dealing with the Chinese over here," Joey Clams admonished.

"Please! I can't tell any of them apart. Chinese, Korean, Japanese, Vietnamese, any of them. I never trusted people when I can't understand one word they say. And they all have big heads, too… no?" Mickey asked, seeking some approval.

"Mick, forget all that. What do you think of the move other than a sneak attack?" Gino asked.

"You can't trust these people as far as you can throw them. Listen to me. Don't think they are paying up because they are afraid or because they feel bad about killing our guys. They are playing a mind game with us. Trying to keep us off balance. They are looking to let us make the next move to set us up for something bigger," Mickey explained.

"Bigger, like what?" Gino asked.

"Like putting a hit on you, for instance. Or maybe making a move on some of our operations. I don't know…gambling…maybe even construction?" Mickey threw out a trial balloon.

"They have a long way to go to get into construction, what with the trades, the unions, the building inspectors," Joey Clams speculated.

Gino held up his right hand while he sipped his coffee. He again paused for a moment to think.

"That's where we have to try to think like an Asian a little bit. They have a different concept of time than we do. We want everything done now, or as we say in New York, 'I want it yesterday.' The Chinese have had many centuries to make time be their weapon and shield. One of my favorite Chinese proverbs, 'If you wait by the river bank long enough, the body of your enemy will float by.' Understand, Cabbagehead and his buddies have had a nice little taste of the money we enjoy in construction, with this Bowery hotel. They are going to want more and more as time goes on. They will move slowly but surely until our bodies go floating by," Gino lectured.

"So, now what?" Joey asked.

"See what he means, Joey? We are thinking of the here and now, and these fuckers are looking way into the future," Mickey stated.

"So now we make a move they will expect, but with a little twist. The Hip Sing Tong and Cabbagehead are expecting us to go in, guns blazing like on the streets of Palermo, shooting up a gambling den or another joint to take our revenge, but not this time. I want to show them how difficult it is to manage a construction site. That job has gone way too smoothly for them so far. Mickey, go ahead and do your thing," Gino ordered.

"Si padrone, subito," Mickey responded.

"I just love it when he talks Italian," C.C. blurted.

"Would you just shut up, fucktard?" Joey countered.

"What? It's a beautiful language is all. My grandmother spoke to me in Italian," C.C. responded.

Joey looked at Gino and all three pals broke out in high school boy laughter, breaking the tension of the meeting.

"Back to business. Gino, I think you cancel that meeting you have tonight at the Waldorf. It's just not safe at this moment," Mickey advised.

"Sorry, Mickey, I don't agree with you this time. I refuse to act from weakness. I promised myself to find a middle ground for this family. Somewhere between bravado and cowardice. If I don't show at the event tonight, it looks like I'm afraid of the Tong. And it makes them think you guys don't have the muscle... or balls to protect me. I want to go to the office today, like I always do, and tonight I will be in my nice tuxedo at the Cardinal's Inner-City Scholarship Fund where I will quietly present a nice donation for the kids to that fat, red-faced Irishman," Gino explained.

It was unfortunate Gino underestimated the electronic genius of

Danny. It had been a good month since he had installed an evesdropping device in Gino's apartment. From his underground office on Doyers street, Cabbagehead was anything but a slow learner when it came to the ways of the streets and its business. He laughed out loud at the amateur way Gino ran his 'family'. He followed his every move and would know exactly when and where he would be this night.

CHAPTER 11

Gino arrived at his office at the late, Carmine Miceli, Sr.'s residence on East Seventy-Ninth Street and Madison Avenue in Manhattan. Carmine, Jr. insisted on not selling the property after his father died and pleaded with Gino that he at least keep his father's memory alive by using his office for family business.

Carmine, Jr. had fully retired now from all facets of the family business and of late had moved to Juno Beach, Florida. Gino rarely heard from his life-long friend, except on major holidays like Christmas and Thanksgiving and August 25th. The old-time Italians put great importance on name days. August 25th was the feast day of St. Louis, King of France, the patron saint of tertiaries. He was, in actuality, Louis XIV. Gino got his early morning 'happy name day' call from Carmine, Jr. every August 25th since he could remember. Gino's real name is Luigino, little Louis in Italian.

Saint Carmine was another story completely. Named after Our Lady of Mount Carmel, Carmine, Jr. never received a call from Gino on July 16th or any other liturgical day for that matter. Gino disliked the Catholic Church from the time he was eight years old and didn't practice the religion in any form except to give gifts on Christmas so as not to be looked upon as a total heathen.

"I think Carmine, Sr. is rolling in his grave over this Chinese thing," Gino announced to Joey Clams. Joey stayed close by Gino, while Mickey Roach was off to visit the Hip Sing Tong.

"Rolling? He's doing cartwheels, Gino. This shit would never happen with the old zips. The East River would be full of those yellow fucks, believe me. If Carmine, Sr. and guys like my Uncle Rocco were still around, Chinatown would be all Italian," Joey declared with a laugh.

"What time is Mickey meeting with Cabbagehead's guy? I feel like going for a walk and having a nice cigar," Gino offered.

"The meeting is at one. And Mickey would shoot me himself if you walked anywhere right now. I have no problem taking you and a few of our guys in the car to Club Macanudo, but no way are you walking sixteen blocks. Let's not even discuss it," Joey warned.

"Car? What car? I though the car was lifted," Gino laughed.

"Real funny, Gino. I gave that car the malocchio, the evil eye. I mention it disappearing and bang, an hour later it's gone. Hot shit!" Joey chuckled.

"No more cars which draw attention. Range Rover? What am I a gangster rapper?" Gino ordered.

"A nice, new Caddy is parked outside for us. Plain, black, nice," Joey stated.

§§§§

Mickey Roach insisted Peter Fong meet him on neutral territory without Fong bringing along his posse of skinny, hard-faced, tattooed forty-nines. The forty-nine Tong number signified members without senior status.

Mickey himself promised to leave his men far enough away not to be seen or heard.

The meeting place was the iconic Katz' Delicatessen on East Houston Street on the lower east side of Manhattan. Always crowded, plenty of cops and detectives grabbing a sandwich for lunch, and a couple of big, black, security guards at the door graced the place. Both men felt as safe as they could in this crowded, Jewish deli.

Mickey Roach, as was his habit with any meeting, or hit for that matter, got to Katz' fifteen minutes early, at twelve forty-five. Mickey took his blue, entrance ticket at the door and surveyed the packed restaurant before going to the counter on the right side of the deli. On the left side, which is reserved for table service only, two of Mickey's men, dressed as UPS truck drivers dug into hot pastrami on rye sandwiches. Not one table was empty and no Asians were spotted in the place. No eye contact was made between the Miceli soldiers and Mickey Roach.

At the crowded counter which was two deep with patrons, Mickey got the attention of a counter man with a ten- dollar bill in his hand.

"Yes, sir, no waiting!"

"Gimmie a pastrami rye, extra lean. That means I don't want to see any fat. Russian on one side, mustard on the other, square knish, open it up, shmear mustard. Diet Cream," Mikey said like a Jewish, Katz' veteran.

The counter man did make eye contact with Mickey and immediately hand sliced the meat with surgical precision and plated the sandwich and potato knish. There was enough meat to feed a family of four on the two slices of rye bread.

"Thanks, pal. This is for you," Mickey handed the ten-spot to the grateful server.

Down the middle of the long restaurant there are tables for those who ordered straight from the counter men and did not want to use a waiter. Mickey made his way to one of those tables, sitting smack in the middle of the deli, and faced the door using the delicious, piled-high sandwich as a prop.

A minute later, Peter Fong walked in alone, took his entrance ticket and looked around the crowded restaurant until he spotted Mickey. Fong carried a brown, leather briefcase and made his way to Mickey's table.

Fong sat down and looked Mickey square in the eyes.

"You want half of this?" Mickey politely asked. He pointed to the stacked high sandwich.

"Never touch the stuff," Fong retorted.

"Me either...not for years, anyway."

"I have something for you," Fong exclaimed and he tapped the briefcase.

"Open it up facing me so I can see green," Mickey ordered.

"What are you afraid of old timer? A bomb or something?" Fong asked with a bit of a chuckle.

"Or something," is what Mickey said out loud. *Fuck you, you Chinese rat,* was what he said to himself.

Fong snapped open the briefcase never taking his eyes off Mickey and held it open a few inches so Mickey could see the cash.

"You will find the exact payment in full plus twenty percent for time. Most people in here don't even make that vig working hard all year," Fong stated.

"What can I say? We're lucky," Mickey said sarcastically.

"Have a nice day," Fong offered and left the table. *Fuck you, you Guinnea fuck,* was what he said to himself as he walked out handing his blue ticket to a waiting woman with small children.

Mickey watched as Fong handed his ticket to the lady near the cashier's counter and exited the restaurant.

The two, UPS backup men took their check and their tickets and quickly paid for their meal, but not before taking the briefcase from Mickey. There was no way Mickey was walking out of Katz' with that amount of cash just in case any pain-in-the-ass FBI were tipped off. A nearby van, filled with Miceli body guards and their AK-47s, was ready in case anyone from Cabbagehead's crew tried to jump, gun down, or blow up Mickey exiting Katz'. Like the predator and prey, Cabbagehead laughed while watching the whole episode take place, Miceli guard van and all, from his underground office far, far away under Doyers Street via his surveillance monitoring system.

Mickey left the sandwich uneaten, paid at the desk and surrendered his ticket.

One of the big, security guards held the door open for the mob's most prolific hit man.

"Sir...you have a nice day now."

"You, too, pally."

Cabbahead's surveillance was two-fold: To obviously keep an eye on Gino's moves, but to also watch his own people to be sure he didn't need to send lower ranking, new members a message by dragging a bloody, bullet-holed, higher ranking member into the street for double-crossing him and skimming off the top.

CHAPTER 12

Detective Matt Baker was in the middle of his turnaround. He worked from four to twelve, got a little sleep at the Fifth Precinct, then started on the eight to twelve shift. He was pounding the streets of Chinatown chasing down leads for the Tea House killings that he and everyone else knew wouldn't amount to a bowl of cold, won-ton soup. Nobody in Chinatown has eyes or ears on normal days, never mind when a major crime is committed. Matt returned to the Fifth Precinct House to get ready to do his fives, the electronic reports on the murders, which were due for his supervisor. The sergeant's test was coming up and Matt still needed to study NYPD procedures. Every spare minute was devoted to study, taking old tests, and reading police procedure. With these homicides, things were starting to pile up, and Matt wanted to be as cool as Dean Martin walking into that six-hour, long exam.

Luis "Fig" Figueroa, the commander of the Fifth Squad saw Matt making his way up the one-hundred and thirty-six-year-old stairway, in the cramped station house, to the second floor Fifth Squad office.

"Baker, take a walk with me," Fig ordered.

"Sure thing, boss. Is there a problem?" Mike asked.

"Yeah, we have a problem. We have one hundred cops in this place, twenty percent women, and only three toilets, and one is always stopped up. I've been shitting at the Dim-Sum Restaurant across the street for three months. That's a problem all right," Fig joked.

Baker laughed as the two made their way to the sub-basement of the building.

"What the hell is that?" Mike asked as they walked toward a small make-shift gym so Fig could have his private talk.

"Oh, that's a morgue slab. Back in the day, when someone was killed or found dead in the streets around this neighborhood, they were brought here before they were taken to the M.E. The ambulances were horse drawn so that's why you see these two grooves in the concrete and stone over here," Fig said pointing to the cracked and faded flooring.

"So the medical examiner would come here to see the bodies?"

"Something like that. Anyway, I didn't want anyone to overhear us, Baker. You haven't been here very long so I need to bring you up to speed on a few things. The Hip Sing Tong has at least one informer in this house."

"What?" the green Matt Baker said a bit too loudly.

"Shut up, and listen up. It's been going on around here since the eighteen-eighties. The money and perks are too good for some knuckleheads to pass up. It's cash, blow, or pussy that makes someone turn. Sometimes it takes all three," Fig stated.

"Holy Christ! Any idea who it is?"

"Suspicions, yes, proof, no. The I.A. is aware, but these things take time. I just wanted you to know to keep your information close to the vest. And, by the way, the O.C.C.B. unit in Manhattan South? They've been asking about you. They see a connection between the tea parlor murders and the Micelis. Give them what they need, Baker. Too bad you don't speak Sicilian; they are looking for a wire guy at the moment," Fig floated.

"Uh, I'm happy right where I am, boss."

"Good, I'm thrilled you're here. I see good things for you after that test. You paying attention?" He patted Matt on the back and gave him eye contact; that was always good for trust building.

"Yes, sir. I'm studying like a third-year, med student."

§§§§

Mickey drove up to Gino's office and brought his boss eighty thousand dollars in cash, just the interest paid by the Hip Sing Tong on the concrete deal.

"I brought the regular payment to our friends. They send their thanks and their respect," Mickey announced.

"It went smoothly, I assume?" Gino asked.

"I'm here in front of you, so yeah, smooth as silk."

"I took nothing away from the table except the cash. This guy Fong is as cold as ice. No reads at all," Mickey said.

Gino laughed.

"Let's see how they react after your next visit. The more I think about it the more I think Cabbagehead will want a sit-down after your big message," Mickey conjectured.

"Let's cross that bridge when we get there."

"Okay. About tonight...I have twenty guys who will be in and around the Waldorf. Six in the lobby, three near you, three outside the ballroom, and the rest outside. The head of security over there is a friend of ours. I stopped to see him on the way up to straighten things out. And the cops outside are ours," Mickey explained.

'Let's not make it look like a Sons of Italy hall, that's all I'm asking... okay?" Gino warned.

"Relax and go have a good time with your Irish friends. I got it all covered."

CHAPTER 13

"Okay, it's three o'clock now. I need a nap and a shower and shave before I put that monkey suit on. The event starts at seven and I don't want to be among the first to arrive. If I get there at seven-forty-five or eight, I'm good. We can all go grab something to eat afterwards. I don't go to these charity things to eat, believe me," Gino pronounced.

"Good. That gives me some time to do a few things I gotta do," Mickey said.

"I don't take naps like old people. You need a driver?" Joey asked Mickey. The nap comment was a ball-breaking dig toward Gino.

"Yeah, sure."

"Careful, Mickey, cars seem to disappear when Clams drives," Gino laughed, tossing some good-natured ribbing back at his life-long friend.

Joey put his middle finger to scratch his forehead. Nothing much had changed with Gino and Joey since 1960. In their minds, they were still teenagers, even though Gino was the head of the Miceli family.

§§§§

"Where to, Mick?" Joey asked.

"McClean Avenue, Yonkers. We gotta' go see an Irishman," Mickey advised.

"Friend or foe?"

"I'm old school, Joey. The Irish were never, ever our friends years ago. They hated us for trying to take their jobs, fuck their sisters, or else they were cops or feds. But this guy is okay. I've used him before," Mickey whispered.

"One of the Westies?"

"Geez, I haven't heard that name in years. Nah, they're all gone now. But I must tell you, those Micks made a big splash for a bunch of years. I swear there were no more than twenty of them back in Hell's Kitchen but they had balls like watermelons. All tough as nails, that crew. They came up against us on the Javitz Center job but it all worked out in the end. They were alright...for Irish."

"What does this guy do?" Joey asked.

"You'll see. He's ex-IRA. Go to Rory Dolan's on Mclean, take a right off the Deegan."

"Remember those Irish girls you tried to bang in your day? I married one of their daughters and went to this joint many times. Food ain't so bad for the Irish," Joey laughed.

Fifteen minutes later Joey Clams pulled the new Cadillac into Rory Dolan's parking lot. A parking attendant came to the car with a yellow ticket. He tried to hand it to Joey.

"Forget the ticket. You just remember Andrew Jackson when you see me. And make sure this friggin' car is right up front when we leave," Joey ordered, handing the kid a twenty- dollar bill. Mickey pointed in a direction away from the front door, and he and Joey walked around to the rear of the building by the dumpsters. Rats scattered in all directions.

"Where the fuck you goin'?

"Just shut up and follow me. I recognize some of those cars parked out front, asshole."

Once safely out of public view, Mickey took his cell phone out of his pocket and texted someone. The glow of his cell phone was virtually the only light out there. A drunk man stumbled out the back door, and vomited what sounded like half his insides out. Mickey signaled to Joey. They walked over to meet his man. Bill Brady looked like he had been there since eight o'clock that morning. Truth was, he got there at seven-forty-five. Short, balding with a three-day beard, nicotine fingers, and rosacea on his face and nose which had three shades of red and pink, Brady's hand shook from the massive amount of alcohol he ingested on a daily basis.

Mickey shook Brady's hand and did the half-hug of old friends.

"Billy, this is Joey; he's with us," Mickey whispered.

"Pleasure, Joey. And any friend of Mickey's...well, you know the rest," Brady coughed.

"Brady, you don't look so good, pally. You okay?" Mickey asked.

"Nah, got a wee bit of the cirrhosis. Me liver is hard as Chinese arithmetic. But what the fook. Gotta die somehow, aye?" His Irish brogue was all that was left of his Irish charm.

"Can you still work?" Mickey asked.

"Fook, yeah. When I get around the wires and powders, my hands are as steady as a brain surgeon's. Jesus Christ on the Cross, I haven't even offered you drink inside," Brady apologized.

We could get drunk off his breath, Mickey and Joey said to each other with no words but only a glance at each other.

"No, not today, pally. We have a job tonight."

Then join me for a wee smoke, will ya?"

The three men stood huddled together trying to block the wind. Joey lit his cigarette with one try. Watching a drunk man try to light a cigarette is material for any comedian. Joey again looked at Mickey with a side nod of as if to say, *Areyoukiddinmeorwhat???*

"So, now then... what's on yer mind, Mickey? And you were right to text me, we can't talk inside that joint. There are more NYPD coppers in there than the nearest precinct at any given time," Brady said.

"I have a job, and I need it done soon. A new hotel in Chinatown," Mickey shared.

"Occupied?"

"No, they open in a month or so."

"That's easier. How many floors?"

"Twenty, twenty one, and a pool on the roof."

"Controlled demolition?"

"What's that?" Mickey asked.

"Do you want it leveled?"

"Hell, no, just a few floors to be smashed up. Delay their opening for three, maybe four, months."

"So you want a fooking I. E.D. job…child's play," Brady croaked.

"I.E.D.?"

"An improvised explosive device…pipe bombs, you retarded fook."

Joey laughed spitting his cigarette into the gutter behind McClean Avenue. Mickey chuckled at Brady's timing and delivery.

"Here's another one for the both of you ignorant bastards. You don't want a U.D. now, do ya now?"

"Go ahead, Brady…"

"A fooking, unintentional detonation. But then ya don't have ta pay me because I'll be with Satan himself."

"Okay, okay, top three floors, and the kitchen and restaurant, 50 Bowery, new job," Mickey ordered.

"I'll go with me boys tomorrow. Give ya a price before noon. Likely do the job in three or four days unless you want to pay a premium, ya cheap fooker."

"That's fine, pally. Turnkey job, Billy. I can't have our signature on this one. Here's five large for expenses," Mickey offered. The Roach tried to hand Brady an envelope filled with five thousand dollars in cash.

"Shove it up yer arse, Mickey. When did I ever ask you for anything before a job? And besides, we don't pass that hat for the fookin' IRA no more."

§§§§

"What a character!" Joey blurted before he even pulled away from the curb as he and Mickey headed back to Manhattan.

"Big time IRA bomber. Lost his only son to the British in Belfast back in the day. Wife died from a broken heart. He's just marking time. From the looks of him I think he's gonna punch the ticket pretty soon."

"Is he still any good, Mickey? Just look at him." Joey asked. Bill was swaying back and forth while talking to the attendant about retrieving his car.

"The best in the business, despite what he looks like. Come to think about it...he's always looked that bad. Even the shaking," Mickey shared.

"What's something like this go for?" Joey asked.

"He'll ask for a hundred, I'll say seventy-five, we'll settle all in at eighty."

"Ironic. The Chinks paid for their own mess," Joey noted.

"That's right, pally."

CHAPTER 14

"**W**e lost one on the ship. Very unfortunate, Miss Ping," Albert Wong almost choked on his words. Wong was the transfer specialist who brought the immigrants to the states from the far east.

"Lost? Lost as in how, Albert?" Suzie yelled. They were in her office on Canal Street. Alison and Diana looked down at their folded hands, held in their laps, awaiting the tsunami.

"We are not sure, Miss Ping. It may have been a suicide. One morning she just did not appear. We searched the vessel and...."

"So you just let her jump off the fucking ship? You moron! Do you have any idea how difficult it is to obtain these girls and boys and how much they're worth over their lifetimes? Now YOU must return the down payment to her family, out of your own pocket, not mine!" Suzie demanded.

"But Miss Ping, this has happened before, when your sister..."

"Fuck my sister, and fuck you! My sister is dead and you can be just as dead as she is, you motherfucker!" Suzie was still screaming at the top of her lungs. Her sexy, leopard patterned dress, at this moment, wasn't beautiful, but made her look like a caged animal as she paced back and forth on her office floor deciding Albert's fate. "I have people here, very serious people I must answer to. And even tougher people in Hong Kong! I can replace you with one call, you idiot!" Suzie screamed.

Wong put his head down in shame. In American culture, a woman could exert her control over a man, rabid as it may be.

"Let me have the manifest, unless somehow you lost that, too?" Suzie hollered, chastising him even more.

Wong passed two sheets of green, accounting ledgers across the desk. Suzie snarled at him. *Bitch,* he thought while he smiled sheepishly and nodded.

"Fifty-nine names. Nine males, fifty girls. I see their destinations listed per our request. Six girls will stay here in New York. Let's see... Miami, Los Angeles, six males and six females to Wisconsin. Those are Vietnamese, correct?" Suzie inquired.

"Yes, Miss Ping."

"Do you think you can get the rest of the cargo to their destinations without losing any?"

"We have tightened our security arrangements."

"Well, that's fucking real good to hear! I will remind you, I run a very lucrative business and I intend to keep it that way- with or without you. Your kind comes a dime a dozen. For Christ's sake! Do you know how many people would kill to have the job you have with me? So, this girl, who is maybe shark food now, you incompetent fool, has to be made up for! She was worth hundreds of thousands of dollars. And you will fucking pay me a tax on the next cargos until you learn from your mistake. Do we understand each other?"

"Yes, Miss Ping," ...*you cunt,* is what he added silently to himself.

"And where are the New York females now?"

"In the designated boarding house. Five from China and one from Thailand. My man has signed them over to your associates."

"Fine. Now, Albert, get out of here while I am still in a good mood. I will contact you when we have the next cargo filled."

Wong stood and half-bowed to the cold, angry, glaring eyes of Suzie. She had just made another enemy.

§§§§

The boarding house was a two-bedroom apartment on Elizabeth Street, a few blocks from Suzie's office. Alison and Diana were dispatched to meet the girls and make them feel comfortable for a few hours until

Cabbagehead's Flying Dragons would take over.

Diana brought a bag of sundries for the girls, passing around female necessities- deodorant, tooth brushes, and American cigarettes, and gum. Alison took their work visas and took individual photographs with her cell phone.

All the girls peppered them with questions, except the Thai girl who spoke neither Chinese or English. She sat wide-eyed and scared.

"Alright, quiet down. Shhh. All of your questions will be answered. But first, you must all be hungry. Let's go to a nice restaurant and a have a walk around Chinatown," Alison stated in a pleasant, sing-song voice so as to build trust with the girls.

The group went to one of the two best Dim Sum restaurants in Chinatown, The Joy Luck Palace. The girls were all fascinated by the long escalator which rose to the second floor of the massive dining room on Mott Street. A short, heavy-set woman greeted the group at the top of the moving stairway and showed them to a large, round table in the middle of the dining room. A good-sized Lazy Susan in the middle of the table was already filled with delicacies. Chicken feet, fried squid, sticky rice, bean curd, fried prawns, a variety of dumplings, and a large bowl of steaming, seafood soup for the famished group awaited them. The smiling, innocent girls also picked small dishes of food from moving carts which circled the tables. In New York City, they simply looked like regular tourists, so the other patrons and wait staff never even took notice of them. After all, don't sex trafficking escapades only happen in dark, back-street alleys?

The abundance of food, the ambiance of the restaurant with enormous, color photographs of China, and the familiarity of all the Chinese faces quietly eating their meals, gave a warm, hospitable feeling to the unsuspecting, young women.

A quick walk around Mott Street and then Little Italy's Mulberry Street with Diana and Alison acting as tour guides followed the sumptuous meal. The girls chatted among themselves, happy to be in their new life.

When Alison, Diana, and the young women returned to the Elizabeth Street apartment, there were four members of the Flying Dragons awaiting their arrival. None of the Dragons were over twenty-two years of age, the youngest being nineteen.

Alison made the introductions, by name, to the friendly boys, all smiling and happy to meet the new arrivals. They sat on worn couches or flimsy, metal folding chairs.

"Okay ladies, we both must get back to our office jobs now. We started out just like you not so long ago. Peter will discuss various job opportunities with you," Diana announced. She and Alison smiled nervously, making a quick exit.

Peter Fong was the oldest of the Dragons. He stood in the middle of the room, in front of the girls.

"The arrangements we made with your families were pretty straight forward. They paid only ten per cent of the fifty –thousand-dollar fee to come here to this country, and you will work off the balance over time. For the time being, this will be your home. In time, you will be moved to other quarters. Any questions so far?" Peter asked. None of the girls uttered a word. The Thai girl still had no idea what was being said; she watched the other girls' expressions to see their reactions to what was being said. Peter's tone so far, hadn't set off any alarms.

"Unfortunately there are no restaurant jobs or office jobs available at this moment. The same with factory work. There are just too many people in need of these jobs and they all came before you." The girls got a quizzical look on their faces and started looking back and forth at each other. The Thai girl sat up straighter in her chair. "Not to worry, though. We have placed you all in good, clean, foot and massage parlors right in this area. You can all start working off your debt tomorrow morning. The hours will be long and you will change locations with each other every two or three days. In time, when you get regular customers they can request you by name and they will be sent to see you. Any questions now?" Peter queried.

"What is the work, please?" one of the girls asked.

"What is the difference? We get you work, you pay your debt, you eventually become an American and live the dream," Peter scolded. His tone discomforted the 10-12 year-old girls.

"What is done in these places?" the girl asked again. Her voice betrayed her suspicions.

Peter walked over to her and towering above her said, "Very simple. You tend to the needs of the clients. If they want their feet rubbed, you rub their feet, if their back is sore, you rub their back; if they want more you get paid more."

"What is more, mean?" the girl inquired and stood up putting her hands on her hips.

"If they want their cocks sucked, then you suck their cocks! Understand? If they want your pussy, you open your legs," Peter explained crassly. Except for the Thai girl, the others gasped. One began to cry.

"That is not what I want to do. I will go back to China," the girl exclaimed.

"And just how in the fuck will you pay for the trip? Use your American Express card?" Peter laughed. "You stupid bitches will do exactly as you are told, when you are told, until you pay the amount your family agreed," Peter demanded.

"Or, my young dear," he said as he pulled down the top of the loud-mouthed girl's t-shirt to leer at her breasts, "your family will suffer the consequences. First," and he moved in closer to her, "we start with your father and mother and then your brothers and sisters. For us, it's a quick phone call, they may have to pay with an arm or leg or an eye or maybe even their lives," the Dragon spewed.

"I refuse to be a prostitute! My father would never allow it!" the girl said.

Peter laughed. "You think your father doesn't know what's really going on?" Peter, without taking his eyes off her, snapped his fingers, motioning the 'go ahead' signal to the other three Dragons, and in one unit, two of them jumped from their chairs, attacking the hapless girl.

One of them dragged her by her long, silky-black hair toward one of the two bedrooms. The other two followed, laughing at the drama.

The other girls were sobbing, now realizing the fate for their lives. Even the Thai girl realized things were not playing out in her favor. She didn't cry, however. She sat with steely resolve, wheels turning in her head.

In the next room, the youngest of the Dragons threw the non-compliant girl onto one of the several mattresses on the floor. One Dragon slammed the bedroom door and the other was on top of her in an instant, tearing at her clothing. He ripped off her blouse and cut the front of her bra with a straight dagger. Her screams were heard through the walls. "Shut up, you stupid bitch!" the youngest pedophile said as he pulled off her sneakers and removed her jeans in one practiced motion.

To stifle her screaming and her pleas for help, they stuffed the remnants of her blouse into her mouth. The young Dragon held the girl's flailing arms down while another one of the others mounted her, jamming himself hard into her, momentarily taking her breath away.

Her virginity was lost in one brutal, violent thrust. The girl continued to plead for the Dragons to stop. They stopped when all three had her. The third of the gang members then sodomized the girl who was now in the state of shock.

"Who wants to be next?" Peter asked the sobbing girls in the next room. The girls all sat frozen, still, and quiet.

"Now do you understand? You will do exactly as you are told, or I promise it will be far worse for you," Peter continued.

The raped girl was left sobbing as the three left her in her bloody heap and returned to the other room.

"Now later tonight other friends of ours will return with us and they will break you in with much less brutality. If any one of you gets it in her mind to go to the police, every one of your families will suffer the consequences. Any questions, ladies?" Peter asked.

The girls all shook their heads in the negative except the Thai girl.

68

Peter pointed to the almost catatonic Thai girl. His hearty laugh rattled the girls.

"And you, my lovely Thai princess, I will take you for myself a bit later."

CHAPTER 15

Cabbagehead temporarily abandoned his office in the tunnel beneath Doyers Street. He reasoned that the place was just too dangerous if the Miceli family decided to react quickly to the tea parlor murders. There was no easy escape from that lower level, and a fire bomb would be catastrophic to the Dragons.

For the time being, the Hip Sing Tong main headquarters would be on the second floor of a building on Pell Street. And aside from his worry about the Miceli clan, Cabbagehead had the constant concern with his competition. The On Leong Tong, now known as the On Leong Merchants Association and their street gang Ghost Shadows was always looking for an advantage, always seeking an edge up on the Hip Sing and the Flying Dragons. The On Leong knew the troubles between Cabbagehead and the Italians could put them in a position of great strength. They lie in wait like a tiger about to pounce on its prey. Only time would tell.

While Cabbagehead and the Flying Dragons were looking over their shoulders, waiting for the Micelis to make their expected move, Gino Ranno was heading from his office to the iconic Waldorf Astoria Hotel, to attend the Cardinal's Inner City Scholarship Fund annual fund raiser. Gino's trip was short, just twenty blocks down Park Avenue, but the traffic was brutal as always. The mile drive would likely take forty minutes.

Mickey Roach was in the lead car, while Joey Clams drove the new Cadillac with Gino in the front passenger seat, two Miceli soldiers in the rear. A follow up SUV had four, heavily armed men with eyes peeled for anything Asian.

"We could be halfway to Atlantic City by the time we get to the Waldorf," Gino quipped.

"I was just thinking the same thing," Joey added.

"Hey, tomorrow is Friday. Let's go down to A.C. in style. We can take a quick flight from Teterboro to the Borgotta, all comped by a friend of ours from Scarpa's crew in Philly. Me, you, and C.C. Like old times," Gino offered.

"And fifteen bodyguards? I don't think Mickey will sit still for this. Let's do it another time when things are not so hot, Gino," Joey advised.

The small caravan pulled up to the rear entrance of the fabulous Waldorf Astoria Hotel on Lexington Avenue. Mickey's men were standing by to escort Gino through the entrance of the Bull and Bear Restaurant to the main ballroom. There was certainly less opportunity for an attack outside the Waldorf's magnificent main entrance on Park Avenue.

Five additional guards, members of the tough, Waldorf Astoria security staff, were there to guarantee Gino was ushered unmolested to his destination...compliments of the head of security, a Miceli associate, of course.

§§§§

"Good evening, sir. Last name please?" A petite and pretty, young volunteer, one of four, at the long, greeting table asked. Sparkling chandeliers illuminated the area giving the place an elegant feel.

"Ranno. Gino, Ranno, Miss," Gino replied with a smile.

"Oh, yes, Mr. Ranno, table sixteen. Cocktail reception is to he left. Dinner is in the main ballroom," the young woman instructed.

Gino made his way to the large room which was packed with New York's moneyed elite. With the men all in black-tie and the women in elegant evening gowns, Gino slowly surveyed the room looking for a familiar face. He never felt comfortable going to these events, even when he was a young, married man. The clergy milling about made him feel even less at ease.

A voice from behind extended a hello; "Mr. Ranno, so nice to see you again." It was none other than Suzie Ping.

"Ah, look who's here! Miss Ping, so nice to see you, too," Gino replied.

Gino tried hard to look at her eyes rather than take an obvious view of her ample cleavage. Suzie wore a figure-clinging, emerald green, off the shoulder Versace gown, with a slit from her shoes to the top of her luscious thigh. Around her neck was a magnificent emerald and diamond broach.

"You look so dapper tonight. You remind me of the famous Italian actor Rossano Brazzi," Suzie declared.

"And you may be the most stunning woman ever to enter the Waldorf," Gino exclaimed.

"You Italians really know how to make a girl feel special."

"It comes from our mothers who train us from birth."

"And what table are you seated at tonight?" Suzie cooed.

"Sixteen, but I'm not planning to stay very long tonight. I have other business to attend to," Gino stated.

"Well, we have a wonderful coincidence. I am also at table sixteen."

"If you are alone, may I escort you to our table?"

"I am indeed alone, and yes, you certainly may, Mr. Ranno."

"Only if you call me Gino, please."

"Of course, Gino, and I am Suzie, Miss Ping is way too formal."

Just then, a waiter walked by hitting the chimes to announce the cocktail hour had ended.

"This is what I get for a late entrance. Not even a cocktail before dinner. Shall we?" Gino offered his arm to Suzie. Suzie put her arm into Gino's and smiled warmly, her sparkling teeth brightening her striking face.

Heads were turning as Gino and Suzie made their way to their table. Gino wondered how many guests were looking at the older man, escorting the elegant Asian woman, or how many were attracted by the mafia gangster. He half-hoped it was the former.

The band was playing as the guests continued to fill the room. Suzie dropped her glittering, black purse on a random seat at the table and took Gino by the hand.

"Can the lady ask the gentleman for the first dance?" Suzie offered.

"You beat me to the punch. By all means. This is 2017, after all."

The exquisite pair made their way, winding in and out of tables to the enormous dance floor.

"How appropriate...Sinatra!" Suzie pronounced.

The couple danced to Summer Wind.

"So, Frank Sinatra's family is from my hometown in Sicily," Gino stated.

"What town is that, Gino?"

"Lercara Friddi, near Palermo."

"Sinatra and you. Famous people from the same town. I'm honored," Suzie flirted.

"We also had an infamous person from our town. Salvatore Lucania."

"Who?"

"In this country he was called Lucky Luciano. His office was actually in this very building back in the day."

"Very interesting!" Suzie exclaimed.

"You know, Suzie, I know you are very benevolent, and that is wonderful, but what do you actually do?" Gino asked.

"I started my own business a few years ago and thankfully it's flourished. I'm in the money exchange business. Mostly from the states to Asia. We are expanding into South and Central America this year if I don't soon die from dealing with the bankers." Suzie was nervous at the question and was speaking very quickly. Gino picked up on that nuance but said nothing.

74

"Bankers are tough, " he said out loud, while the voice in his head was screaming, *there must be more to that story!*

"I don't have to ask what you do, Gino; I think I already know," Suzie whispered.

"If you choose to believe what the tabloids say, 'So say good night to the bad guy; it's the last time you see a bad guy like this again," Gino did his Cuban accent impression of Al Pacino in 'Scarface'.

Suzie laughed out loud as the song ended. Gino did not immediately release her from their embrace.

"Or you can get to know me as a person and understand what I really do. My family does have many legitimate business interests, Suzie," Gino uttered.

"I meant no offense, Gino. And I do want to get to know you better, no matter what you do," Suzie whispered.

"Let's get back to our table," Gino smiled. *Do I actually have a shot at this beauty?* he thought.

As they made their way back to table sixteen through the maze of tables, a booming voice came from behind them.

"Two of my favorite people, Miss Ping and Mr. Ranno, welcome! So very nice to see you both," Cardinal Dolan declared.

"Your Eminence, so happy to see you!" Gino lied.

"Hello, Cardinal Dolan. What an amazing turnout," Suzie replied.

Gino thought to himself, *He looks like a cherub capped crusader, with a red hat and an even redder face.*

Suzie thought, *Phony.*

"The truth is we have a great group behind us who really embrace the idea of inner-city education. And you both have been extraordinarily generous. My sincere thanks for caring about the future of these young people," Dolan emoted.

"You are very welcome, Cardinal," Suzie said.

Gino smiled. "Cardinal, I wanted to discuss something further with you on that. I have a close friend, an author, Louis Romano, who has written a book, especially to encourage inner-city children. It's called ZIP CODE, and I would personally like to donate 1,000 of those books to schools in the area." Gino knew the coward catholic church hated that author because of the previous books he'd written about a serial killer murdering pedophiles in the church.

Dolan laughed nervously. "That's very generous of you. Well, I have to make my rounds; have a great time tonight."

The Cardinal quickly shook Gino's hand and planted a quick kiss on Suzie's cheek.

Yuk, Suzie thought.

"Suzie, I want to be candid with you. My job is done here. I saw the man; he knows I was here. And knowing these fucks, I'm sure the check has already cleared. Luckily for me I got to dance with the prettiest girl in the place. And besides, I hate these things. How about let's just go have a real nice dinner somewhere?" Gino asked.

"I thought you would never ask, but what about your business meeting?" Suzie asked.

"Well, let's see…I punch my own time clock. I can do it!"

"I'll get my purse!"

CHAPTER 16

Scabby the Rat, a thirty foot high, inflatable, dark gray rat, replete with sharp, white, buck teeth, long fangs, unblinking red eyes, festering sores, and engorged nipples looks directly at the new Chinatown hotel at 50 Bowery.

Scabby had been filled with air every morning since the owners of the property began demolition of the old tenement building, to make way for the new construction just about eighteen months ago. When word got back to the various union trades that the job was to be done by non-union workers, scabs as they are called, Scabby was inducted to help protest the job.

The Hip Sing Tong Association, the real money behind the project, couldn't care less about hiring non-union workers, Why inflate the cost of construction, and take many more months to finish the job? Besides, the Hip Sing wanted to hire their own. Chinese laborers, plumbers, carpenters, electricians, and the rest of the trades would not have had a chance to work if the unions were awarded the work. That just wasn't going to happen anymore in the heart of Chinatown. So basically, the unions, and the Italian mob who had infiltrated the unions for decades, were being given the middle-finger by Cabbagehead and his Hip Sing crowd.

Traffic on Bowery had been a nightmare since the project started, with double and triple parked trucks delivering all the needed construction equipment. The traffic and the union workers who stood blowing whistles and screaming obscenities from across the street made Bowery a living hell.

Now, Scabby was losing her effect as the building was near completion with the hotel's opening day being just around the corner.

"Lots o' hustle and bustle, eh?" Billy Brady mentioned. The burly Irishman was standing next to Scabby looking up at the shiny, new hotel, with two of his band of bombers. They were all rapid-fire, chain-smoking Pall Mall, unfiltered cigarettes. All three men were former members of the Irish Republican Army who never fired a weapon against the British. Bombs were their stock in trade.

"Billy, it's an easy in and out, don't ya know? We don't want a bloody scene now, do we?" Pat Ring asked. Pat was like a brother to Billy, and between the two they likely killed over sixty of the seven-hundred-sixty-three soldiers and police who were lost during 'the troubles' in Northern Ireland.

"It's gotta' be at night, boys," Billy announced. "My clients don't want anyone killed unless we have to. It's not like the old days, Paddy."

"Three on each floor, all on the same timer. Purely gunpowder and a wee bit of nitro. We don't want the whole place fallin' down now," Billy advised.

"Just create havoc; make a fookin' mess o' the place," Ricky Bendix noted. Angus Richard Bendix, short, bald, and red in the face, did nine years in prison for his weapons trafficking in Northern Ireland for the IRA.

"All we need to know is how much security they keep after hours, then it's glass and metal all over the fookin street," Pat Ring said with glee.

"Yeah, unless some of these crazy fookers work around the clock, it's a tit job," Bendix said.

"Who wants to come back later and check things out? I'll be too smashed from the drink after three," Billy declared.

"Fook that, Billy. I need to get these pipes set up. Got shit to get for the job and yer gonna damn well help assemble this time! Last time ya said ya had to go to church and do the stations of the cross with yer mum. All the while youse were at Erin's Pub with that floozie, red-head," Pat Ring alleged.

All three men got a good belly laugh, slapping each other on the back.

"I'll come back, then. I need a good massage and happy ending anyhow. There's a wee place on Baxter, all young Chinese lasses," Bendix uttered.

"So how much are we gettin'?" Pat Ring asked.

"Chinese pussy?" Billy joked?

"No, ya dumb bastard, money for the job."

"Oh, the job. A three-way split. I'm askin' a hundred. He'll say seventy-five, we'll take eighty," Billy pronounced.

CHAPTER 17

Matt Baker was at the Fifth Squad office, both hands propping up his head, his elbows on his cluttered desk.

"You look like I feel," Luis Figeroa affirmed.

"How many homicides do you think have gone unsolved in this precinct house since it opened?" Matt queried.

"Christ knows. I think you're better off asking how many have been solved, Baker."

"We have two dead bodies, no known motive, ballistics, but no guns, and no one saw anything. I mean, really, I'm not a quitter but..."

"You have a lot more than you think, Baker. Look, two Italians with known mob affiliations come out of Nom Wah Tea Parlor... dead, a known hangout of the Flying Dragons, then the hatchet thing. This is real mob versus gang stuff. We haven't seen this kind of thing down here in a very, long time.

The problem is, even if you get some intel on why these guys were offed, you still only have a one percent chance of backing into who the killer or killers are," Figeroa said.

"I was thinking about asking the O.C. unit if they can get me an interview with Gino Ranno."

"Probable cause?"

"Don't really have that. Just a talk to see what's happening between the two branches of the service."

"No way he will talk with you. No fucking way. But ask anyway, what the hell? You're new, you're young, you're dumb; hide behind that for four or five years! That's how I came up," Figeroa advised.

§§§

While the cops were trying to figure out who killed who, Gino had other things on his mind. The leader of the Miceli mob family, the Don, was smitten by Suzie Ping. Not since his relationship with Lisa, when he nearly got himself killed and chipped to pieces at the Amagansett Fish Farm, had Gino fallen for a woman like Suzie. And Lisa was way back before he was part of Carmine Miceli, Sr's. Cosa Nostra. Back then he was just a dear friend of the family.

Gino waited until almost noon, the day after their impromptu dinner date, to call Suzie.

"Hi, Gino! I had such a great time last night, thank you," Suzie whispered.

"It was fun, wasn't it?"

"More than fun and you were the perfect gentleman…damn it!" Suzie joked.

"I'm good like that, especially on the first date. I'm still just a little old school," Gino quipped.

"I had a hard time answering the bell this morning. You know I have a business to run, Gino Ranno," Suzie teased.

"I fell back asleep on the treadmill this morning."

"That was my first time at Rao's. What a place!"

"Indeed it is. Who would have thought Madonna would be at the next table?"

"And she was so friendly. And the table of FBI guys and the district attorney? I thought they were going to just flip out when you walked in."

82

"Anyway, I have a proposition for you. My dear friend the undertaker, Anthony Magenta, gave me his house in Montauk for the weekend. Frankly I'm thinking about buying the place. How would you like to join me? We can take the helicopter from the East Thirty-Fourth Street heliport and be there in just about forty-five minutes. A few of my guys will be there too, to chaperone us," Gino joked.

"I would be delighted. This is a rare weekend I'm not so crazy busy, and I can work a bit if there is Wi-Fi."

"Well, if there isn't, I'll see that there is." Gino continued, "How about I pick you up at three in the afternoon tomorrow?"

"Let's make it easy on you, Gino. I'll meet you at the heliport at three. Is that okay for the old school Italian?" Suzie asked.

"Perfect. Bring your bathing suit."

$$$$

Billy Brady, Pat Ring and Ricky Bendix, the IRA connection, were ready to do the piece of work Mickey Roach had ordered.

Billy and Mickey agreed to terms: eighty-thousand cash and a five-grand kicker if no one was hurt. Mickey agreed Friday night it would be a go. He knew Gino would be out of town, out in Eastern Long Island, so the timing was absolutely perfect.

CHAPTER 18

"Suzie, you look absolutely fabulous!" Gino declared.

Suzie stepped out of an Uber car at the heliport, her overnight Louis Vuitton bag in her hand. She was wearing a tight, white, V-neck tee shirt with black, skin tight, leather pants and spiked, black high heels. Her jet-black hair was pulled back in a bun, highlighting her striking, angular features, her eyes hidden behind gold-rimmed, Gucci sunglasses.

"Sorry if I seem a little nervous, Gino." Suzie whispered. The wind from the east river swirled around the entrance to the Blade Club, tossing Gino's salt and pepper hair in every direction.

"Did you have a hectic day?" Gino asked. He took her bag and gave her a peck on the cheek.

"Honestly, I'm nervous about the helicopter ride. It's my first time."

"First time? I promise to be gentle," Gino quipped. Suzie laughed.

"I like it rough!" Suzie responded with a grin.

"Believe me, it's no big deal. After the take off, it's very smooth. We'll be at the house on Lake Montauk before you know it. The place is just a mile or so from the airport and a car will be waiting. Right now, let's have a nice drink in the club house to settle you down before we take off."

Joey Clams, Mickey, C.C., and two soldiers were already in Montauk, having taken an earlier flight. Two of Mickey's handsome, Sicilian imports were booked on the same flight with Gino and Suzie. They were dressed in tan, Italian linen slacks and blousy Tommy Bahama shirts to hide their weapons. Gino pretended not to know them as they all sipped chilled, rosé wine and munched on lobster rolls.

The Sikorsky S-76, Blade Ultra service helicopter took off smoothly giving the well-heeled passengers a quick view of the east side of

Manhattan before heading due east toward Long Island. Suzie held tight to Gino with her left hand, digging her nails into her seat with her right.

"It's okay Suzie, I'm here. There's nothing to be afraid of," Gino whispered.

"I read up on helicopters last night. I was almost going to call you and cancel," Suzie uttered.

"These pilots are highly skilled and trained to get us to our destination without trouble."

"So what if the engine stops? Will we plummet to the ground like a rock?" Suzie asked.

"Absolutely not. These helicopters are designed to be able to get down safely if that happens, but that's very unlikely. These pilots are not hacks. Relax and enjoy the view. Have some wine," Gino advised.

"So then tell me how come there's been seven incidences in New York City in the last sixteen years?"

Gino laughed out loud. "Sixteen years? Well you have done some research now, haven't you? So, can you tell me how many car fatalities have there been on the Long Island Expressway in those years?" Gino queried.

"It's not the same, silly…besides…"

"Besides, did I tell you how stunning you are?" Gino reached over and planted a long kiss onto Suzie's pouty lips.

Suzie removed her sunglasses and smiled sweetly at Gino.

"Maybe we should make out for the rest of the trip. That will settle me down I think," Suzie whispered.

One of the two Sicilian bodyguards poked his elbow into his partner's arm to bring his attention to their boss and his hot, Asian lady.

"That's a pretty nice idea, Suzie, but it may disturb the pilot and the other passengers," Gino quipped.

"Okay, how about a rain-check?"

"Deal!" Gino blurted.

Suzie had now acclimated to the ride and had calmed down to the point where she was enjoying the view of the beaches on the right side of the craft.

"That's the famous Jones Beach right there," Gino said.

"I've never been there."

"Too crowded. I think you will love Montauk, Suzie. It's a great place to kick back, relax, and enjoy the ocean."

"I have to say, Mr. Gino Ranno, you are a very, sweet man. And in my humble opinion, you are a very handsome, sexy guy."

"You must tell that to all the Italian men you know."

"You are the first Italian man I have dated if you must know my past. Besides, I am very turned on by the way you look at me, and the kindness in your big, dark eyes. If you must know, the power that you have excites me. There, I said it," Suzie admitted.

"Suzie, this is the beginning of a beautiful friendship," Gino said in a poor, Humphrey Bogart impression.

"I know that line from Casablanca, you nut! Except Bogey said it to Louie who, by the way, was played by Claude Rains; I'm such a huge movie buff."

"So am I, Suzie. I think we will soon find that we have an awful lot in common."

"You have no idea!" Suzie reached over and kissed Gino softly on his mouth.

Gino got a tingling in his nether regions, unable to recall the last time he felt that way.

CHAPTER 19

"We need to fill the ranks of the Dragons with fresh blood. Pure, Chinese blood. I hear that the Born to Kill…those Vietnamese maniacs, want to make a return to New York from New Orleans. These BTK or Canal Boys or whatever the fuck they want to be called again can be useful to us…but they can never step on our toes like they tried with the Ghost Shadows…never," Cabbagehead proclaimed. He was meeting with Peter, his right-hand man and six other high ranking Flying Dragons. Multi-colored tattoos ran up the necks of all of the Dragons from below their necks up to their jawlines. Snakes, and dragons galore.

"The BTK were different years ago. They were all immigrants and first generation from Viet Nam. They had blood in their mouths when they came here, and their violence knew no boundaries. They have a new leader since David Thai went inside for life. His name is An Phan. In Little Vietnam in New Orleans, they call him Andy. I hear he has a head on his shoulders and more reasonable than his uncle David," Peter informed the group.

"I want to meet with them soon. In the meantime, what are we doing to bring in some 'blue lanterns'? We need new blood," Cabbagehead asked.

Peter pointed to Lee Chen, an eighteen-year-old up and coming Dragon who was recruited three years ago at Bronx High School of Science, where the best and brightest students attend.

"We are working at the better high schools. Finding smart, Chinese immigrants is our focus. We must infiltrate the schools, like Stuyvesant and Bronx Science, and one or two good, charter schools and find the young students who have a need and desire to make money. We look for the loners, the discipline problems, and relatives of other Dragons," Chen advised.

"Any prospects, now?" Cabbagehead asked.

"Several. We are vetting them now, checking family roots here and in Hong Kong to make sure of no police infiltration. We want boys with clean records and balls," Chen said.

"Like you?" Cabbagehead blurted. He smiled at the young Dragon.

"Thank you, Danny," Chen responded.

"Good. We will have some important work for them to do very soon. After their thirty-six oaths and they are tatted and become our brothers, we will give them a few small jobs at first, and then I'll have some special tasks to be done by the cream of the crop," Cabbagehead hinted.

The thirty-six oaths are similar to the Sicilian mafia's initiation ceremony. The Sicilians burn a holy picture in the hands of a newly, made-man while he recites various pledges. The Chinese Triads conduct a ceremony at an altar, with an animal sacrifice and burning incense enveloping the room. The new member, 'a blue lantern' passes beneath an arch of sharpened swords after drinking the animal's blood and wine while reciting the promises. The oaths are written on a sheet of paper and then burned at the altar.

"After having entered the gates I must treat the parents and relatives of my sworn brothers as my own kin. I shall suffer death by five thunder-bolts if I do not keep this oath.

I shall assist my sworn brothers to bury their parents and brothers by offering financial or physical assistance. I shall be killed by five thunder-bolts if I pretend to have no knowledge of their troubles.

When brothers visit my house, I shall provide them with board and lodging. I shall be killed by myriads of knives if I treat them as strangers.

I shall not disclose the secrets of the family, not even to my parents, brothers, or wife. I shall never disclose the secrets for money. I will be killed by myriads of swords if I do so."

CHAPTER 20

The Sikorsky S-76 landed smoothly at Montauk Airport on East Lake Drive. The small strip is nestled between Lake Montauk and the Block Island Sound, far enough away from the busy town of Montauk during the summer months to even be noticed. It's the perfect place for the head of a New York mafia family to get away for a few days with nearly complete anonymity.

Suzie was so thrilled to touch down in one piece on the grass which served as a heliport at the tiny airport. She thought of a photo she once saw of a pope kissing the ground upon landing in a foreign country. Instead, the extreme heat from the asphalt and the sound, and gusts of air made by the whirling blades of the helicopter distracted her initial impressions of Montauk.

Gino and Suzie approached the brown bungalow which serves as, for lack of a better term, the Montauk airport terminal building, complete with a brown picket fence and a two-person wooden bench. The bench is dedicated to a local pilot who was killed on a flight from Teterboro, New Jersey.

A blue and white Cessna 182 Skylane had just landed on the twenty five hundred foot runway and taxied slowly near the bungalow. The pilot opened the plane's door for a handsome, athletic young man and a great looking blonde in a tight, green jumpsuit. The woman held a small dog in her arms and the jock had the two overnight sized bags. The two body-guards made it their business to get themselves between Gino, Suzie, and the couple, just in case.

Joey Clams and Mickey Roach were in the small gravel parking lot to meet Gino and Suzie in a sparkling new, deep blue, Maserati Quattro-porte. The car came with the house for the weekend courtesy of Gino's undertaker friend. The two, soldier bodyguards from Mickey's crew sat in a rented Kia Sorento directly behind the Maserati. Then the two,

Sicilian guardians hopped into the Kia.

Suzie noticed for the first time that the two, quiet, handsome, young men were on the helicopter to protect Gino.

"Mickey, Joey, say hello to my friend, Suzie. She is my houseguest for the weekend."

Holy shit...look at this one, Joey Clams thought to himself. He smiled shyly at Suzie, trying not to stare at her ample tits.

"My pleasure, I'm sure," Mickey exclaimed in his old school, polite manner.

"What a car! Can I drive it to the house?" Gino asked.

"Of course but the ride is so close you won't even be able to open it up," Joey warned. He opened the door for Gino as Mickey jumped to open the passenger door for Suzie. The two men jumped into the back seat of the Italian sports car.

Joey was right. Gino had no idea of the precision and power the car was capable of in the short drive to the lakeside house, although he left the Kia far back in the Maserati's rear view mirror as he sped along the windy and bumpy East Lake Drive toward Route 27 and then quickly onto West Lake Drive.

"Here we are...home sweet home...if for only a few days," Gino announced, as the car's tires crunched on the gravel driveway.

"My goodness, what a beautiful place!" Suzie commented.

The Kia, minutes later, finally pulled into the driveway almost fishtailing onto the gravel.

"Let's get a drink and I'll show you around the place," Gino suggested.

Joey took their bags into the house ahead of them while Mickey went to the Kia to give the bodyguards their orders.

"Gino, would you mind if I took a look at the lake first?" Suzie asked.

"'Course not. C'mon."

Gino took Suzie by the hand down a bluestone, garden path, past a row of honeysuckle bushes, around a long row of Emerald Green Arborvitae, and several, Red Dragon Japanese maple trees toward Lake Montauk's edge.

"What is that amazing aroma?" Suzie queried.

"Ah, we do have a lot in common. That is my favorite scent from nature on the entire planet. It's honeysuckle. That smell brings me back to when I was a kid at my father's aunt's bungalow in Long Beach, New York. What great moments we had there," Gino reminisced.

"And that salt air! It sure beats that fishy smell of Mott Street. I have to get out of Chinatown more often…this is magnificent!" Suzie extolled.

Suzie bent slightly in her tight, leather pants, picked up a few stones, tossing them into the lake. She stopped for a moment and stared at the warm, late afternoon sun low on the horizon, taking in the tranquility of the large lake.

"Gino…thank-you so much for inviting me." She took her eyes from the gorgeous panorama and moved into Gino. The kiss she gave Gino made his knees wobble.

§§§§

No one was working at 50 Bowery that torrid, summer evening. It seems even Chinese scabs need some down time, especially given the recent sweltering weather in Chinatown. There was only one security guard on duty that night in front of the glittering, new, gray steel and glass hotel.

Billy Brady, Pat Ring and Ricky Bendix drove up to 50 Bowery in a lifted, old, Ford Econoline van. If they planned right, the van would be back with its owner in a few hours. If there was a mess up, the van would either be smithereens or impounded by NYPD's Traffic Control Division.

Bendix, being the youngest of the three, handled most of the pre-made pipe bombs in the large, gray, luggage bag with wheels. The weight of twenty, steel pipe bombs easily exceeded ninety pounds. Billy handled the electronics in a Regis High School gym bag. Regis is known for its brainiac students, and Billy couldn't get in the door if his father had endowed the school with a new gymnasium. Truth be told, Billy didn't see the eighth grade in Ireland. He used the Regis bag to throw off the police in case they were spotted by any pain-in-the ass witnesses. Billy was uneducated, but brilliant in battle.

The third guy of the crew, Pat Ring, carried a knap-sack with incidentals. Tools, flashlights, a nice billy-club, some cookies, candy, and some orange juice in case Brady had one of his diabetic episodes.

Pat approached the guard booth and saw a very old Chinese man sleeping inside. The man resembled the former President of the Republic of China Chiang Kai-shek but with a smaller head and scraggly whiskers. The only thing this old man could do is chase some nearby project kids away if they decided to have some fun breaking the hotel's windows with pieces of brick or stones. Pat decided to let the man sleep. One good whack on the old guy's head with Pat's billy-club would cost the trio the promised five-thousand-dollar bonus Mickey offered if no one was hurt.

Billy was an expert lock picker, so he had the flimsy, contractor-grade door's, Yale lock opened in seconds. The three Irishmen were inside the dark hotel headed for the lobby's bank of elevators. Fortunately, one of the lifts was operative.

The trio went to the top floor.

"Jesus fookin' Christ, if I had to walk twenty-one stories yu'd be callin' a priest fer me," Billy whispered.

"Ya old fart, ya been smokin' like a fookin chimney since yer twelve. No wonder yer shot," Pat half-joked.

The ding of the elevator alerted the passengers they had arrived at their destination.

"Floor twenty-one! Ladies undergarments, nylon stockings, and the like," Pat announced.

"Okay, quit the jokin', will ya? Let's get this floor set up, PDQ, so we can move to the three others. Shouldn't take more than eight minutes per floor like we planned," Billy commanded.

The three men moved like they were all young again setting the pipe bombs in strategic places on each of the top three floors in under the time allotted. Wrapping the steel devices around beams with copper wire, while humming Irish pub songs, then breaking into song all at the same moment was reminiscent of a Quntin Terrantino movie, complete with its staccato dialogue.

Brady ya moron, don't ferget what we're here for. Your singin could make a freight train take a dirt road fer fook sake,' Pat laughed.

"I'll sing at yer funeral ya fat fook just before I piss on ya grave ya koot,"

"Quiet will yas, what was that noise?" Billy held a finger to his lips.

"That's Patrick passing wind, don't ya know,"Brady joked.

"Just make sure the charges are set facing away from the wall is all. I don't want a single dud fizzin' out on us," Pat announced.

"The only dud here is you in bed with the missus. Yea, she told me the long high hard one is no longer hard nor long," Brady choked before going into a fit of coughing.

Back on the elevator after the top floor was finished, Billy was panting and out of breath.

"I need a smoke," Billy blurted.

"Never ya mind with that now. Just the lobby and the kitchen and we're the fook out a here," Pat demanded.

"Yer a hardon, Ring. Ya know that, don't ya?" Billy cursed.

The last of the devices were set up in the lobby and kitchen in just about five minutes. Pat Ring clicked off his flashlight as some light from a Bowery Street lamp gave enough elimination to see their way out.

The men exited the construction site with nothing in their hands, as was their plan.

"Thank baby Jesus I can light up," Billy coughed. His hands trembled from the lack of nicotine in his depleted system.

"Let me go see if the Chinaman is still sleeping," Pat said.

"Well, the Ford is still there. That's a bonus!" Bendix stated.

"We can have it back up to Yonkers before the band starts at McKeon's," Billy quipped.

Pat went to the security booth to the right of the entrance of the hotel. The old man was just coming out of his nap. He was startled by the red-headed, white man's face looking through the plexi-glass cut out in the door to his shack.

"Hi ya, buddy. How would you like a drink with me and me pals over there?" Pat offered.

"The man, not even fully understanding a word of the English he was speaking said, "You go. You go, now!"

"Ah, that's not being hospitable. Here's a couple o' bucks for you to enjoy to yer heart's content." Pat offered two, crisp, fifty dollar bills.

"You go! You go, now!" The old guy repeated flailing his arms at Pat.

Pat stuffed the bills into the old man's shirt pocket with his left hand and clobbered him on the side of his face with a roundhouse right. He caught the poor, old Chinaman before he fell.

"Did ya have to hit the poor soul, Patty? What the fook?" Bill asked.

"No choice; let's get going."

Pat gently placed the Chinaman in the rear of the Econoline and hopped into the driver's seat. All three of the bombers climbed into the van through the two, front doors.

Pat drove the van past the corner of Bowery and Houston Street, pulling over to an empty spot which was reserved for a fire hydrant.

Billy pulled a complicated looking electronic device gingerly from under the front seat.

"May I have the honors, boys? I have a feeling this will be my last," Billy asked.

Bendix nodded in agreement. Pat's eyes filled with tears. He knew his old friend wasn't wrong.

Billy turned the device on with two switches. A green light and a red light slightly lit up the interior of the van. With his trembling, nicotine-stained, right hand, Billy mashed the red button.

The sound of the explosion rattled the van. The force of energy was so great it blew out many of the windows in buildings which surrounded the hotel. A storm of glass and steel rained down upon both the sidewalk, and part of the asphalt of Bowery. Car alarms and screams peppered the still, summer air. Smoke from the lobby billowed onto the street like a vertical mushroom cloud. The old man's vacant, security booth was flattened like a Mexican tortilla.

The old man was taken from the van and placed on a park bench along Houston Street. He would forget how he got there and how he got the two fifties.

Cabbagehead and the Hip Sing were awakened from their sleep by the deafening explosion. Danny knew instantly he'd received the Sicilian's reply. He squinted a few times, got up, wearing nothing but his boxer shorts, and looked at his monitors to see where his tracking device placed Gino at the moment.

CHAPTER 21

Cabbagehead had been having his way with the two, new Chinese girls who were brought in by Sister Ping, aka Suzie, when the blast rocked his sparse apartment on Elizabeth Street. The stark apartment only had an old, white refrigerator and a barely used, four burner stove which hadn't been cleaned too well in years in the tiny kitchen area; a few worn couches were in the small living room. Nothing adorned the walls except peeling, green paint. There were mattresses on the floor in both bedrooms, and the rusty toilet and an ancient, four-legged tub with a make-shift shower and no curtain made up the bathroom. The young girls were already nauseous from having their virginity and innocence stolen from them, and the putrid smell from the mold and mildew in the bathroom was overwhelmingly stomach-churning, causing the girls to vomit repeatedly, while tears streamed down their faces, causing their once pretty hair to become stuck to their faces.

Cabbagehead had abused them in a brutal manner in which they never contemplated was possible. It was only minutes after Cabbagehead heard the blast he heard the pounding of footsteps coming up his stairs. He reached for his Sig Sauer, forty-millimeter handgun inside a holster on the belt of his slacks, which was draped over the doorknob of the room's closet.

The two, wide-eyed and horrified young girls began screaming and crying at the sudden mayhem, clinging to each other for any support they could muster.

"Shut the fuck up or I will shoot both of you," Cabbagehead commanded. Loud banging on the apartment door was followed by shouting from Peter and the Flying Dragons.

"Danny! The hotel was hit bad. The top floors and the lobby are destroyed. Danny!!!" Peter yelled.

Cabbagehead went to the front door with his Sig. He flung open the door pointing his pistol at Peter.

"What? What did you say?" Cabbagehead hollered.

"Someone blew up the hotel! Glass is everywhere! The place is a complete disaster," Peter declared, a shortness in his breath.

The piercing sounds of the sirens of police, fire, and EMT units filled all of Chinatown and Little Italy faster than a speeding bullet.

"Those fucking guineas. They will pay with blood! Now we are in all-out war. Go there and wait for me. All hands on deck, Peter, and I mean everyone!" Cabbagehead ordered.

"I am leaving a few of our Dragons to cover you. They may be looking to hit you tonight."

"I fucking hope they try. Okay, Go!"

The maniacal Danny Chu, the one everyone in Chinatown feared, the Cabbagehead cold killer, could feel his blood pressure pounding behind his eyes. The veins in his bald head looked like a pulsating, red roadmap. He went back into the bedroom to dress and saw the two girls cowering and whimpering on a mattress on the floor.

"I told you to shut the fuck up!" Cabbagehead screamed. Before he dressed and went to survey the damage at 50 Bowery, Cabbagehead pulled the thick, black belt from his pants and began to beat the girls unmercifully, leaving welts and bruises on their young, tender skin. The black and blue marks wouldn't heal for a long time, leaving them open to be abused even further by their 'clients' now as well.

§§§§

The chef at the Montauk house was serving home-made cannoli and espresso to Gino and Suzie as they sat together on a wicker divan on the rear deck, overlooking Lake Montauk. The meal the chef prepared for them was as good as any five-star restaurant in Manhattan.

Suzie wore a pair of tight, white, spandex shorts with flip flops, and a sexy, green bathing suit cover up over a black, bikini top. Gino looked handsome in a pair of white, linen shorts and Cuban shirt which draped over the shorts. His Panama hat with a black band, and black, alligator skin loafers finished the look.

"You are going to make me fat, Gino. Nothing can be worse for you than a fat, Chinese lady," Suzie joked.

"Did you enjoy the meal and the Sassicaia?"

"That was the best wine I've ever tasted. How do you pronounce it again?"

"Sass-e-kiya."

"It almost sounds Japanese," Suzie joked. She placed her hand inside Gino's thigh and squeezed ever so slightly. Gino was sipping his espresso and nearly choked on it.

Mickey Roach knocked on the weather-worn, cedar shingles at the rear of the house.

"Gino, pardon me. I need a second please," Mickey asked.

Gino put his hand on Suzie's which was still on his thigh and removed it tenderly.

"Hold that thought, please." Gino smiled and waited a few seconds for his erection to dissipate before standing up and walking behind the wall to Mickey.

"What's up, Mick?"

"Just wanted you to know that the piece of work on the Bowery is done. Good results. The place is wrecked," Mickey whispered in Gino's ear.

"Any casualties?"

"Only the building."

"Good; it's good that we're out here," Gino stated.

"Padrone, just be careful with this lady, will you? Remember blood is thicker than water. She is Chinese first, then she is a woman," Mickey warned.

"Thank you, consigliere. I think I have it covered."

"Carmine, Sr. would always say, 'un pelo pubico ha la forza di venti cavalli. Ma e vero. And it's true, Gino," Mickey advised.

Gino chuckled, "One pubic hair has the strength of twenty horses. I remember that expression from the old timers. Mickey, non si preoccupa il mio amico. Don't worry," Gino said. He kissed Mickey on both cheeks.

I think in this case it may be one hundred horses, Mickey thought.

CHAPTER 22

"It's going to be a bloody war, maybe the biggest ever," Matt Baker offered. He was speaking to his direct supervisor Luis Figueroa, First Deputy Commissioner Frank Byrne, and Chief of Detectives, John Esposito.

Matt was called into the 'Puzzle Palace' commonly known as One Police Plaza, the headquarters of the NYPD, to report directly to the brass. They were in the First Deputy Commissioner's office on the twelfth floor of the thirteen-story, red-brick, rectangular building near the Brooklyn Bridge in lower Manhattan. PP1, as some call the complex, is more like a fortress than an office building, with tight security every-where.

First Dep. Byrne's office is decorated to suit his larger than life ego. Photographs of Byrne with every president, pope, mayor, ball player, judge, and celebrity took up much of the walls in the twenty-four-foot by twenty-four-foot corner office. A collection of antique police badges, hats, night sticks, and other memorabilia from around the world were displayed in glass cabinets, much like a museum.

"What makes you think there is going to be a huge, gang war, Detec-tive? We have no intel on that at all. What makes you think you know something we don't? You and Little Miss Suzy take a roll in the hay?" Byrne asked.

Matt ignored the comment and turned his focus to the other two. "The two homicides at the Tea Parlor on Doyers Street was a hit related to the building of the hotel at 50 Bowery. Evidently there was a non-pay-ment issue which was due the Miceli clan."

"Detective Baker, I don't like the word 'evidently'," Byrne chided.

"Sorry, sir. May just be a poor choice of wording on my part. Our intel came from two separate sources- one on the Miceli side, from a perp facing a twenty-year sentence for narcotics sales, and one from a Flying Dragon member facing a rape charge," Matt informed.

"Go on, Detective," Byrne ordered.

"The real money behind the hotel is the Hip Sing Merchants Association. They refused to use any union workers on the job- that's how the Micelis got involved. The only non-union show in town for pouring concrete is Global Sand and Concrete in College Point, a company with ties to the Miceli family. There are other concrete companies, but they were all told to stay away from this job leaving Global Sand as the only source for the builders. The official owners, Chinatown-Bowery LLC held back paying for two-thirds of the concrete job. The two deceased from the Tea Parlor are known members of the Miceli crime family per O.C.C.B. intel," Matt reported.

"So, how do you tie this bombing to the Micelis?"

"Sir, that is an assumption I came up with in conjunction with O.C.C.B. It makes sense, but there is always the possibility of..."

"Please don't say the word 'terrorism', Detective! We'll have the God damned White House, the mayor's office, the global media, and every other swinging dick waiting for us to proclaim the T word. The mayor wants the federal money so he's probably already on his way here now, God-forbid," Byrne screamed.

"Sir, I was going to say, there is always the possibility of a competing Tong. Perhaps the On Leong, but we highly doubt that in this case," Matt calmly corrected the Deputy Commissioner.

Chief of Detectives Esposito let a tiny smile form on his mouth to express his pride in his young detective.

"Johnny, if you don't have an objection, I would like to put Detective Baker here on loan to O.C.C.B. Manhattan South," Byrne queried.

"Of course, whatever it takes, Chief," Esposito declared.

"Good. Do your best, Detective. I understand you're a candidate for the sergeant's exam."

"Yes, sir. I'm preparing for it now," Matt answered.

"Good luck, Baker. We need bright, young men like you coming up the ladder, so study up," Byrne pronounced.

§§§§

"So you are telling me Gino Ranno is conveniently out of town? That coward fuck is not hiding from the cops...he's hiding from me! Ranno knows I will gut him like a fish, that faggot bastard. He has some big balls to do what he did to me- to us. Those greedy guineas want everything for themselves: the unions, the construction, gambling, everything they can put their greasy hands on," Cabbagehead rambled. He and a crew of nine Flying Dragons were meeting at his office in the Hip Sing office on Pell Street.

"We are trying to figure out where he is, Danny. His office in Manhattan in dark. No bodyguards, nothing at all hanging around. The Club Macanudo where he puffs away hasn't seen him in a few days. His apartment in the Bronx, same thing. The doorman hasn't seen him in days. It's like he took off for Sicily like he's done in the past," Peter replied.

"Great. All this surveillance equipment to track him, and you lost him? What the fuck? And don't involve our people in Palermo if we find out he is there- not for now at least. I don't want to fight a war on two fronts. We are in a great position with the Palermo mob. Most of our smack comes through them and the Camorra in Naples and I don't want to interrupt our flow of product. These Italians stick together like we do. For the most part that is," Cabbagehead ordered.

"Got it," Peter agreed.

"Hit the streets, hard. Ten g's for information on where Ranno is. I want this so-called Godfather dead; do you hear me? Dead!"

"Already done, Danny. If he shows up, what then?" Peter asked.

"We will plan accordingly. Remember what Sun Tzu said; 'He will win who knows when to fight and when not to fight'. Maybe we ask for a sit down first and see what the true cost will be," Cabbagehead reasoned.

"I'm told by our people the damage to our hotel will delay the opening for at least six months," Peter informed.

"Unacceptable!" Cabbagehead started pounding his fist on the table and his crew knew what that meant. Peter opened a cabinet and took out a glass and a bottle of Hennessy. He poured a drink handing it to Cabbagehead to calm him down. "God-fucking-damn it! I expect a faster turnaround. Right now, I want you to find that old man, the so-called security dude, and bring him in so I can lean on him," Cabbagehead commanded. He took the and threw the glass, water and all, into the sink. The glass shattered.

"He is the grandfather of a 426. We shouldn't lean too hard," Peter said.

"Bullshit!"

"Danny, who would have thought Ranno would attack our place? The old man was just a…."

"A what? He was hired as a favor. You buy cheap, you get cheap. I want four, armed Dragons around the hotel starting tomorrow."

"Already done," Peter responded.

CHAPTER 23

Suzie and Gino were dancing closely to one of Gino's all- time favorite ballads by Dean Martin.

I've grown accustomed to your face
She always makes the day begin
I've grown accustomed to the tune she whistles
night and noon
Her smiles, her frown, her ups and downs…

Suzie interrupted Dino's melodious voice, "It's been such a lovely day and night Gino. First the helicopter ride, then the drinks and antipasto, a fabulous dinner with amazing wine, and now, getting to be here with you and enjoying the lake. You really know how to treat a lady."

"It really was extraordinary, wasn't it?" Gino whispered.

"But now I think it's time for bed," Suzie cooed.

"Oh, I'm sorry. The time just seemed to slip away. C'mon, let me walk you to your room," Gino offered.

Suzie's cellphone made the rushing sound of a waterfall.

She left Gino and went to the wicker coffee table on the deck. Suzie checked her screen and saw it was from her assistant, Alison.

"Excuse me, I need to take this call."

The conversation was taking place in Mandarin Chinese, and Gino could not make any sense out of what was being said, which bugged him. Suzie's face was not at all animated.

"Yes, go ahead!" Suzie blurted as she answered the phone. Alison could tell she was not happy about the interruption.

"I-I'm so sorry, Miss Ping but there has been a major development we thought you should know about," Alison offered.

"Tell me," Suzie snapped. Suzie paced, keeping a fair distance away from Gino. She pressed the phone tight to her ear so he hopefully wouldn't overhear the conversation.

"Someone placed bombs in the new hotel. The top floors and the lobby and kitchen are virtually destroyed! And your friend over here is going wild... and he is blaming the Italians... and he came by to speak with you..."

"Alison, slow down. You're rambling."

"O.k., O.k." She let out an audible sigh, then continued, "Anyhow, I told him you were away, and I was not aware of where you were or when you were coming back," Alison uttered.

"Very good, I will be home on Monday. My friend doesn't have this number so don't give it. Anything else?"

"Uh, yes. Your friend broke two of the new vases. I took them in for repair."

"Fuck! Shit!" Suzie was furious but didn't want Gino asking any questions when she got off the phone. "Okay, good job. Stay close to the situation and call me if you need," Suzie replied. Her voice was more conciliatory.

Suzie hit the end call button and lay her phone back down on the table, face down. "So sorry. Now, where were we?" Suzie asked Gino.

"Is everything alright? Gino asked as he drew his China doll close to him.

"Just some silliness with a bank in Hong Kong; the bane of my existence," Suzie lied.

"Well, you were saying it was bed time. Let's say good night to the boys," Gino whispered as he gently stroked Suzie's hair. He could feel himself starting to get hard.

The aroma of cigar smoke and the shuffling of playing cards made

Gino think twice about saying goodnight. *Who the hell need the looks-those hairy eyeballs I'm going to get?* Gino thought. He took Suzie by the hand and changed direction toward the stairs.

The pair laughed as they walked slowly up a winding, maple wood staircase to the second floor which was appointed with modern, Italian, white furniture, fresh flowers in long, elegant, lavender vases which stood atop marble buffet tables. Four, Giancarlo Impiglia original art deco prints, hung on blue and black silk wallpaper. The flooring was a combination of Persian rugs and white and gray porcelain tiles.

There are four-bedroom suites on the second floor, spread out comfortably for privacy. The lower level had three smaller bedrooms where Joey, Mickey, C.C., and the bodyguards would retire after their boss was comfortably settled in. They planned to take four-hour shifts-two men awake at all times as a security precaution. The Sicilians were armed with Beretta shotguns and Smith and Wesson .45 automatic handguns. They took the first shift.

Mickey, Joey, C.C., and one of the other bodyguards played Pinochle on a round card table in a study off the large living room.

Gino walked past his bedroom to the suite where earlier, Suzie had freshened up and changed from her traveling clothes.

"I'm sorry I was rambling on; I should have realized you were tired," Gino whispered.

Suzie looked at Gino and moved closely into him. She looked softly into his eyes and smiled, exposing her perfect, white smile. Suzie kissed Gino on his mouth separating his lips with her soft, damp tongue. She pressed her hot body against his until she felt his erection against her thigh.

"First-of-all, who said I was tired?" Suzie whispered, her hot breath sending a chill up and down Gino's spine.

Gino reached in again for another passionate kiss. Suzie purred her appreciation sending Gino's heart into overdrive.

"Your place or mine?" Gino asked. He felt his voice quiver like a teenager on his first date.

"You pick."

Gino took his first Chinese conquest by the hand into his room, while Suzie followed her first Italian conquest to his bed.

CHAPTER 24

The morning after the blast, Cabbagehead, his right-hand Peter Fong, and two other high ranking Dragons took a tour of the damage at 50 Bowery. The job's construction manager and two civil engineers joined them. The FDNY had not yet given clearance to enter the building, but Cabbagehead made his own rules.

"It looks like they planted the bombs to do the most damage without encouraging an implode. This could have been a lot worse, gentlemen. They could have effected a total property collapse," Andrew Lorenz, one of the engineers said.

"They did do some structural damage to the top floors though. Nothing major, however. Some of the corner beams are bent, but can be replaced to code. When we go down to the lobby and kitchen we will show you the damage is mostly equipment, ceilings, walls, and flooring which are totaled. No damage to the structure at all," the other engineer, John Chung noted.

"And how long will all this take to repair?" Peter asked.

"Better part of six, seven months, for sure," Chung said.

Cabbagehead let out a farting noise with his lips, his serpentine, dagger eyes showing his disapproval.

"That is way too long, gentlemen. We have partners in the Far East we must answer to. They were expecting a huge opening next month, with all the bells and whistles. How in the fuck can we explain this may carry over into next year?" Peter explained.

"If we put crews on around the clock, perhaps we can shorten the time by better than half that six months. But that's costly, and we will need local variances. The city is not enthusiastic about those kinds of things. Christ, then there's OSHA!" Lonny Sung the construction superintendent stated.

Cabbagehead made the farting noise again.

"We will deal with the god damn city and OSHA. They are the least of our problems! Your job is to go balls-to-the-walls and get this place opened in eight weeks," Peter demanded.

"I don't think that's possible with...," Sung blurted.

"Just fucking get it done! Peter interrupted. "Work with these two, engineer guys and make sure everything is fucking perfect," Peter said.

Cabbagehead cleared his throat rather than make the crass farting sounds. His face was red as he had been holding in the furious emotion he was feeling. *I am surrounded by fucking idiots!* he said to himself.

"I want you all to pay attention to what I'm about to say." He spoke clearly and succinctly and everyone knew he was trying not to blow. "We must show whoever the fuck did this to us that we do not fear them. You hear me? One, I want the construction to begin immediately. Demolition and repair right now." He was now speaking quickly as his mind was racing. "We are self-insured so we have no reason to wait for some corporate, insurance assholes to have ten meetings to find a reason not to pay us! Everyone who worked on this job should be brought back... at lower rates. Do you hear me? Lower rates. Everyone-everyone must share in our loss or they will never work on another one of our jobs, or in Chinatown period. Put that word out. If we need twenty-four-seven workers, then so be it. I've had enough of our people being excluded in this country, and I've had enough of looking at this mess. Peter, call the circle and have them meet us at Pell," Cabbagehead commanded, sweat now pouring from his forehead.

Peter followed Cabbagehead back to the office on Pell Street making the appropriate calls on his cellphone to the top Hip Sing crew members. Peter could tell that Danny was about to erupt.

Within thirty minutes, everyone convened as Cabbagehead demanded. The old man security guard was waiting in the office when Peter and Danny arrived.

'What happened, grandfather?" Cabbagehead demanded.

"I am so sorry for this…I am an old man and I fell asleep. There haven't been any problems in a very long time. I…"

"Enough!" Cabbagehead slammed his clenched fist on his desk. "Just tell me what you saw! Who did this to us?"

"I don't remember much. I saw three men and yelled at them to go… to get off the property. One man slammed me on the side of my head and then I woke up on a park bench somewhere. I don't remember how I got there."

"What did they look like? How old?"

"I'm sorry; I don't remember the two very clearly except they seemed like old men. All white people look similar to me, but they seemed older, not as old as me… but the third one, the man who hit me, looked like maybe a Viking. His hair was red; his beard was red, too."

"If you saw this man again, or his photo, would you be able to say it was him?"

"Perhaps, yes. Perhaps no."

"Grandfather, I will take pity on you because of your age and your grandson. I respect age and family above all else. And I have taken a sacred oath to protect all our families. That is why you have not been thrown from the roof of the building. Anything else?" Cabbagehead queried. He stared through the old man.

The old man put the two, fifty dollar bills on Cabbagehead's desk with trembling hands. "I found this in my pocket."

Cabbagehead looked at the money and stared for a few seconds. He burst into bellowing laughter.

"Grandfather, you take this and go straight to the mah jongg table. I think today is your lucky day."

The old man, bent with age, wrinkled like a yellow prune, took the cash and left quickly.

Cabbagehead addressed his men, "Contact our people in Palermo and Naples. I want our shipments doubled for the next few months. Make sure our gambling rooms raise their income. Peter, you and I must meet with Baby Sister. She needs to bring in more product for us. I want more action here and in New Jersey. We need to pay for this loss with our own wits. Any other ideas?"

"Maybe we should lean on the restaurants and stores a bit harder," a Dragon leader offered.

"No. They are already into us enough. But this gives me an idea. All imports we can get our hands on? We will tax an additional five percent. Have our boys look for ways to raise more cash. They will be amply rewarded and recognized. Cabbagehead was feeling better now. He loved to fight, loved the challenge, and had his plan. In his mind at this point, Gino was fucked. He laughed as he lit a Camel cigarette and smoked it. It was now time for him to find one of the girls and "relax".

CHAPTER 25

The morning after Gino and Suzie spent their first night together was promising to be magnificently, glorious weather in Montauk. The keow, keow, and ha-ha-ha-ha sound from the seagulls flying over the lake house woke Suzie just after dawn.

The fragrant and distinct bouquet of honeysuckle wafted up into the bedroom. The sound of a fishing boat horn off in the distance of Montauk harbor and the scent of the lake water were all foreign to Suzie. She had spent the formative years of her life in a landlocked town in Northern China, most of her adult working life in the cities of China, and for the past few years, in New York's Chinatown. Life had never been easy for Suzie and her family, at least until her sister, Cheng Chu Ping, Sister Ping, had made it big in the United States.

Suzie woke Gino with a tender kiss.

"Gino, sweetie, I am going for a run around the lake. Would you like to join me?"

"What? Oh, good morning! Did you say run? After last night, I don't know if I can even walk," Gino teased.

"C'mon, silly man. You need exercise to stay fit, my love." Suzie kissed Gino on the lips, neck, and continued down to his manly chest, ending with a swirling of her tongue insinuating he would need his strength if she continued to go lower.

Gino's body tensed with excitement, and he let out a heavy sigh. "I think you're right. Normally, every time I feel like I need to exercise, I lie down until the feeling goes away," Gino quipped.

"Would you please come on? It's good for you."

Gino put his hand on her hip, pulled her in closer, and kissed her forehead. "I'm good! Sleep is good for me, too. I'll wait right here for you,"

Gino whispered as he turned and pulled the sheets over his head.

Suzie laughed. "Okay then. We can shower together when I get back."

"Now that would be VERY good for me!" Gino joked.

Suzie bounded down the stairs in her sneakers and black, Nike exercise outfit- tight, lycra running shorts, a two-tone pink sports bra, and black, Nike sneakers. Her iPhone Seven ear buds were already spewing out her music. Hearing the sound of steps from the stair case, Joey Clams and Mickey who were in the kitchen having coffee and cigarettes, went to see what was going on.

Suzie, momentarily startled, pulled the buds from her ears.

"Good morning! Sorry if I disturbed you!" Suzie declared, all smiles.

"Not at all Miss Ping; we've been up for a while," Joey replied shyly.

"Would you care to join me for a jog?" Suzie offered.

"Our running days are way behind us, but thanks for asking," Mickey replied trying not to stare at Suzie's in-shape body.

"Okay, see you in a bit!" Suzie said as she bounced toward the door.

"I don't like this one bit," Mickey blurted.

"I don't either...I'm very jealous," Joey joked.

"I'm fucking serious. I already have feelers on the street. This broad can be a total set up. I don't trust these Chinese motherfuckers as far as I can throw them," Mickey cautioned.

"She's just a piece of ass, Mick," Joey whispered.

"Nah! Do you see the way Gino looks at her? I tell you he's smitten. He thinks he's in love again."

"You know what they say about Chinese pussy, right?"

"Cut the shit, Clams. I'm as serious as cancer over here."

'Why are you so crazy over this, Mick?"

116

"Why? Areyoukiddinmeorwhat??? Gino is not acting like a Don. He's making the same mistakes as other bosses I've known. Look at Castellano with his maid! He was banging the fucking, hired help, for god's sake. Big Paul lost all respect from the guys he was supposed to be leading. They saw him as weak- a man who thought with his dick."

"Do you really think Gino is being looked at this way? Even after he took his revenge on those Chinese bastards with his job at the hotel?" Joey asked.

"That was leadership...yes. But this spells absolute, fucking danger for Gino and for all of us. Trust me on this one, Joey."

"So, now what?"

"I don't know yet. But if and when I do, I'm going to have a real, old fashioned sit-down with our boss."

CHAPTER 26

Matt Baker was at the Organized Crime Control Bureau office at Manhattan South precinct for a briefing on the Miceli family's criminal activities. The mood was tense as the team of investigators, cops, and inspectors tried to sort through all the crap to see who they could haul in about the Bowery blow up. The room was filled with chain smokers except for Matt who rubbed his eyes every so often, but never said a word about it.

Just like in all the FBI movies Matt had ever seen, on one of the walls there was a pyramid-shaped, organizational chart of the Miceli Crime family. At the bottom were photos and names of the many Soldiers who reported to the Capos. Next came the Underboss, then the Consigliere then the Don, with a recent photo of Gino Ranno affixed to the top of the chart.

"Since Carmine Miceli, Sr. died, there has been a vacuum in the Miceli Family. The Feds have Carmine, Jr. by the short hairs, and Ranno has no real street experience," Inspector Mike Abbate proclaimed. Abbate, a first-generation Sicilian who speaks fluent Italian and Sicilian, has been the head of O.C.C.B., the Organized Crime Control Bureau, for eight years.

"Would you say the Micelis are almost done here?" Matt asked.

"They're not putting a going out of business sign out just yet. Just because they are not as visible as they were under Gotti, doesn't mean the ballgame is over by any means. I'll go over their various cash flows with you in a minute. Suffice it to say, Ranno is not a true gangster, and that's a problem with the rank-and-file. He did get lots of street cred on the war with the Brighton Beach Russians and if your theory is correct, his stock just went up big-time with this hotel bombing. By the way, I do think your opinion on the matter is right on point. However, we have no proof right now, and that's why you've been assigned to us for the time being," Abatte stated.

"Thank you, Inspector. I'm happy to help in any way I can."

"Construction and the unions are the main focus the Micelis have. Here is a list of companies and unions they own or are in control of. Their bread-and butter is still illegal gambling, loan sharking, and extortion. Drugs seem to be out of the income stream largely on the advice of Mickey, the Roach, Ranno's consigliere, an old timer from Sicily with the old guard values. He came up with Carmine, Sr. and was his number one button man. Roach has major contacts in Italy and Sicily from way back, and it seems he imports strong armed zips when he needs a special piece of work done."

"Did he bring in the zips for the hotel job?" Matt asked.

"I doubt that very much. You're young, but have you ever heard of the Westies?"

"Yeah, you mean the Irish gang from Hell's Kitchen from back many years ago?" Matt replied.

"Yes, correct. They were a small group of crazies Mickey Roach worked closely with to blow things up when the Micelis needed to send a message, or needed a hit with a car bomb. A few years ago, these knuckleheads blew up a pizza shop up in the Bronx. It had the Westies M.O. written all over it, however we didn't have a collar on that one. These guys are pretty much stealth operators. Former IRA members do their grunt work. It's an assumption, but the hotel job looks like their work."

"Really? So what do you think we should do now?" Matt asked.

"We have intel from an Irish bar in Yonkers. One of our undercover boys spotted The Roach around there a few days before the bombing. No proof and no probable cause, but it's a start. We're keeping our eyes on a William Brady, but he has one foot in the grave and another on a banana peel. He is a sick guy with a big drinking problem. To answer your question, we need to decide if we call The Roach in to shake things up a bit or go right to Ranno," Abatte said.

"I think they may start fighting on the streets with this Cabbagehead's crew in Chinatown, don't you think?" Matt queried.

"I do. Unfortunately, the Chinese don't open their traps up much. They don't have the bravado like the Italians do, and we've never had any luck getting someone inside their organization. The mafia has this omerta thing which has gone the way of the dodo bird; The Chinese, however, wrote the book on silence."

CHAPTER 27

Billy Seragusa, Larry Pieroni, and Joey "Shades" Piccirelli, three, made-men in the Miceli crime family, all members of Joey Clams' crew, and all top earners on the construction side of the borgata, the family in mob parlance, were having lunch at Enzo's restaurant in the Morris Park section in the Bronx. The three wise guys met once a week to discuss business and to let off some steam. Sometimes their lunch would last three hours at their favorite haunt.

"We need to have eyes behind our heads these days. What with the Chinks spitting in the boss' face and then that loud noise at that friggin' hotel, who knows what's next?" Joey Shades remarked.

"Another good reason to stay away from downtown for a while," Seragusa added.

"Me? I don't give a fuck about these slope-eyed bastards. I think this thing will be settled very soon. I hear rumors that that fat Cabbageface wants a sit-down," Pieroni blurted.

"It's Cabbagehead Larry, but, you know? Come to think of it, he does have a Cabbageface now that you mention it," Seragusa laughed.

All three raised their glasses in a toast.

"Here's to Hop Sing!" Shades pronounced.

"It's Hip Sing Joey…Hip, not Hop," Seragusa corrected.

"Who's talking about that? I meant Hop Sing, the Chink on that old T.V. show Bonanza…remember with Pa Cartwright and that fat Hoss and the other two?" Shades reminisced.

"You are one sick dude," Seragusa added.

They clinked glasses and laughed.

"By the way, I really appreciate Gino didn't sit down after they whacked our guys. I was close to Vinnie from when we were kids. That was a bull-shit thing that happened," Larry said.

"You never know when your number comes up in this life. You go into the wrong place at the wrong time, or say the wrong thing, and bam! Lights out," Seragusa said.

"That's what I'm saying. We need to have eyes everywhere," Shades added.

"Question. When they start rebuilding that hotel, do we put the rat out again?" Larry asked.

"Fuck no! That ship has sailed. Unless Clams says so, and I doubt it, we should just let them finish so we can try to get a piece of the action after they open," Seragusa stated.

"Not gonna be easy. The Chinks are really pissed off, I'm sure," Larry said.

"So that's what we should get at the sit-down. An agreement as to what our take will be going forward," Shades recommended.

"That's if the boss will even make a sit-down with these shit heels," Seragusa argued.

"No way Gino goes. No chance. He'll leave that to The Roach," Shades challenged.

"I got a grand that says Gino goes. He's never gonna show fear to those slope heads… guaranteed," Larry said.

"You got it. A grand…you want in, Billy?" Shades asked.

"I'm gonna sit this one out."

"Let's eat and then I got a surprise for you two," Larry announced.

"Lemmie guess…those three Russian whores on Eighty-Forth Street, right?" Shades asked.

"You prick! It was gonna be a surprise!"

"I'm not even hungry; let's blow this place. Besides they always have a nice spread over there," Seragusa said.

Let's go. I got this." Larry put a fifty and a twenty for the drinks on the table.

The trio said their good-byes to the owner and to the waiter, all three kissing the owner on his cheek.

"I can't wait to get that twenty-three-year old Vanessa's legs wrapped around me!" Larry announced.

"Oh, nooo…she's my one and only love. Maybe we have to choose for her like in a stickball-game," Shades laughed.

Shades held open the door of the restaurant for Larry and Seragusa. He lit a cigarette and the three made-men stood in front of Enzo's for a moment.

Suddenly the side door of a cream-colored van which was parked at the meter next to Enzo's on Williamsbridge Road was flung open.

Three Flying Dragons, one with an AK-47, one with a Mossberg 500 pump action shotgun and one with an AR-15 assault rifle opened fire on the unsuspecting wise-guys. They silently opened up on the unsuspecting targets.

Part of the storefront windows of the restaurant came crashing down from the hail of rounds. The shades and draperies on the windows flew back in the torrent of fire. Some of the bullets went through the trio and some missed, going through to the restaurant's back walls. Larry was flung back through the plate glass window by a blast of the Mossberg. Seragusa fell into a heap clutching his barrel chest, his blood flowing rapidly onto the concrete sidewalk. Shades was hit through his sunglasses, stomach, and legs, collapsing to the concrete pavement in a bloody mess. He moaned once before gasping his last breath.

The door of the van was snapped closed quickly. The vehicle drove away slowly, as if they were out for a Sunday drive toward Pelham Parkway.

The bloody war Detective Matt Baker predicted was in full swing.

CHAPTER 28

Suzie returned from her forty-minute jog and found Gino sitting Indian style on the bed, working on his laptop.

"How was the run, Sweetie?"

"Great! I freakin' love this place. If you don't buy it, I swear, I will!"

"After this weekend. I'm sold also," Gino agreed.

"Maybe partners then?" Suzie asked. She realized her remark sounded a bit forward considering the timing of their relationship.

"Well, I mean…as a business proposition. I don't want to scare you off, Gino," Suzie added.

"I can't think of anything that could scare me away from you, Miss Suzie Ping. Now, you said something about, um, a shower?"

Suzie laughed and made her way toward the shower. Gino heard the shower turn on and saw something flying at him from behind the bathroom wall. It was Suzie's damp, jogging shorts.

Gino, unsure of how he would perform with a twenty-year younger woman, had swallowed a twenty milligram Cialis pill while Suzie was on her run. He wasn't certain if it was Suzie's gorgeous face and body or Cialis that made him perform like he was a twenty-eight year old the night before, but what Gino did know was that the performance enhancing medication gave him morning wood again like he hadn't had in years.

"May I see your driver's license for a moment?" Suzie asked when the fully erect Gino entered the shower. The shower could have easily fit eight people, with a wrap-around marble bench, and black and white spotted tumbled marble tile which went from ceiling to floor. Suzie was standing under a seven-jet shower, the water hitting her luscious body in every direction.

"My driver's license? What for?" Gino asked.

"You mentioned, not that I asked, but you mentioned you were in your mid-sixties. After last night and seeing that thing coming at me this morning, I simply don't believe you," Suzie teased.

The shower was suddenly steamy... and lasted the better part of an hour.

§§§§

The chef prepared a brunch of eggs Benedict with a killer, fresh-caught, crab hollandaise sauce, cold, lobster salad with a cold curried vermicelli pasta, and an assorted fruit platter. The house, which was on two acres of lakefront property, was surrounded on three sides by a virtual forest of greenery, including a seventy-food strip of sand on Lake Montauk. The chef served the delightful meal on a bistro table for two, under a huge, royal blue umbrella on that waterfront beach. The two Sicilian bodyguards made themselves scarce but milled around the property with their weapons in full view.

Suzie looked ravishing in a sleeveless red and yellow short floral sundress. Gino could hardly take his eyes off her. "What's on our agenda today?" Suzie asked.

Gino shook himself back into reality and cleared his throat. He smiled at his lovely lady. She stared back into his eyes and smiled back. "I hadn't planned too much. Thought maybe we would enjoy the sunshine and maybe take a boat ride around the lake." *I can't believe I find myself without words around her!* Gino thought to himself.

"Sounds perfect! But if it's okay with you, I have some work to get done on my laptop, first."

"Absolutely, I have some things to catch up on, too. I guess your day is twenty-four seven with the time difference in the Far East."

"And those bankers seem to have no perception of time. Calls, e-mails, faxes, texts at all hours of the day and night. It's almost inhumane," Suzie proclaimed.

"I hate to mix business with pleasure, but why are you dealing with banks and not private investors or factors? Are your credit lines so large?"

"No, they're not so large that I can't use private funds, but banks make things easier when you borrow from them, especially in China. Besides, I don't trust private investors, they always seem to want to butt in and run things," Suzie exclaimed.

"I get it. I get it. It's just that I have friends with deep pockets...lots of cash...who are looking to park their funds here and there. Strictly passive investors."

"Gino, if you mean you and your connected friends...yes, I'm all ears. Except, well, I wouldn't want things like money to get between us. I'm feeling I can get very used to being with you," Suzie purred as she moved in closer to Gino. She fed him a sliced, fresh strawberry from her fork.

"I'm at the age where I'm counting how many Saturday nights are left. I'm not sure if what I'm feeling about you at the moment is infatuation or something deeper that's always eluded me."

"So I think we need to explore those mutual feelings over time. We can discuss business if and when we are both sure about each other. Is that fair to you?" Suzie queried.

"More than fair, Suzie. The more I get to know you the more I'm falling for you," Gino admitted.

The two love birds, the mafia Don and the human trafficking queen, passed the hours under the umbrella, chatting, having a few drinks, working on their individual business interests, and stopping for a few passionate kisses.

"Gino, can I have a minute...inside the house?" Mickey Roach inquired. Gino knew from the sound of Mickey's voice there was a problem.

"Subito, let's go," Gino responded.

Mickey led the way from the lakefront to the house. The two Sicilians suddenly showed themselves and followed close behind. Two of the other guards were on the house's deck, eyes scanning the property, seemingly ready for action.

"What's up, Mick?" Gino asked.

"Hold on 'til we get inside, Gino, please."

Once inside, Gino could see from the look on Joey Clams' face there was real trouble.

"Gino, I just got off the phone with our detective friend in the Four-Nine up the Bronx. Three of our guys, in my crew, where hit outside Enzo's less than an hour ago," Joey reported, his voice shaking with anger and sadness at the same time.

"Who?" Gino shouted, with an exhale like he was punched in the stomach, "Tell me, now!"

"Shades, Larry P., and Big Billy."

"Billy is Carmine, Jr.'s brother-in-law. Fuck!" Gino blurted. "Who the fuck...?"

Joey interrupted. "Our cop friend could get nothing from any of the people inside the fucking place or anyone even around the neighborhood. I called Enzo. He said all they know is three Chinese guys in a cream-colored van did the hit. His place is in shambles! He's hysterical, cuz you know, bad publicity and all."

"Alright, alright. Jesus Christ, alright! Mickey, send word to Enzo that we will cover his costs. The publicity we can't help him with. It's probably better for business in the long run. Fucking people love this shit. Look at Sparks. They killed Big Paul there…can't get in the fucking joint now."

"Jesus Christ, Gino, with all due respect who gives a fuck about Enzo? What are we gonna do here?" Joey demanded.

"Relax, pal. I know you are bleeding for your guys…me too. I want to think about our next move, okay? Shooting from the hip is not a plan, right Mick?"

"The boss is right, Joey. Let's just calm down and think this over. Gino, let's send the broad home," Mickey advised.

"Mick…first off, she's not a broad. Second, no…she stays until we leave, as planned, tomorrow. Third, contact Sicily. Perhaps we'll need some friends here," Gino commanded.

"Understood," Mickey replied.

"Call an emergency meeting of the other families for tomorrow night. They need to hear from me about this shit," Gino continued.

Gino lovingly patted Joey on his bald head and turned for the back door and the lake. When he was out of ear shot, the conversation continued.

"She stays? Va fa en cuolo. We are at war with these fucking Chinks and…this broad…this lady stays? See what I mean, Clams? This is not good," Mickey whispered to Joey.

CHAPTER 29

Suzie took a call from South Africa as Gino was returning from the house to the lakeside table. She signaled to Gino that she had a call and walked away from the table for privacy. Gino went to the table and stared out onto the Lake, thinking about his just murdered associates.

"This is Suzie Ping."

"Miss Ping this is Asanda Mjongile. I was given your name by mutual friends."

"Yes, I was expecting your call. What a lovely name!' Suzie exclaimed.

"Why, thank you. Every South African name has a meaning. Asanda means addition to the family. My last name means looking at you"

"How lovely!" Suzie stated politely again.

"I understand you are looking perhaps to do business here. I can tell you we have already done business with the Chinese. Your product is very popular here," Asanda declared.

"Well, it comes down to how difficult it is to export my products and what price we receive. We are doing quite well in the United States. What kind of inventory are you looking for?"

"The market here is quite wide open. I have outlets in Johannesburg where I am, Cape Town, Durban, and Bloemfontein. Plus, the ukuth-wala in the outskirts of the cities."

"I'm sorry, but I'm not familiar with that term."

"Forced marriage. Very lucrative, Miss Ping."

"I see. And boys?" Suzie kept pacing back and forth so she could keep an eye on Gino to make sure he didn't overhear her.

"They are used for a variety of jobs. Mostly agricultural but also for street vending in the cities, begging, and other activities which involve the police," Asanda advised.

"What are the ages you are looking for?"

"Nine and older. The work we have done with other Chinese is similar to what you have now, but we pay a premium price, as you will learn."

"I am certainly interested in learning more. Would you allow me to send my representative to have a face-to-face meeting with you? He is my cousin and runs our production from China," Suzie queried.

"That would be excellent. I will text you my contact information."

"Please do that, and I will reply. I am returning to my office in a day. I will contact you again," Suzie advised and ended the call.

Suzie returned to the table, kissing Gino softly on the back of his neck. Gino didn't move.

"Are you okay, my love?" Suzie asked.

"No, I'm not really. Some distressing news from the city."

"Oh, my. Want to talk about it?"

"No, sorry, not at the moment."

"Do we need to return?"

"Not until tomorrow, unless you need to go?"

"I will stay here with you, if that's okay?"

"Of course it is. I'm sorry, I just need a few minutes to gather myself."

"I have more work to do. I'll leave you to your thoughts," Suzie whispered, kissing Gino gently on his cheek.

§§§§

Back at the Hip Sing office on Pell Street in Chinatown, Cabbagehead was reveling in the successful hit on the Miceli family.

"Those guineas know they have a fight on their hands. I will make sure they agree to pay for what they have done to us if I have to turn this city on its head," Cabbagehead announced.

"Danny, let's not go too far. You are always quoting Sun Tzu and I have one for you to remember: 'A good commander is benevolent and unconcerned with fame', Peter said.

Peter was close enough to dare say what Cabbagehead needed to hear.

"Yes…you are right. We cannot get ahead of ourselves. Let's plan our next step as General Tzu would. You know the cops and the feds will make life miserable for both sides after this."

"What about asking for a sit-down? Possibly offer a truce?" Peter asked.

"Perhaps that will show weakness. Or perhaps the Italians will see that business comes first. This may be a brilliant tactic," Cabbagehead pronounced. He stood up from the black leather chair and stared at an ornate mirror behind his desk. He seemed to be happy with what he saw, studying his round, bald head by the centimeter.

"With your permission I will reach out to the Micelis through our regular channels," Peter said.

"You do that. In the meantime, advise the Dragons to lay low and watch their backs. And get that Andy Phan up here on the next plane out of New Orleans," Cabbagehead commanded.

"Already done, Danny."

CHAPTER 30

After a short time, the mood changed. "I have to go back. I'm to-tally distracted and I will be crappy company for you. We can do this again another time. I hope you understand?" Gino asked Suzie.

"Of course I do, Gino. I could see it in your eyes. Whatever happened must be real bad and needs your attention," Suzie responded.

"I chartered a helicopter for all of us to return. We're boarding in an hour."

"I'll be ready in ten minutes, honey. I'm behind you all the way," Suzie whispered.

"That's comforting, believe me," *but no woman can be ready in ten minutes,* Gino added just in thought.

An hour later, Gino's entire entourage boarded the Sikorsky and were whisked back to the Thirty-Fourth Street heliport. Suzie showed no fear this time but still held onto Gino's hand the entire forty-nine-minute flight. A dozen Miceli bodyguards awaited the aircraft in several, black SUVs. One of the vehicles was to bring Suzie back to her apartment in Chinatown.

"Suzie, once I can, I'll call you. I hope in just a few days," Gino explained.

"I'll wait for you as long as necessary."

"You are the best! I'm sorry, Sweetie."

Suzie put her hand on Gino's mouth and smiled as if to say there was no need to apologize.

Gino kissed her on her sweet mouth and helped her into the car. Suzie opened the window blowing a sweet kiss to Gino.

"Okay Mickey...let's get back to Seventy-Ninth Street," Gino said when he was in the safety of his car and the caravan of bodyguards.

"Gino! Are you paying attention? We can't go there. Christ, Gino! There are a bunch of media trucks around the place. Your apartment, too! The word is we got hit, and the press is making this their lead story, those attention seeking, mother-fuckers. No, we gotta go to your friend Louie's house in Westchester. He's in Italy, so it's ok. Don't worry, it's all set up," Mickey advised tersely.

"Sinatra called the media two-bit whores. Now I know why," Gino blurted.

"The press will make this a war, for sure," Joey Clams spouted.

"I think this Cabbagehead has already seen to that, don't you think?" Gino asked.

"We got a call from his people. They reached out to Charlie Lib and our friends on President Street. They want to talk. The cops called, too. They want to see you immediately," Mickey stated.

"When were you going to tell me all this, Mick?"

"With the lady around, I didn't get the chance. Jesus Christ, Almighty, Gino, I'm telling you now!" Mickey blurted.

"Sorry, kiddo. I'm on edge. What do you advise?" Gino apologized and asked his consigliere for his counsel.

"I say we get Atkins the lawyer to meet us up at our friend's joint is Eastchester; he said he'd close early for us. We call the cops then and let them know where to meet us. Not at Louie's house. No way. I don't trust these cocksuckers one bit," Mickey said.

"The Chinamen?" Gino queried.

"Them least of all, but I'm talking about the cops. Ten minutes after we tell the cops where we are, those Chinks will be called. That Fifth Precinct has a leak like a macaroni strainer.

No way will Cabbagehead try anything in Eastchester. If they do, believe me, we are more than ready," Mickey explained.

"Did you call our friends overseas?" Gino asked.

"They are already here and waiting for us at Louie's. The house is totally secure. I may be old but I can still get things done, Gino," Mickey declared.

"Never doubted you for a second."

"His fastball may be a bit slower, but his curve is still amazing," Joey Clams added. Mickey didn't get the analogy.

§§§§

The procession of vehicles moved quickly up toward Westchester County. Mickey called Saul Atkins from his cell-phone. The world-renowned lawyer was on his way to Armondo's Restaurant in Eastchester.

Mickey advised Gino to personally return the call to Mike Abbate of the NYPD, O.C.C.B. Gino complied.

"Inspector Abbate this is Gino Ranno. I understand you wish to talk with me," Gino said coldly.

"Yes, Mr. Ranno, thank you for returning my call. There is an urgent matter we would like to discuss with you," Abbate proffered.

"I can't imagine what this could be about, however, I have cooperated with law enforcement all my life. I can make myself available tonight, but it will need to be up in Westchester. Is that a problem for you?"

"That would be fine, although we would prefer if you came to our office, sir," Abbate offered.

"On the advice of my attorney, he thinks it's always better to meet on neutral ground. I'm sure you understand, Inspector."

"Okay, name the place and time, Mr. Ranno."

"My lawyer will be present of course, so how about in an hour or two at Armondo's in Eastchester. Nice food if you're hungry," Gino laughed.

"No, sir; I've already had my dinner. We will be there in an hour or so, depending on traffic."

"Okay, Inspector, no lights and sirens, please. I wouldn't want to disturb the rich people in Eastchester." Gino ended the call without waiting for a reply.

§§§§

Atkins was already at Armondo's when the convoy arrived. Gino walked into the restaurant passing a few of his bodyguards. He was casually dressed in a pair of blue linen slacks, a blue and gray Nat Nast shirt which hung smartly outside of his trousers, and a pair of brown, Italian loafers without socks. Atkins, in a full suit and tie, hugged Gino in the foyer of the elegant establishment.

The two men walked down three, marble steps and onto a plush, green carpet with gold speckles which made an interesting, swirling pattern. Atkins held onto the gold-colored banister which ran along the staircase.

"I may have to lay off golf for a while. My back is killing me," Atkins announced in his bellowing voice. His five-foot-six, athletic frame fit perfectly in his tapered, gray, Canali suit. The white shirt, loud red and black, woven-silk tie, and French cuffs put the lawyer in a class of affluent distinction. Atkins looked many years younger than his seventy-three years in spite of his thinning, gray hair.

"Stretch, Saul…ya gotta stretch before and after you play," Gino advised.

"Stretch, smetch. I barely have time to take a good crap in the morning anymore. Anyway, what does this inspector want? You aren't going to say shit anyway and he knows it."

"I guess he has to tell his bosses I met with him and I was intimidated or who knows what these guys think anymore?" Gino conjectured.

140

"Okay, you know the drill. Pleasant, not friendly… if he asks you a question I don't like, I will put my hand on your arm, and I will respond so try not to answer so quickly. Wait before you answer to give me a chance to digest and react. If he goes too far with his questions I will be firm with him so don't show any sign of surprise. Got it?"

"Got it!"

CHAPTER 31

Happy Family Therapy Center on Mott Street in Chinatown is owned by Cabbagehead through a maze of LLC's, none of which has the name Danny Chu attached.

Suzie Ping's new, young asset from Thailand, now called Mindy, and duly broken in by Cabbagehead and several members of the Flying Dragons, was on duty for any walk-ins who wanted a full body massage, a foot massage, a scalp message, or any sex act the client desired.

Her roommate, one of the two, new Chinese girls brought in by Suzie, was in Roosevelt hospital recovering from the rape and beating handed to her by Cabbagehead himself. She was dropped off at the emergency room by two of the Green Lantern rookies who told the attending nurses they found her in the street. The girl, now called Jen Woo, knew better than to tell who her actual assailant was. Her family in China would be slaughtered, she was told, if she opened her mouth.

The other roommate, broken in by the Dragons but otherwise unharmed, was sent to Flushing, Queens to a brothel which specialized in serving Hasidic Jewish men. She would soon pray for her day off, which began on Fridays at sundown due to Jewish tradition. Thank God these men were so religious.

Every patrolman, sergeant, lieutenant, and detective at the Fifth Precinct knew that Happy Family was off limits to them, either for personal service or for a collar. Happy Family was a favorite place for NYPD brass to go and relax and enjoy the comfort of the young girls who worked there.

"Hello, sir, so nice to see you again," the counter man greeted an Inspector from 1 PP. It was early morning, a favorite time for regulars who knew the girls were fresh at that time.

"What's new?" The 'Full Bird' queried. The inspector was assigned to

143

the license division at the Puzzle Palace'.

"I have new girl from Thailand, young and fresh, and very pretty. Very thin, like you like. She is free now. I call her…you see for yourself."

The counter man went behind a multi-colored, beaded curtain, returning in seconds with 'Mindy'.

"This is Mindy. She take good care of you. She cost a little more but worth it…you see. If you no like, you no pay."

"Very nice. I want my regular room," the inspector demanded.

The counter man blurted something to Mindy in broken Thai, who dutifully took her john behind the curtain and into a small room with a massage table and a single bed. Posters of the human anatomy, all in Chinese characters hung on the faded, light-blue walls.

The inspector stripped naked from his skivvies and lay face down on the massage table.

Mindy wore a pair of tight, black shorts and a plain, white, see-through halter top. Her nipples shown through and the inspector knew he was going to enjoy this fresh, new girl.

The girl began to massage the burly man, in his late fifties, on his neck and shoulders. She rubbed him from shoulders to toes, holding up a towel to shield his privates when he turned onto his stomach. He laughed, pushing the towel aside as he had no modesty.

Mindy worked the inspector's chest with her strong hands, slowly working her way down to his thighs and calves, avoiding his now semi-erect penis.

"Okay, baby girl, let's get started," the inspector stated. He grabbed her hand and pulled it on to his cock.

"Ohhh, you so strong! You so big!" Mindy announced in the few English words which were drilled into her.

"Wait until I ram it into you, baby girl," he laughed.

Mindy chuckled shyly not understanding what was said.

The inspector began to rub the girl's pussy through her shorts. Mindy stiffened at first, took a deep breath, and relaxed for fear of a complaint to her Flying Dragon boss. She knew any discipline for poor performance would be more brutal than the john could deliver. She squeezed her eyes shut trying to shut out the inevitable.

The inspector, a highly decorated member of the NYPD upper echelon, hopped off the table and pulled Mindy to the bed. He forcefully removed the girl's shorts, throwing them on to the massage table. Pushing Mindy down onto her knees, he pushed his fully erect member into her mouth. When she gagged, the cop grabbed her by the back of her neck, thrusting himself deep into her throat. The young girl gasped for air with each plunge.

The inspector held himself back from orgasm. He brought Mindy to her feet, turned her around and tried to insert himself into her.

"Condom!" Mindy demanded.

"No condom, no condom," he yelled.

"Condom! Necessary. Must have condom!" Mindy pleaded with her limited language skills.

Pushing the tiny girl's torso down onto the bed, the decorated inspector, hired to serve and protect, jammed himself into her, ignoring her loud pleas. The counter man heard the poor girl's cries and laughed aloud from the front of the store. Money over honor.

Mindy put herself into a trance hoping for a quick ending to her pain.

When the inspector finished, he wiped himself with a white, terry-cloth hand towel. Mindy fell back onto the bed in a heap, holding back her tears.

"Pretty good, baby-girl. I'll tell my friends about you."

As one of the thirty-five-thousand of New York's finest, the inspector dressed quickly, opened his wallet, and tipped Mindy with a twenty-dollar bill.

He left the room and met the counter man in an adjacent room.

"Sixty for massage, one ten dolla for the extra, with your discount," the counterman stated.

"And ten for you, my friend. See you next time."

After the inspector left, the sweaty counter man opened the door where Mindy was now sitting on the bed, in total disgust of her new life in America.

"You get money?" he asked, rubbing his fingers together with the international sign of cash.

Mindy showed the counter man the twenty. He promptly ripped the bill from her hand.

"This for me. You get paid later, after what you owe." He turned his back and walked out of the room.

CHAPTER 32

M att Baker and Inspector Mike Abbate arrived at Armondo's Restaurant in Eastchester within the time promised. Matt had driven his superior, as was protocol.

The two cops were not surprised at the show of force outside the two-story building which was reputed to be a mob hangout for decades.

"The feds tried to wire this place a couple of times. Struck out after the bugs were found. I think the owner sweeps the place clean twice a day at least," Abbate theorized.

"I was at a wedding here a few years ago. It was like a Who's Who in LCN," Matt said, alluding to the members of La Cosa Nostra.

Abbate led the way into Armondo's under the watchful eyes of Joey Clams, C.C., Mickey Roach, and a small platoon of Miceli soldiers. Mickey thought better about being at the meeting with Abbate. Nothing good could come of Mickey's presence with the head of the NYPD O.C.C.B.

A bartender, in full tuxedo, stood on duty behind the long, dark green, marble and mahogany bar. A similarly dressed waiter stood a fair distance from the table where Gino and Saul Atkins sat awaiting the police, but at attention, just in case one of the four guests would want something from the bar or kitchen.

Gino and Atkins were already at a square table for four; a cup of espresso and a bottle of Marie Brizzard anisette sat in front of Gino, Atkins a large ginger ale, no ice.

Out of respect for the law, both Gino and Atkins stood as Matt and his boss walked over to the table.

Gino addressed Abbate, the obviously older man, and offered his hand, which the inspector accepted.

"Inspector Abbate, I presume? I'm Gino Ranno. Do you know my attorney, Saul Atkins?" Gino asked.

"Only from television and the newspapers. My pleasure, Counselor. Please meet Detective Matt Baker. He is new to my staff," Abbate offered.

"Please, gentleman, sit down. May I offer a cocktail, an espresso, something to eat?" Gino offered.

"We are good on food, thank you, but I would love a cup of American coffee, light and sweet," Abbate requested.

"And you, Detective?" Gino asked.

"A double espresso would be fine, thank you," Matt responded.

Gino waved at the waiter and gave the order.

"So tell me, Inspector, what's on your mind?" Gino asked without tone.

"Mr. Ranno, we are concerned there is potentially a powder keg which is ready to blow between the Chinese Hip Sing Tong and the Miceli family. We are here to discuss the recent events, including two hits on Miceli family members and an explosion at 50 Bowery. Are you aware of these events, sir?"

Atkins put his arm on Gino's.

"Inspector Abbate, with all due respect, my client knows nothing of these events other than perhaps reports he saw on the nightly news or in the New York Post. Mr. Ranno is a retired real estate developer and a philanthropist. You can ask Cardinal Dolan to verify his generosity," Atkins noted.

"I know about Mr. Ranno's generosity, Counselor, however it's common knowledge Mr. Ranno holds an important position with the Miceli family," Abbate added.

"Of course he does, Inspector. The late Carmine Miceli, Sr. was a dear, family friend of Mr. Ranno's father and grandfather going back to their small town in Sicily many years ago. Mr. Ranno, at the request of both

Carmine, Sr. and Carmine, Jr. entered their business, their legitimate business I may add, to help manage the family finances and expand their real estate holdings, of which Mr. Ranno has some expertise," Atkins added.

"Mr. Ranno, are you familiar with the names Joseph Piccarelli, William Seragusa and Lawrence Pieroni?"

"Yes, I know their names," Gino answered.

"Were these associates under your employ, sir?"

Atkins again touched Gino's arm.

"Inspector Abbate!" Matt jumped slightly at the lawyer's loud response. "Your snide use of the word 'associate' has me puzzled," Atkins bellowed.

"I will rephrase that. Were these three gentlemen under the employ of any Miceli owned company?"

"Yes, they were and I was shocked to read they were murdered in cold blood yesterday," Gino responded.

"What did they do for the company?" Abbate queried.

"They were three, very good, long-term employees who worked as construction supervisors for Miceli Realty and Development, and I must tell you that this came as quite a shock to us," Gino answered.

"Were you in town yesterday?" Abbate persisted.

"No, I wasn't."

"Where were you then?"

Atkins quickly interrupted. "Excuse me, sir...." Just then the coffee was served. Atkins waited for the waiter to distance himself from the table. "My client is not under a subpoena nor is he under an indictment, and his whereabouts are a private and confidential matter. Suffice it to say he was out of the city yesterday."

"Forgive me, I was just trying to determine your whereabouts, Mr.

Ranno."

"May I, Inspector?" Matt asked. His boss nodded his head.

"Mr. Ranno, let's cut to the chase. I'm the new guy on the block so I will get my ass reamed later, but I want to say how things look to us. You were seen with two men at Forlini's Restaurant on Baxter Street the night those men were gunned down on Doyers Street, then a few days later a huge explosion rocked Chinatown in a building which had a long-disputed union problem. Then the hit yesterday on your construction employees. To me, to us, this looks like a turf war in the making. All we want to do is see it doesn't become a systemic problem in our city, pretty simple," Matt stated. Abbate looked at Matt like he was from a different planet, and with some pride at the young detective's direct approach.

Atkins jumped in once again. Young man…Detective, now you hold on just a minute, now. If you think we're going to sit here and take this nonsense, you both need to leave. My client agreed to see you gentlemen as a courtesy, and in no way, is he involved with these nefarious criminal acts. Your assumptions are baseless and without merit. Inspector, I'm surprised you would allow this kind of personal attack on a man who has no criminal record and is one of the pillars of our community," Atkins seethed.

"Calm down, everyone. Detective Baker, is it Baker?" Matt nodded. "I happen to meet with many people during my work week. I happen to enjoy the food at Forlini's. Been going there for many years. That doesn't mean I have anything to do with any killings or bombings or DWI's for that matter. I understand your concerns, and as a citizen of our great city I also am concerned about violence in our streets. This activity isn't good for anyone, especially in the business of buying and selling real estate properties. Nonsense like this hurts valuations, believe me when I say that. I've seen neighborhoods collapse over fear. However, there is nothing I can do for you as I am not the man you think I am," Gino articulated.

"Mr. Ranno, Mr. Atkins, I apologize for Detective Baker's zeal. I think we're all in agreement these types of horrible deeds need to stop. I appreciate you seeing us and sincerely thank you for your time," Abbate offered. The two policemen rose as one, shook hands all around. and left the table.

"That kid is some cowboy," Gino whispered to his attorney.

"Are you kidding me? That whole thing was planned. Classic good cop, bad cop. They got their message to you. They want you to settle this thing with the Chinese and be done with it," Atkins advised.

Matt got behind the wheel of the unmarked police car, Abbate on the passenger side.

"Great work, kid!" Abbate lauded.

CHAPTER 33

Cabbagehead enjoyed exercise and loved pushing himself at the gym. His daily routine included lifting free weights at Ludlow Fitness on Delancy Street or playing a pickup, half-court basketball game at the Chinatown YMCA at 273 Bowery. Known as Mr. Danny to the entire staff for his generosity to the Y and for his friendliness to everyone who utilized the facilities, Cabbagehead had carte blanche of the place, including being able to close the pool or gymnasium while he and his Dragons swam or competed on the courts.

This day, six Dragon bodyguards stood outside the gymnasium entrance to ward off the neighborhood kids and any interlopers who had bad intentions toward their boss.

Cabbagehead, Peter, and four of the best basketball players among the Flying Dragon's ranks had a three-on-three match, complete with unlimited hacking without making a foul call, except for the boss, of course. Cabbagehead took as good as he gave in a physical game, which was a cross between basketball, hockey, and martial arts.

The match was held on one of the four side courts which boasted new NBA-approved, Plexiglass backboards, donated by Mr. Danny.

Six-foot high, blue pads behind each net cushioned any body blows when the players made a hard layup. The polished, light-brown hardwood floors gleamed with a fresh, water based urethane finish Mr. Danny insisted be added every few months, at his expense. The overhead LED lights, also a Mr. Danny donation, shone brightly and reflected off the floors and white walls, giving an almost too bright effect.

"Danny, the Micelis will see us. They have two requests, one, that you personally attend the sit-down, as will Gino Ranno, and two, that it be in neutral territory. I see no issues with either," Peter announced. The group was practicing their shots before the match began.

"That's why my number is higher than yours, my dear Peter. What is neutral ground for the Micelis? They fucking have a piece of everything. We have Chinatown, and not all of it, by the way. Those wops have long memories that go along with their long reach. The Italians are still determined to get the heroin trade back from us. They know how much money is involved in distribution and they are weak in other areas. That is not up for discussion. Fuck them Peter, no way, no how," Cabbagehead spouted as he made a layup, crashing into the cushions for effect.

"You have to realize the organized crime cops were at our office today to give us a clear message. The powers that be want this fight between us and the Italians to go away. To tell you the truth, I don't believe a war like this, with the Micelis and possibly the other families, will be in our best interests," Peter reasoned. The second in command took a three-point shot...all net.

"Do you believe we can win?" Cabbagehead asked. He walked up in Peter's face with a serious scowl on his face.

"Win? If the cops and the feds shut down our operations, the swag, the girls, the gambling, and other things, is that winning? If they throw you in prison what have we gained? Is that winning? I don't think so."

One of the bodyguards opened the gym door and raised a cellphone to get Cabbagehead's attention.

"Hold that thought, Peter," Cabbagehead ordered. He took the phone and brought it to his sweaty head.

"Yes? ... Yes, go ahead!... Was this verified?...hmm...they stayed together?...very good. Come and see me when you can...there will be a nice bonus for you," Cabbagehead pronounced. He smiled broadly, shook his head looking down at the court and handed the phone back to the bodyguard.

"I'm disappointed in you, Peter. You just haven't found our opponent's weakest spot... but luckily I have! Sometimes, like in basketball, I would rather be lucky than good," Cabbagehead declared. He took a three-point shot making an air ball, missing the rim and backboard.

"What do you mean?" Peter asked.

"You should have brought the Baby Ping situation to me before I was told by someone else."

"Ping situation?"

"That call just now was from our friend at the NYPD. Inside the Fifth.

It seems our dear friend, Suzie has been seeing one dago, Mr. Gino Ranno. This Ranno asshole is making the classic mistake of thinking with his dick. Now do you believe we can win?"

"Hmmm…that opens a different door for us," Peter admitted. He stood looking at his boss rather than take any practice shots. Cabbage-head made a reverse layup like he hadn't a care in the world but to score points.

"So who will take over for the Miceli family with Gino out of the way?" Danny asked.

"What do you mean out of the way?" Peter queried.

"Fucking dead! With all the security around Ranno, Baby Ping can poison the fucker, or slit his throat while he is banging her or something like that. Are you asleep, Peter?" The boss took a shot from the foul-line sinking it with help from the backboard.

"I…I…that never dawned on me, Danny. But how sure are you she will do a hit like this?"

"She will have no choice. Baby Ping is into us too deep not to go along with my plan. We can bury her and she knows it. She will be giving happy endings in one of our parlors when I'm finished with that bitch. On the other hand, we can drop a dime on her with the feds and she will end up like her sister. Dying in a federal prison, all dried up and ugly. Okay, let's get this game going. Twenty-two points wins!" the boss commanded.

"Poison will be a good way to off him, now that I think about it. But then she possibly will give up her life," Peter rationalized.

"Peter and you two, against me and these two. Then we round-robin…

Cabbagehead selected the teams for the first game. One way or another Peter, my friend, she is fucked unless she does things right. Ranno is not young, it can look like a heart attack, she killed him in the muff from that great, Chinese pussy of hers," Cabbagehead laughed.

"Do we call her in now?"

"Not just yet. Let them get cozier with each other. Remember reading about how the CIA was going to assassinate Fidel Castro so many years ago with poison? Go find out how they were going to poison the bearded one. He outlived all of them, and died in his bed, the shrewd bastard. I need you to start thinking ahead, like in a game of chess, four, five moves ahead," Cabbagehead decreed.

"You guys have the ball!"

CHAPTER 34

"I know the girl is not supposed to call the boy, but I miss you, Gino," Suzie said softly. She couldn't believe the deep feelings she was having for Gino. Gino was still at the safe house in Westchester. Suzie was at her desk in Chinatown but used her cell phone to call in case her office phone was being monitored, which is how the FBI nailed Sister Ping... tapping the phone in her small store.

"I miss you too, Sweetie. It's only been a few days but it feels so much longer," Gino replied.

"How are things? I've been following the events in the press, and I feel awful for you."

"Nothing I can really talk about here. How about we get together tonight? Unless you have a better date planned, then I would have to kill myself," Gino laughed.

"I thought you would never ask! If I were going to the White House to see the president I would cancel to see you," Suzie spouted. Her voice was serious. She felt a tingling in her stomach.

"You say that to all the old men in your life."

"First of all, please stop saying that about yourself! You don't behave or perform like you are old, um, if you get my drift." Her voice trailed off. Gino could feel her sex appeal through the phone and felt himself getting excited. Suzie continued, "Besides, I've decided that I'm off the dating market now. Not that I ever really was. If you don't feel the same, I really don't care. I'm yours exclusively and that's that, Mr. Ranno."

"We can discuss that tonight over dinner. May I send a car to bring you to where I'm staying?" Gino asked. "I'm kind of laying low for a while."

"I will walk if I have to. And if it's real far, I have a bicycle."

They both laughed.

"Okay, my driver will pick you up at six at your apartment. Is that OK?"

"No, silly. I don't want anyone to be following me, for your sake. Make it four o'clock at Balthazar's in SOHO. I have a meeting near there at two. Is that okay with you?"

"Perfect!" Gino blurted.

"And Mr. Ranno," Suzie teased, "please give your driver the night off. He can take me back to my office in the morning."

CHAPTER 35

Gino was sitting on a wood and wrought iron bench in the backyard of his friend Louie's home in Westchester enjoying a Monte Cristo Number Three, Cuban cigar and a Jack Daniels on the rocks. He took a slow, long drag, tipped his head back, and let the aromatic smoke billow into the air. He smiled thinking about his later plans.

A few of Gino's men strolled around the manicured lawns and flower gardens which complimented an old Weeping Willow tree, and made sure the only trouble around the house were the two, plump blue-jays who were arguing over whatever it is blue jays fight over. The scent from a lavender, Sunday lilac tree, his late mother's favorite, made him think of his mom. He knew she would not be proud of what he was doing with himself at this point in his life. The life of a mobster was not what Carmella Ranno had in mind for her son.

This cigar break is just what I need after dealing with all that fine print, Gino thought to himself. Gino had just gotten off the phone after working on a building purchase with his lawyers and accountants. I don't need any more stress today at all.

Unfortunately, Mickey Roach and Joey Clams approached and interrupted Gino's few moments of quiet.

"Sorry, Gino, we need a minute with you," Mickey announced.

"These two birds have been going at it for the past twenty-minutes. They are really pissed off at each other," Gino noted. In his own way, he was letting his top two guys know he wanted to be removed from the life, if only for a few more minutes.

"Gino, we got word from the Chinaman. He wants to meet in a public restaurant in Jersey tomorrow night. We suggested a few places. They are getting back to us tomorrow afternoon. Evidently they don't want to give us time to set them up," Mickey said.

"Give them my word nothing will happen. Just don't make it south of Newark. Who needs to smell that foul, New Jersey Turnpike?" Gino answered.

"Okay, I'll suggest near the bridge, but there's something else you need to know," Mickey said. The old hit man nodded his head to Joey.

"Buddy…It's…it's about your friend, Suzie," Joey stuttered.

"What about her?"

"Do you know what she does for a living?

"What is this Jeopardy? A fucking, game show? What's My Line? Tell me what you need to say, Joey," Gino hollered.

"Suzie Ping has a large money transfer business in Asia. Very clean, very profitable, she does okay with it. She is looking to expand in the Carib and South America…you know…and Mexico…Costa Rica…like that," Joey stammered again.

"Pal-o-mine, when you start that hesitating bullshit of yours, I know something really big is on the way. You've been doing that since we were ten. Spit it the fuck out, will ya?" Gino ordered.

"Okay…fine…Her nickname is Baby Ping. Her older sister was called Sister Ping. The older one died in Federal lock-up for human trafficking. You know…sex slaves, shit like that! They bring in the kids, girls and boys, Gino, poor kids who already have nothing, and they turn them into hookers, drug runners… the whole nine. "Suzie" is the biggest in the business here and in China!" Joey blurted.

"You're shittin' me?" Gino exhaled. His moment of relaxation shattered, and his romantic evening looking like it wasn't going to happen now, he continued to listen.

"And she is ruthless with her business. She does a lot of work with the Tongs. Yeah! Guys like Cabbagehead are her customers and her protection. She's in big with these cocksuckers, Gino," Mickey added.

"Sorry, Gino...but you... we had to tell you...ya know...it's..." Joey mumbled.

"There you go, again. It's okay; I get it," Gino said.

He threw the cigar stogie under the willow and drank the remainder of his JD in one gulp.

"I'm falling in love with her," Gino announced.

"What the fuck did you just say? Gino, it's too dangerous right now. Who knows where her loyalty is? Put the ego aside for a minute and think. Maybe this whole thing with her is a set-up, just to get to you and to us," Mickey shot back.

"Man, if that's true she could win an Oscar. Holy Christ! I've been taken by women before but certainly nothing like this," Gino lamented.

"Buddy, I've seen you with more women than I could count in the past fifty-six years. Some good, some not so good. This one can cut your balls off and feed them to you with macaroni. She is the real deal gangster my friend. I say dump her now before you get fucked, and I don't mean in a nice way either," Joey proclaimed without one stammer.

"Hello!!! The last time I looked, I'm a real deal gangster too, unless you believe that philanthropist, pillar-of-the-community nonsense. Remember, Polonius said, 'to thine own self be true.' I don't want to start believing my own bullshit gentlemen," Gino roared.

"Who?" Mickey asked.

"Polonius...in Hamlet. You were around when Shakespeare wrote that weren't you, Mickey?" Gino joked.

"Fuck that, Gino. I couldn't care less how she makes a living. Just look at it for a minute, though, will ya? Suzie Ping may be part of that whole Tong thing." Mickey spoke in an almost whisper. "Those same people... who now suddenly want to eat our lunch and move in on our biggest action. The fact that you are falling for this broa...sorry, this woman, is just pure insanity," Mickey argued.

"It's just too risky, Gino. You are letting your emotions rule you and that is not good on any level. You have an entire family to look after," Joey Clams uttered.

"Look, I never wanted to be doing this damn thing we do. I stayed away my whole life and then all of a sudden, because of happenstance and loyalty, bam! I'm hiding out in Westchester afraid to be assassinated by a Chinatown maniac and his gang. For what? Money? Power? Is this what I wanted to do with my later years? Hell, no!" Gino bellowed.

"Like it or not, you are the Don of the Miceli clan. You command this family from here to Sicily. And now, you are infatuated with a forty-something year old Chinese woman who can take our whole borgata down? What am I missing over here?" Mickey reasoned.

"I finally found someone who may be the love of my life and I have to let her go because of business? Maybe I should retire like Carmine, Jr. did. Just quit the life I never wanted in the first place," Gino bemoaned.

"And give it to whom? You are the last stop on the A-train, my friend. I never seen you run and hide before, and you ain't gonna do that now, buddy," Joey yelled.

"Okay. Let's just see how it plays out. She's still coming late this afternoon. I'll keep my eyes open. Sorry, guys. I see what you're attempting to do, and I love you both for trying to protect me and the family. I really do, from the bottom of my heart," Gino said quietly.

"Gino, forgive me for saying this, please, but you need to start acting more like a Don than a scene from Romeo and Juliet. Mickey looked at Gino with a grin. See? I know Shakespeare, after all," Mickey boasted.

They all three laughed out loud. Joey lit a cigarette.

"I'm going inside and coming out with a bottle of JD, some ice, and three Cubans. Let's just have an hour together and go over old times.

CHAPTER 36

"**W**ord is the Micelis and the Hip Sing are meeting tomorrow night. It seems our talk with them worked...well, at least we got them to the table," Inspector Mike Abbate proclaimed.

Abbate and Detective Mike Baker were at the 'puzzle palace' for a briefing with First Deputy Commissioner Byrne and Chief of Detectives Esposito in Byrne's office. First Dep. Byrne stood up behind his desk to stretch his back. "The commish, and the mayor, and that freak of a governor up in Albany are all over me on this thing. The mayor and that presidential hopeful asshole want to be the first to jump in front of the cameras on this. That's the last thing we need because it will only give more life to this so-called turf war. Look, we have enough going on in this city and a mob war will only make us look like wide-open Dodge City to the rest of the world. The media will turn this from 'I love New York' to 'I fear New York'. The politicians will point their slimy fingers at the NYPD for not keeping the streets safe, the liberals will call for the commish to resign, and then the president will come to town and it will be a national disgrace, and on and on. I, for one, want to put my head on the pillow at night and not have to worry about fifty dead Italians and Chinese, and innocent bystanders dead in the gutter," Byrne declared. "I'm not looking forward to this at all."

"Frank, these two guys have done a yeoman's job getting the Micelis and the Tong to sit down. We can't predict what's gonna come of their meeting, but at least they're talking. It may not be the cure we need but it's all we have right now," Esposito interjected.

"Our intel tells us they will meet in Jersey, neutral territory, so if there is a shoot em' up at least it's not here," Abbate added.

"May I, inspector?" Mike asked. Abbate shook his head in the affir-mative.

"I don't believe that will occur. Both sides are looking for an out -

a peaceful settlement. They know we can hit them both hard in their pockets," Mike advised.

"Correct, Detective, and we will. Espo, start planning to break their balls. If we need to, I want to hit every gambling room in Chinatown, every bookie joint in all the boroughs, every rub and tug place everywhere. It's time these knuckleheads know we mean business," Byrne ordered.

"Yes, sir. We have the uniform and detective division manpower to start this action at a moment's notice," Esposito declared.

"The only wild card is this loose marble Cabbagehead. Danny Chu is very unpredictable and flies off the handle at the drop of a hat. He wants to be the king of the hill and that may pose a big problem, but Ranno and his boys have been through this kind of thing before and they know how to negotiate and settle disputes," Abbate said.

"Yeah, and I'm not so sure the Micelis will sit still for any crazy, maniac antics. Remember, they blew up half of Brooklyn with their problems with the Brighton Beach mob, and the Russians went whimpering back to Moscow. Those Ruskies have been very quiet for a while," Esposito countered.

Mike Baker nervously cleared his throat.

"You have something to add, Detective?" Esposito asked.

"Yes, sir, I do. I'm concerned by a bit of intel we received today. It seems the Vietnamese leader of the former BTK gang, An Phan, a/k/a Andy, from New Orleans is in town. Word is he is meeting with Chu. As you all know BTK has a history of unbridled violence. At least that's how they did things years ago," Matt reported.

"Do we think Chu is importing them to have backup for a big fight in the streets, Detective?" Esposito inquired.

"Sir, we are not certain. I mean, they could be meeting about other criminal activities but I don't believe in coincidences," Matt pronounced. Matt spoke with a practiced politeness that was unique among his fellow detectives.

"And neither do I. I want 24-7 surveillance on this fuckin' Andy character. If he takes a shit we need to know about it. First sign of anything to do with this issue, find a reason to lock him up," Byrne commanded.

"Yes, sir. I'll put our best men on it."

"Do we have any undercover Asians we can use on this?" Byrne asked.

"One man in the Fifth. His name is Sam Lee. He speaks several of the Chinese dialects, but the problem is it's always nearly impossible to get close enough to these Chinks to find out what's going down," Esposito replied.

"If I may, sir, there is another Asian detective, not undercover though. His name is Kevin Wang and he speaks Chinese, as well," Matt added.

"He is a known entity, Detective. The Tong knows he's on the job. There is no way he will be able to infiltrate this gang," Esposito stated.

"I don't want to ask the FBI boys for help. They like the limelight even more than the mayor and governor. Next thing you know, the case is theirs, and we will look like smacked asses," Byrne added.

"We may need them on this one if things start to heat up, sir," Abbate spouted.

"Listen carefully. Only as an absolute last resort do we bring the feds in on this case, and I want the final say, understood?" Byrne bellowed.

"Yes, sir, absolutely," Abbate replied.

"Anything else on your minds?" Byrne inquired. The scowl on his face brought a slight chill down Matt's spine.

"One more thing, sir. There seems to be some added activity with respect to human trafficking in Chinatown and Queens. Do you think…" Matt was interrupted.

"Let's not get ahead of ourselves, Detective. You young, up and comers need to learn a bit about the virtue of patience. One thing at a time, Detective Baker. The trafficking problem is like trying to slay a dragon. Right now, we need to concentrate on keeping these assholes in check,"

Byrne advised.

I think what I really need is lessons in the virtue of politics, Matt thought to himself.

CHAPTER 37

At two-minutes before five o'clock, a black Cadillac Esplanade SUV, with two Miceli soldiers sitting in the front seats, pulled up to the safe house in Westchester County, New York where Gino Ranno was carefully entrenched.

Suzie Ping stepped from the rear of the vehicle looking like a veritable movie star. Dressed in a short, brown, leather skirt, brown, Jimmy Choo, four-inch high heels with a thick, ankle strap and a colorful, Versace original blouse, Suzie was an absolute knockout. Her long, jet-black hair and high cheek bones, confirmed the fact that she was Asian even though the Chanel Bijou Cat black and gold sunglasses partially veiled Suzie's eyes.

None of the Miceli bodyguards would give more than a quick glance to take in Suzie's sexy saunter into the house, for fear of offending Gino or his girl.

The driver of the SUV carried a small, overnight bag and a small, green, gift-wrapped package which boasted a wrap-around, black-silken ribbon.

Gino met Suzie at the door. The couple embraced for what seemed like ten minutes. Suzie kissed Gino squarely on his lips.

"Sensational is not even a close enough word to describe you," Gino uttered as he stepped back to get a look again at the magnificent woman before him.

"You don't look so bad yourself, young man," Suzie replied. She boasted a beaming smile as she threw her arms around Gino again and gave him another smooch.

Gino had on a pair of tan, front-pleated slacks with a royal blue blazer and a powder blue, open-collared, button-down shirt, Italian loafers sans socks, and with his salt and pepper hair slicked back, it gave Gino a GQ look that would turn many a ladies' heads.

"I hope you like what I got for you, my love," Suzie whispered in a voice that dripped with a sexual undertone. She handed the box to Gino.

"Now I feel like a real spilorcio."

"A what?"

"A cheapskate. I have nothing for you, sweetie. I'm embarrassed now," Gino admitted.

"You silly man. I just saw this and thought of you, that's all. I just hope you like it and it fits," Suzie hinted.

The couple walked into the study, Gino's hand was around Suzie's taut waist. She propped her Chanel's on top of her head, smiling like a school girl.

"C'mon, open it, baby," Suzie spouted.

Gino fumbled opening the package, feeling his face flush. With his dark olive complexion blushing wasn't possible.

The chef walked into the study carrying a silver tray with a bottle of Dom Perignon Champagne and two, long stemmed flutes. He left the tray on Gino's desk.

"Trying to get me drunk this early, Casanova?" Suzie laughed.

Gino handed one glass to his guest and took his, raising it for a toast.

"To the most beautiful girl I've ever seen," Gino proclaimed.

They wrapped their arms around each other, glasses in hand in an intimate fashion, looking deeply into each other's eyes.

"So sweet, Gino…now please open your present, will you?"

Gino finished opening the box and looked inside with an amazed face.

"My God, I always wanted one of these but would never get one for myself," Gino admitted. He kissed Suzie on her full lips, placed the gift on his desk and removed his sports jacket, trading it for the Sulka, blue silk, Jacquard smoking jacket.

"Perfect fit!" Gino proclaimed.

"You look amazing!"

"I'm using this tonight after dinner."

"What time is dinner?" Suzie asked with a coy smile.

"Usually around seven."

"Do you think we can make it eight?" Suzie requested. She moved her curvy body into Gino.

§§§§

After their passionate reunion, the couple remained under the sheets enjoying the touch of each other for what seemed like eternity. Finally, Gino spoke.

"Sweetie, this is probably not the time or place, but I need to talk with you about something," Gino began.

"Yes is my answer. Yes, I think I'm in love with you, Gino."

Gino was momentarily stunned.

"Well...I...I think I'm feeling the same way, but that's not what I wanted to discuss, Sweetie, and, um, I don't want you to take this the wrong way."

Suzie sat bolt upright in the bed. "What? What's wrong?"

"Relax, please. There is absolutely nothing wrong. I just want to be totally honest with you, Suzie. I'm just going to say what I need to say. Look, I know you told me about your business... the money transferring venture, but I've been told you are in another business that, well, let's say, is not so legitimate, for lack of a better word."

"I was eventually going to tell you, my love. When I thought the time was right," Suzie stated.

"Look, who am I to judge anyone? And I'm not judging you, it's just that I don't want our business worlds to collide and ruin something beautiful, something that may have the chance to last forever."

"I assume your people have done their homework and are warning you to stay away from this Asian, gangster broad. I've known all along what you do, who you are, and what you are, but it doesn't matter to me at all. I know you as a dear and loving man, a powerful man who I find amazingly sexy and smart. Can't that be enough for us, my love?"

"Of course, it's just that your business is quite dangerous and I would hate to lose you."

"And what about you? Look at where you are right now! Almost in hiding. You always will have a bull's eye on your back, so what about me losing you?" Suzie blurted. Her tone was defensive.

"I understand, and I get it. We are who we are, and we take the good with the bad."

"Gino, I don't like how that sounds. I just told you I love you. I have never said that to another man in that way, and I don't take my feelings lightly. Look, I know it's very soon for that word but I've never felt this way about anyone…ever!" Suzie admitted.

"Maybe I need to hear how you got into this thing you do," Gino offered.

"It's a long story."

"I have the time," Gino replied. "Come here." The couple settled back in the bed, Gino's arm around Suzie. Her head rested on his shoulder; her hand streched across his broad chest.

"My life was pure shit in China. You probably never experienced true poverty. I hope not, anyway. The pain from hunger is… indescribable.

Can you imagine the kind of poverty where your parents would be forced to sell you for food and shelter? There is something to understanding the Chinese world; my people have survived starvation, disasters, war, and ignorance for over five thousand years." Suzie took a deep breath and continued. "Obtaining food was a daily struggle in my world. It still is where I come from, so much so that in my dialect the words for hello are 'have you eaten today?' Have you ever in your life gone to bed hungry night after night after night? That was my life! So I make no excuses that I have and for how I have become a wealthy woman. There are more Chinese on this earth than any other nationality, and survival is for the strong, the smart, and the shrewd. Our population is both our greatest strength and greatest weakness, and I wasn't going to live as a prostitute in that shithole. I was taught in school, like most Chinese students, to memorize, but I chose to use my own brain and think instead, so I came here to follow my sister's business which has brought us some money and freedom, and I do what I do. Maybe you would be happier if I was a mathematician or doctor like a good China lady?" Suzie asked. Her temper was beginning to get the best of her.

Gino pulled Suzie even closer to him, kissed her on her forehead, and stroked the soft skin on her arm with his strong, but loving hands.

Gino let out a sigh. "I am sure that I love you, now more than ever, Suzie," Gino proclaimed.

"Wait, Gino, I'm not finished. I believe crime is a human behavior. Everyone has some criminality, some transgression in their hearts and in their souls. Those are the facts of life. I chose my business to get what I wanted in life, and I will not apologize to you or anyone for the path I have chosen. Just know one thing…I will never do anything to hurt you my love…never!"

CHAPTER 38

On Baxter Street in Chinatown, a few doors down from Forlini's restaurant, one of Gino Ranno's favorite Italian places in New York City, is Nha Trang One Vietnamese restaurant.

Cabbagehead selected Nha Trang One, which is named after a beachside village in Vietnam, to host the New Orleans visitors, Andy Phan and two of his associates, Nguyen van Hoang, who they called Van, and Will Phan, Andy's first cousins. Van had a cachectic, almost skeletal look. A deep, darker skin color than the others, resembling more a Filipino than a Vietnamese. Will Phan, appeared more Hawaiian than a typical person from the Philippines, with a rounded, chubby face and small beady eyes. Andy Phan was killer handsome, with a sharp angular face and slicked back, jet black hair. The average American would be scared shitless if these three were walking toward them on the street.

Cabbagehead had Peter sitting next to him at a large, round family style table in the rear of the crowded and not so fancy, real deal, Vietnamese eating place. None of the china plates or inexpensive, flat silverware on the table seemed to have any relation to one another. It was well known; If you want fancy, don't go to Nha Trang One. If you want great food and not a backbreaking check, this is the place.

The owners knew Cabbagehead so no menus were offered for the group of five men. The owners also were aware there would be no check given as the Flying Dragons never paid for food or drink anyway. On top of that, their weekly tribute for protection to Cabbagehead was just about due.

Several Flying Dragons sat at a nearby table, loaded for bear to protect their 489, while others remained outside the restaurant, milling around just in case their services were needed.

"This is your first time here, Andy? I mean here in Chinatown?"

Cabbagehead inquired. Danny Chu was trying to be as affable as he knew how. Warming up his guests for a while before they discussed any business dealings. Everyone had glasses at their place on the table, with a variety of booze and rice wines.

"I was born here, Danny. I have a lot of family history in New York, but I was a little boy when we left for Louisiana, so my memory is a bit cloudy," Andy replied in perfect, non-accented English.

"Probably much like my family history. When did your family get here?" Danny asked.

"That's an interesting story. My grandfather was one of the Binh Xuyen in our country. The name of the mob in Vietnam was named after Binh Xuyen where my family was from. It's a small town very near Cholon where many of the, let's say, hoodlums came from. Grandpa was a pretty big deal gangster and had a lot to do with smuggling and manufacturing a variety of illegal substances."

Suddenly, four waiters arrived at the table with plates and platters, balanced from their hands to their elbows. The food was placed family style on the table, in silence.

A platter of golden fried, crispy squid, perfectly folded spring rolls with pork, or shrimp, or just vegetables, a small mountain of barbequed, boneless pork chops, two, monstrous, whole fried, snapper fish, a large bowl of steamy seafood soup, hollow vegetable dripping in a spicy, garlic sauce, and enough rice to feed most Asian families for a week.

Andy continued, "This looks like my grandma's house in New Orleans."

"I hope it meets with your approval," Cabbagehead uttered.

"Are you kidding…this is authentic Vietnamese food. I can tell from the aroma. Anyway, as I was saying, the Binh Xuyen went with whatever side they could made a buck. The French, the Diem regime, the Americans, the Viet Cong, whoever. The wars made them rich and then the communists made them suffer. My grandfather was killed, shot in the head in front of his entire family, while two of his daughters were taken as comfort women for the soldiers and found a week later in a ditch, bayonetted to death. So my dad, the arch criminal he was, decided fighting against the tide was folly. He came to New York with my mom and grandma and made the best of it."

"Wasn't he one of the original Canal Street Boys?" Peter asked. His tone was a bit coy. He already knew the answer to the question.

"Yep, one of the founders. I hope he didn't piss any of your parents off," Andy offered.

"Those days are long gone, Andy. We are looking to the future now," Cabbagehead announced.

"So when things got hot here, lots of killings and the like, we moved south and now we have a nice little thing going on down there."

Andy reached for the platter of fried fish, exposing a large, colorful, snakehead tattoo on his forearm.

"How is business for you?" Peter asked.

"It's a grind. The NOPD are redneck motherfuckers who don't let us breathe. They shake us down more efficiently than we ever could shake down our clients. Every month we must pony up to several layers of these pricks. Naturally, we pass that cost along to our patrons," Andy admitted.

"It's a cost of doing business. We have that here on a daily basis. We do the right thing by our cops and they go easier when there is a bust. It's the cat and mouse game which has been played for both our people for a very long time my friend," Cabbagehead declared.

"Honestly, I am bored, Danny. There is no creativity in what we do. I must tell you, I see very little growth in our business to the point that we can't even bring in new recruits. The big easy ain't so big and it certainly ain't easy."

"That's why I called you to come visit, my friend. Would you consider doing some special work for me here, on a needed basis for a while?" Cabbagehead inquired.

"It depends on the work and the rewards. If it's just contract work, I must be honest, I am not so enthusiastic about that. If we could come to an understanding about a piece of the apple down the road, I would be all ears," Andy replied.

"I have a situation with the Miceli family which may require a certain expertise. A certain, out of town influence we can count on in a pinch."

"Danny, please forgive me but I need to add my voice on this. Years ago, we were known for getting jobs like this done with swift and certain strength. That was when our country was being torn apart by war and our people here had nothing to lose. Brutality was a way of life. The Vietnamese generation before us were without shame when it came to violence. Today, breaking store windows, splitting heads, burning cars is ordinary work for us. The kind of work you are looking for brings great risk and is costly," Van admitted. He was Andy's right hand man and enforcer in New Orleans.

"Danny, why not use your own people?" Andy asked.

Danny took out his surveillance monitor and swung it around for the others to see. A photo of Gino getting into his vehicle popped up. "This is why. We are talking about a very big job, here. My Dragons have many younger members now. Some just don't have the instincts needed right at this moment. When a job is done, we send them away to cool off for a while. You understand, I'm sure," Cabbagehead added. His tone and demeanor changed to a less than friendly tenor.

"Look, gentlemen…let's cut to the chase." Peter spoke rapidly. "If we need you to do some work, and you do well with it without breaking the bank, we are prepared to get you boys back up here for a portion of Canal Street. We have a big footprint here, and we have expansion plans but none we are ready to discuss with you yet. If we band together, as Asian brothers, there is plenty of money to be made. And money is the game, am I right?" Peter asked.

"Naturally. And how about the powder business? We just don't want to paint the streets red, shake down a few stores, and sell pussy. What about the real money, the horse?" Van asked.

Cabbagehead started to show his temper. The veins in his bald head started to redden and swell. He gritted his teeth as he began to speak.

"Gentlemen, we will let you know if we need you." He banged his pointer finger on the table with such force people at the nearby tables started to notice. "If you want to prove yourselves to us and get back up here, you will need to work for it!" He leaned in closer to stare Andy in the eyes. "Otherwise, stay where the fuck you are and play small ball!" Cabbagehead yelled. He was now pounding his whole fists on the table, which was his M.O.

Calmly, Peter said, "Gentlemen, think things over. Please eat and drink and enjoy yourselves. Our people are expecting you to come around the corner when you are finished. The fresh, young girls are our gift to you for the evening. We will be in touch." Peter handed Andy a card for the Happy Family Therapy Center. Cabbagehead abruptly stood and left without shaking anyone's hand or saying goodbye. The meeting didn't go at all according to his plan. The other Dragons followed their boss out the door and onto Baxter Street.

"He is one sick and crazy bastard," Andy whispered to his cousins.

CHAPTER 39

It was seven thirty in the morning and Suzie needed to return to work and get back to the city. She had an important telephone meeting about her expansion plans into South Africa, and a backup Skype meeting with her cousin about a new selection of young people to fulfill her nefarious business needs.

Gino and Suzie walked hand in hand, taking small steps so their time together seemed longer. The adoring couple walked toward the glimmering, Cadillac SUV and the two, strong-arm bodyguards.

"I never dreamed I would ever in my life be this happy, Gino! You have hit me like a bolt of lightning from the sky. One day I'm happily single and busy with my business, and the next day, wham, I'm... I'm in love to the point of distraction," Suzie whispered.

"I'm glad we were able to discuss things last night. It seems like a heavy weight has been lifted from my chest, because I don't see myself without you, Sweetie. Strange, because we don't really know each other completely."

"We have plenty of time for that," Suzie said.

"Unless I drop dead from the sex!" Gino whispered in her ear.

"You'd better not! Maybe one of those steaming hot, Eye-talian babes will win you over, and I'll be left crying in my won-ton soup," Suzie laughed.

"Go ahead, shoot me. You'd be doing me a favor," Gino did his best Humphrey Bogart impression, lisp and all.

"Rick...The day you left Paris, if you knew what I went through..If you knew how much I loved you...how much I still love you...," Suzie did a perfect Ingrid Bergman impersonation.

The two of them kissed fervently like Rick Blane and Ilsa Lund did in Casablanca.

"I absolutely adore you, Suzie Ping. More and more by the minute," Gino gushed.

"I am beyond the luckiest girl in the world, Gino! Thank-you for a great evening. I'll talk to you later," Suzie whispered as she planted a passionate good-bye kiss on her man.

Suzie reluctantly climbed into the SUV.

"Where can we take you, miss?" The driver asked.

"My office is fine. Corner of Mott and Elizabeth.

§§§§

Gino returned to the house under the watchful eyes of the Sicilian bodyguards. The aroma of freshly brewed espresso and anisette toast drew Gino into the kitchen.

"That little love scene outside doesn't make me feel like you are taking our advice," Mickey Roach proclaimed.

"Mick…can you get off my case about this? I know what I'm doing, and besides, I checked her out thoroughly, if you know what I mean. Now do me a big favor, will you? I need to get back to the city and get back to work. I've been here long enough," Gino said. Mickey looked at his boss and shook his head. They both laughed.

"We are waiting for the name of the sit-down place in Jersey, and I just don't trust these Chinky bastards. I feel like we are being surrounded on all sides. I just feel like we're being watched. I can't pinpoint this feeling I have. Gino, maybe I'm getting too old for my job and you need someone else, someone who can understand this opera that you are starring in?" Mickey lamented.

"Cut the shit, Mick! My mother died years ago, and I'm not falling for your Sicilian guilt game," Gino hollered.

Joey Clams and C.C. heard the commotion and rushed into the kitchen. "Jesus Christ what's the hell's going on?" Joey asked.

"You sound like an old, married couple in Boca having a fight over the early bird special," C.C. added.

"I'm just pissed off, that's all. I guess I have cabin fever being in this place. I have to get back to real life," Gino offered.

"So, let's go! Let's drive back to the city. The press is already gone from your apartment and the office. Let's meet with that fuckin' chink fuck and bring this thing to a head, one way or another," Joey yelled.

"And let Tokyo Rose put two behind your ear one night?" Mickey bellowed.

Mickey knew what he said hurt Gino. Gino looked up at the ceiling, holding any comment back out of his respect for the older, mob icon.

Mickey opened his arms and walked toward his boss. "Gino, forgive me…I was out of line just then," Mickey offered.

They hugged, Gino kissing the aging hit man on both cheeks.

"Tokyo Rose was Japanese, Mick." C.C. whispered.

"He has a problem telling Asians apart," Joey murmured.

"Mick, guys…I know you mean the best for me…and for the family. Understand something about me that maybe you missed over the years. I am pretty much compulsive at times. That shows with Suzie especially. She makes me feel like I'm twenty-five again and I don't mean only in the sack. It may sound crazy to you because we've only know each other for fifteen minutes but we are both in love with each other and maybe for the first time in our lives. I'm not stupid. I know she runs a criminal enterprise, and it could backfire. She can also be taken away from me in a heartbeat…she can wind up dead or in jail. Everything in life is fleeting, and all three of you know that. And thankfully, because of you guys, I have my eyes and ears open. I promise you, if I see or sense something is wrong, I will send up the white flag and then you can do what you have to do," Gino articulated.

"Mencia, the Don and the Mama San. Can you imagine if they had any kids?" C.C. joked.

"Charlie, I don't think we have to worry about that." He kept his eyes still staring at Gino. "Let's just all be weary of everything around us and make sure we come away from this Cabbagehead confrontation all in one piece," Mickey proclaimed.

CHAPTER 40

David Wong, owner of Hop Wong Chinese restaurant on Mott Street came from Hong Kong just over nineteen years ago. He worked as a dishwasher, bus boy, and waiter working himself up the ladder by putting in eighteen, grueling hours a day, and for the most part, raising his family the best way he could. One of his daughters was now enrolled at New York University School of Law. This was just a part of the American dream David and his young wife had moving to New York... hope for their family. David also sent money every month back to his younger brother in China who eventually brought his family to America with the same dream.

Aside from the pride of his brilliant daughter, David boasted of having the best won ton and sweet-and-sour soup in all of Chinatown, a fact to which even a New York Times restaurant critic agreed.

David was in his restaurant kitchen early, dressed in his white, kitchen uniform and a netting around his hair. He was showing his twelve-year-old nephew the finer points of slicing roast pork. David's brother, the nephew's father, worked the restaurant until two o'clock that morning and would awaken to come help with the lunch crowd at around noon. David, a very thin man, was several inches shorter than his five-foot, six-inch nephew.

"Nephew, always keep your fingers tucked in on the pork so you will prevent cutting yourself. Remember the blades here are sharp like razors. Let me show you and then you will try."

David grabbed a large piece of roast pork, plopped it on the butcher block, curled his fingers into the palm of his hand, and sliced a healthy swab of meat with a razor-sharp cleaver. David turned the thick slice of pork on the bias, and made uniform chunks with the practiced eye of an expert.

"These chunks are for flavoring in the won tons, in the fried egg-rolls, and in some dishes, so we keep them aside in a bowl for when your aunt and your mother come in to help make the mixtures. Here, now you try it, but remember, very sharp," David instructed.

The young man took the cleaver gingerly from the butcher block and tentatively approached the ample piece of roast pork. Just as the tip was about to slice into the meat, the young man was startled by loud sccreaming.

"What the fuck, Wong! This is the third time we have had to come here to collect our organizational fee! No more sending our people away with a promise of next week…next week…" A Flying Dragon enforcer and two of his Green Lantern trainees had kicked their way through the back door and into the small, sparkling clean kitchen.

David blocked his young nephew by putting his arm across his chest. "Look, I always pay, just sometimes business is slow, taxes are due, it's difficult," David pleaded. His nephew raised the cleaver over his head just in case he had to come down and slice the intruder's head open.

The enforcer quickly grabbed the nephew by the arm and snatched the cleaver from the now, more-than-nervous nephew.

The enforcer now held the cleaver up over his own head. "How diffi-cult would it be to remove this hatchet from this kid's arm? Or his head?" One of the Lanterns moved behind the two, who were now defenseless.

David kept one eye on the man with the cleaver and one eye looking behind him. David was also checking the kitchen for any other knives lying out that he might possibly be able to grab quickly. "Please, don't hurt him. He is only a boy. I don't want trouble. Please, I will pay later today. I will pay," David blurted.

"Fuck that shit. You will pay now! One thousand, and the same amount is due every week, otherwise, well, you know what will happen," the enforcer hollered.

The Lantern behind them grabbed the nephew in a full-nelson, wres-tling hold. The other trainee punched the pre-teen in his solar plexus.

The nephew doubled over and then fell onto the cold, tile floor in a heap, sucking wind to catch his breath when the enforcer let him go.

"I should beat the living shit out of you for making my boys here hit this innocent kid. Where is the money, Wong? Where is it? Get it now! " the enforcer threatened.

"I don't have it here. My brother will bring it at noon, I swear," Wong begged.

The enforcer, with lightning speed and surgical accuracy swiped the razor-sharp cleaver across David's right hand spraying the restaurant owner's blood all over the roast pork and his unsuspecting nephew who was still crumpled on the floor.

David grabbed a white kitchen towel and quickly wrapped his wounded hand, the blood soaking through the cloth instantly.

"We will be back at noon, and now it's twelve hundred to pay for my travel time. You should be back from the hospital by then."

The enforcer turned and walked from the kitchen, the Green Lanterns on his heels.

§§§§

The same morning of the Flying Dragon's assault on the Hop Wong restaurant, Suzie Ping was dropped off at the corner of Mott and Elizabeth Streets. She was up in her office by eight forty-five.

Suzie walked into her office to find Alison and Diana trembling and pale from fear.

"What's wrong? What happened?" Suzie demanded.

"Cabbagehead and three of his boys were here fifteen minutes ago. They demanded to know where you were and when you were returning. When we said we didn't know, those creeps grabbed us, touching us all over and saying filthy things," Alison cried. "We thought you said this would never happen to us anymore, Suzie!"

"They said they would come back every half-hour and do much worse to us if you were not here," Diana stammered.

"Leave… both of you go home until I call you. I'm so sorry that you had to endure these animals," Suzie ordered.

The two, horrified girls fled from the office and down the stairs like Olympic athletes.

Fifteen minutes later, Cabbagehead and his crew, this time along with Peter, barged into Suzie's empty office.

"Are you fucking kidding me, Danny? You come in here and terrorize my girls? After all we do together, and you bring your crazy shit to my doorstep?" Suzie fearlessly demanded.

"So what are you going to do now, call your wop boyfriend, Gino to come and beat me up? I run things in Chinatown, and don't you forget it! And soon I will run this entire fucking city, not him!" Cabbagehead screamed.

Suzie was shocked and made speechless by Cabbagehead's revelation about her and Gino.

"And two of Ranno's fat goons have the balls to drop you off in our territory? Mocking us? Spitting in my face because he is fucking you? I can't have this!" Cabbagehead hollered.

"It's none of your business what I do in my private life! Whoever I decide to fuck is my affair, you lousy, dirt bag," Suzie raged. Cabbagehead had all he could do to not slap Suzie in the face.

Peter stepped forward and spoke in a low, matter-of-fact tone. "Here is how we see things, Miss Ping. Either you are Chinese, or you're not. Either you are one of us, or you are one of them. You crossed over the line, pretty lady, and you will have to decide where your true loyalty lies," Peter uttered.

"If you want to stay in business, and if you want to keep that beautiful face of yours, and if you don't want to wind up dying in federal prison like your fucking, stupid sister, you will have to first take a bath, and then do what you are told. Got it? And remember your family who is left in China? We will deal with them like we deal with all pig traitors. Their lives will depend on your loyalty to the Tong. We will no longer stand for the exclusion your white friends have laid on us," Cabbagehead warned. He looked at the three, Flying Dragons and shook his head yes.

The three goons began to toss the furniture and files all around the office, upending anything which was moveable. One of them pulled a switchblade knife from his pants pocket and tore open the beautiful, leather couch. He sliced at the silk draperies like a maniac, tearing them to shreds. Cabbagehead lit a cigarette and watched the mayhem ensue.

"I think you understand our message, Miss Ping. Soon we will come back, and we will tell you how you will be of use to the Hip Sing. One word of this to anyone, especially that Ranno jerkoff, and you will lose two blood relatives," Peter boasted.

Cabbagehead and his group of maniacs left the office laughing.

Suzie put her hands to her face and began to sob.

CHAPTER 41

David Wong called his brother waking him from a sound sleep to tell him about the Flying Dragons' visit to his restaurant. He was told to bring twelve hundred dollars to Hop Wong, clean the place up, and calm his son down.

David hailed a taxi on Canal Street and took the ten-minute drive to New York Presbyterian Lower Manhattan Hospital to have his hand attended to. The cuts were quite deep and David knew he would require stitches and medication. Going to the local acupuncture physician or a Chinatown holistic Chinese pharmacy was not going to work on the wound he had.

Checking into an emergency room in New York City, unless you are having a heart attack, can be a many hour ordeal, and this day was just like any other. Check in, take a number, sit down and wait.

Something is David Wong's eyes and story told the trauma nurse, Peggy Roach, that this injury was much more than the mundane kitchen accident which she was told on David's intake. She decided to make a call to a dear friend of hers at the Fifth precinct in Chinatown. Peggy called Matt's cell phone knowing she had only a thirty percent chance of him answering the call. Matt saw Peggy's name on his display and answered on the first ring.

"So, are you ready to marry me, Peg?" Matt answered. They had dated for a while when Matt was in new on the job, in undercover narcotics up in the Bronx.

"Would you knock it off, you nut? You had your chance and blew it," Peggy laughed.

"What's up, Irish?"

"It may be nothing Matt, but a man just came into the ER with a pretty bad knife wound to his hand. He said it was a kitchen accident but I don't think so. He's a real sweet man, and even shorter than me, if that's possible. He owns the Hop Wing on Mott Street right near you," Peggy explained.

"You mean David? David Wong? I eat there at least once a week. He does the right thing for all the cops in the Fifth. I'll be there in ten," Matt promised.

"Hey cowboy, no lights and sirens okay? I don't want to scare ten of our methadone clinic patients half to death," Peggy joked.

"I swear! What are you doing later?"

"Shut up, stupid!" Peggy ended the call.

As promised Matt walked into the ER and went directly over to David who was sitting with his head down, hand wrapped in a bloody towel and dealing with the pain and worry.

"Hey, David, what the hell happened to you?" Matt asked.

"Hello, my friend. What you doing here?"

"I had to see a sick pal and say hello to an old girlfriend while I was here," Matt lied.

"You handsome guy! Always with the girls. Maybe a girl every week, I think," David tried to laugh.

"What happened? Jesus Christ, what a freakin' mess."

"I had a fight with a fat piece of roast pork. After all these years, I should be more careful."

"Hey, this looks like a long wait. Let me see what I can do. I know a few people here," Matt offered.

"No…no detective, no fuss. I wait my turn. There are many sick people here."

"Just sit tight, David. What are friends for?"

Matt went to the desk, showed his gold badge, and was buzzed into the hustle bustle of the busy emergency room. Peggy was working with a young, Wall Street type who looked like he was about to implode from the stress of his job. Her back was facing the door.

"I never forget a great ass," Matt whispered into Peggy's ear.

"Maniac! Sit over there while I get this kid stabilized, will ya?"

A few minutes later Matt embraced Peggy as old friends do.

"Thanks for calling me. This David is a good guy and I think you're right about his injury not being a kitchen thing. I need a favor Peg. Get him in to see a doctor asap. I'm going to stay with him for a bit, if that's okay?" Matt asked.

"Of course not! This 'patients rights' and HIPPA laws bullshit will get us both thrown out, but I know you; you never take no for an answer, so let's go get him," Peggy winked at Matt when she said he would never take no for an answer.

Matt followed the petite, redhead to the entrance of the waiting room.

"Wong…Mr. David Wong, please!" Peggy announced.

Sheepishly, David walked into the ER.

"I'll have a hand surgeon look at you in a few minutes. Please go into room eight and lie down. You look like you need a rest Mr. Wong," Peggy advised.

Matt followed David into the room and helped him get on the bed. The detective pulled the semi-circular, white and blue curtain around the bed for privacy.

"Thank you, my friend. This hand is throbbing. Very painful."

"David, do me a favor, will you? Tell me what really happened to you."

"Just as I told. I was cutting some roast pork with my cleaver and I looked away, and the knife slipped. So stupid!"

"That's a pretty weak story, my friend. Just between us now, who sliced you?" Matt asked.

"Nobody. I think I was tired and lost my…"

"Okay, I can't make you tell me the truth because I know you will never tell me. So how is your family? Your wife? Your daughter still at NYU?"

David's demeanor changed. His eyes filled with tears and his lower lip trembled. The tell on his face told Matt all he was going to discover.

"This world is so bad, my friend. So bad! Please for my family, just let me wait for the doctor to fix me so I can go back to work," David pleaded.

"Of course, but listen to me, if you need anything, I want you to call me at this number, anytime day or night," Matt offered. He put his card in David's left hand, patted him on his shoulder and left.

Motherfuckers, Matt thought, *God damned animals.*

CHAPTER 42

The next morning, promptly at eight-thirty in the morning, Suzie was back in her office with Alison and Diane, rearranging the overturned furniture, fixing the company files, and assessing the damage done by the Dragons. Suzie had postponed her conference call meeting between Chung Leung in Hong Kong and Asanda Mjongile in Johannesburg until ten o'clock this morning. If the numbers worked, Suzie's cousin would be able to deliver a healthy load of young women and boys to South Africa from China within a month's time.

For the last three days, Chung Leung was working his contacts in Hong Kong by day and partying all night. Chung liked to dabble in very young girls, no older than twelve, crystal meth, and Ketamine, the Special K that boasts hallucinogenic effects which can last as long as two hours. Chung enjoyed the drugs in small doses, using the crystal meth to stimulate his nervous system making him feel euphoric, and the Special K to bring him the out of body experience that he came to crave.

Two, preteen girls had died in Chung's bed within the last year, their bodies never recovered.

Chung knew that he had to be clear of mind by eleven o'clock that evening, ten o'clock in the morning, New York time, and five p.m. in Johannesburg, so he stared his debauchery early.

Through a contact to whom Chung sold many girls from mainland China and Vietnam, he negotiated to spend the next three days with an eleven-year-old Cambodian virgin. His wholesale price, directly to the parents of the little girl, was nine hundred British pounds, just around twelve hundred dollars. Chung truly believed that taking a young, virgin girl would give him extraordinary, physical powers and reduce the effects of aging on his bloated body.

The girl was brought to Chung's hotel by his intermediary who knew just what to do to get the nervous child up to the lavish suite. Never seeing such opulence and wealth in Cambodia, and seeing the teeming streets of Hong King for the first time, added to the girl's extreme anxiety. She was trembling from head to toe.

Dressed in tiny, denim shorts and a red, Mickey Mouse blouse with common, brown sandals, the girl's long, black hair flowed past her waist, and was the only indication she was not a boy. Her thin body and sharp features were accented by her large, black, almond eyes which seemed to be absorbing the world around her with nervous anticipation.

Chung's partner greased the right palms in the hotel lobby and took the quaking girl to the bank of elevators. Once inside the cab, for comic relief, he wrapped a red bow around the terrified, pre-teen's neck. She would be a present to Chung.

The girl was taken to the door of Suite 1910. The man, barely containing his laughter, rang the doorbell and moved quickly to the stairwell, to be out of sight of the expectant Chung.

Chung opened the door in a terrycloth bathrobe that had the hotel's ornate logo embossed on the upper left breast plate in gold.

"Well, look at you, my little angel. All gift wrapped for me and everything. Come inside, please, and we can enjoy the beautiful sights of the great city of Hong Kong."

The apprehensive youth could not understand a word of the Chinese that Chung spoke. The pedophile reached out and gently took the pre-teen by the shoulder and into his room.

The child was in awe of the panoramic view of the city which she never dreamed of seeing. Chung wasted no time and dropped some crystal meth into a Coca-Cola with ice, motioning for the juvenile girl to drink up. He knew that within ten minutes, he would be having his way with the semi-comatose virgin.

Chung took her to a divan facing the view, her body still quivering in fear. The suite's doorbell interrupted the moment.

Chung opened the door expecting perhaps a gift from his partner from room service. Instead, he was greeted by three Chinese men in their twenties. Two with spiked hair and muscle shirts, one with a Mohawk haircut, died in several colors. A petite, Chinese woman was behind them, dressed in a white and blue nurse's uniform.

The Mohawk pushed his way into the room, smashing his fist into the portly Chung's stomach, dropping him to his knees.

One of the other men smacked the wind sucking Chung hard on the side of his face, sending him sideways onto the plush gray carpeting. The third went to the wide-eyed girl, tossing her cola onto the ground. The woman ushered the now crying girl out of the suite, telling her in broken Cambodian not to worry and that she would bring her back to her mother.

"You fat piece of shit. Instead of having your fun with that baby, we will have some fun with you," the Mohawk announced as he pulled Chung by his hair, into the living room.

"I did nothing wrong. Here, take my money, there on the glass table… and drugs, I have some K and other stuff. Coke, H, it's all yours, and my Rolex, is yours," Chung pleaded.

"Certainly we will take all those generous gifts you so graciously offered. But first, I must make a call from your cell phone. Where is it?" Mohawk asked.

"There…on the table. Who are you calling? What do have against me?"

One of the two, spike-haired goons removed a hatchet from the small of his back and held the weapon behind his leg.

"I am not calling anyone. It is you who is making the call. Dial your lovely cousin, Suzie Ping. I'm certain she is awake in New York by now, I'm absolutely sure she will happily take your call," Mohawk spouted.

The now terrified Chung took his cell phone from the hovering Mohawk and quickly pressed the speed dial for Suzie.

"Well, hello, dear cousin. Our call is much later, you…." Suzie was interrupted with sound of Chung's quivering voice.

"There are three men in my room…my God, what is going on? I'm…I'm…" Chung blurted before the Mohawk ripped the phone from his hand.

"Miss Ping? Are you there?"

"Yes! Who is this? What is the meaning of all this?" Suzie demanded.

"Oh, nothing too severe, my dear, Baby Ping. We are just here to kill this piece of garbage cousin of yours while you listen.

The spiked one with the hatchet, reached over Mohawk, burying the blade into Chung's clavicle bone, spraying his blood onto his white robe, the sofa, and the ceiling. Chung screamed in agony.

The second, spiked hood went behind Chung, clicked open a nine-inch switchblade and removed his right ear with one swipe of the knife. Chung pleaded with them to stop.

Mohawk took a nine-millimeter Beretta, fitted with a silencer, from his waist and fired a shot into Chung's left knee. Chung fell from the sofa sobbing.

"What are you doing to him? Stop please! I will pay you to stop," Suzie pleaded to anyone who was listening on the other end.

Mohawk pointed to the top of Chung's head. The hatchet man buried the weapon deep into the victim's head, rendering him very dead. Mohawk took the cell phone from the sofa, held it to his ear, and listened to the sobbing Suzie.

"Baby Ping? It looks like you need a new partner. This is just a sample of what will happen to your family if you utter one word to anyone. As they say in America, 'have a nice day.'

Cabbagehead sent his ruthless message to Suzie.

CHAPTER 43

Gino texted an 'I miss you message' to Suzie and didn't receive a reply. After an hour or so he called her cell number.

"Hi, Sweetie. Did you get my text about missing you?"

"Hi, my love. I'm sorry. I did, but I got involved with a few issues and was waiting until later to reach out," Susie replied. Gino could sense a tightness in her voice.

"Is something wrong? You really don't sound yourself."

"I'm fine. Just a few business issues. I had to put my expansion plans on hold for a while. Complications with personnel."

"Anything I can do for you?"

"No, I have to work things out. Not a great time for me," Suzie quivered.

"Hmmm. Am I getting the bum's rush? Are we moving too fast for you, Suzie? Are you getting cold feet?" Gino asked. His intuition, and the sound of her distressed voice was telling.

"Oh, baby…not at all. Just give me a day or two and we will get together, okay?"

"No worries, Sweetie. I'm pretty involved with a problem, as well. I'll wait for you to call."

"I love you, Gino." Suzie ended the call, not waiting for a response from her lover.

§§§§

That evening, Gino, Mickey Roach, and Joey Clams sat in the rear of a black SUV heading up to Rockland County, a mostly suburban county north of New York City. Two Miceli soldiers were in the front seat, armed with assault rifles and .45 millimeter handguns.

Behind them in an identical vehicle were C.C. and six bodyguards including two of Mickey's Sicilian hit men. Both cars stayed at the speed limit, in the middle lane of the Palisades Interstate Parkway, which ran from the George Washington Bridge in Fort Lee, New Jersey all the way to Bear Mountain, near the West Point Military Academy in New York. Gino and the group would be exiting well before Bear Mountain.

"I thought we were going to meet in New Jersey?" Gino asked.

"We were all set to meet at a joint along the Hudson in Edgewater, but the Chinks pulled a last-minute change which we agreed upon. They felt Jersey was covered by our friends in Newark and didn't trust it," Mickey responded.

"The Sparkhill Steak House, owned by an Albanian kid. Our Albanian friends in the Bronx say he's clean. No ties to anyone. They are sending a few of their men to mill around the joint, you know, work in the kitchen, like that. Just in case," Joey added.

"Listen to me. I don't want to break bread with Cabbagehead and his people. A nice meeting, maybe some drinks or coffee is all," Gino stated.

"The Albanian kid, Carlo, is setting up a private room downstairs for us to meet. Nobody, from either side will be able to go down the stairs or get through the fire exit. My guys will sweep the place for bugs, and for anything else in the room, and the bathrooms. We are each allowed two men outside the room. I'm putting the Sicilians close to us. Anyone going into the room will be wanded for weapons, including us and any Chinks who will be at the table. That's the agreement," Mickey informed.

Twenty minutes later, the two SUVs slowly rolled into the large, parking lot off Route 304 in Sparkhill, New York.

"Hmmm. Sparkhill. I had Dominican Sisters of Sparkhill when I was in grade school. Is this the same place?" Gino inquired.

"There aren't that many nuns around anymore because being a lesbian is now politically correct," Joey laughed.

"Yeah, it's the same place. They had an orphanage here when I was a kid. The nuns are still here. Show some respect, Joey," Mickey admonished.

Gino's thoughts were racing in his mind as quickly as the trees were passing by in the rear seat window of the SUV. He kept playing his last conversation with Suzie and how poorly she sounded.

C.C. and the bodyguards exited their vehicle and checked out the area. The real deal steak house is in a large, two story colonial house with purple shutters and a beautiful arched window which graces the front of the building. Accent lights beamed up at the house giving it an even grander appearance. A fifty-foot wood deck faced Route 9W and a heavily wooded area. Mickey thought about a sniper for a moment then realized they would be entering the front of the building away from the dense trees.

Once inside, Carlo met the group, shook hands with Gino and ushered the entourage to the bottom level. The keen eyes of the Sicilians scanned the room for possible problems.

The bodyguards fanned out and made themselves inconspicuous.

The upstairs dining room and rectangular bar were busy but not jam packed.

There were no signs of Albanian mercenaries except for a large, sunken eyed waiter with an oversized head, who just seemed to be standing around in a tuxedo which fit him poorly.

Ten minutes later, Danny Chu, Peter, and two bald and burly Chinese men walked in the front door. Four other Flying Dragons, dressed in black business suits stood outside the restaurant.

Carlo quickly escorted the four men down a wide staircase passing an amply supplied wine cellar and into the private room.

Everyone in the room wore suits and ties except Cabbagehead and

Gino, who wore their suits with open collars.

Gino was standing behind the long, oak table. He walked up to Danny and extended his hand. Danny grasped Gino's hand firmly and gave him a broad smile.

"Danny, it's good to finally meet you. I hope we can settle our differences tonight," Gino stated.

"Mr. Ranno, I knew the elder Mr. Miceli for a while several years ago and he had my utmost respect. We did some work with him which suited us both very well. I hope that respect will continue with you," Cabbagehead replied.

"I hope so," Gino answered.

Gino, Joey, and Mickey sat at one side of the table, Cabbagehead and Peter at the other. The Sicilians seemed to blend into the walls at the two heads of the dark table. The Chinese bodyguard stood behind Peter and the boss. No one asked and no one offered even a glass of water. Both sides wanted to get to business and forgo the social graces.

"If I may begin...this whole thing began over the union dispute at 50 Bowery. With all due respect to my late uncle and to you, if he were alive today that job would have been done with our union people and work would have been given to some of the local trades," Gino declared.

"And with all due respect to you, Mr. Ranno, without a union book, no Chinese worker would have put one nail into that building. You know it as well as I," Cabbagehead responded.

"You make an excellent point. The time for us to have discussed that was during the demolition of the old building. Union books could have been granted to select workers. If we would have communicated, like we are now with each other," Gino articulated.

"So, we got spiteful and didn't pay for the work your people did with the concrete, and you blew up our property," Cabbagehead replied. His bald head began to show a pinkish hue.

"I don't know anything about that incident Danny, but you are leaving out one vital bit of information. Your people gunned down two of our friends, basically setting them up to be slaughtered. If that was a message, it was a pretty bad way to show respect to us, don't you think?" Gino bold face lied.

"You ask for respect yet we were pushed aside like Cooley's in our own neighborhood. And by the way, we are still trying to find out who hit your men," Cabbagehead lied.

Gino chuckled. "You deny, I deny, but there is no denying the fact that you and Hip Sing are trying to muscle into our bread and butter affairs. The construction industry has been our mainstay, our blood, since the turn of the last century. Do you think for a minute that we will just allow you to walk all over us, Danny?"

"Allow? Who are you to allow anything in this city? I call what you do exclusion. Just like we were excluded since the eighteen hundreds." Cabbagehead stood up and slammed his hand on the table.

Gino smiled across the table bearing his pearly white teeth.

Cabbagehead's cranium was now a scarlet red, his famous veins popping a quarter inch above his scalp.

"Gentlemen, may I interject here?" Peter requested.

"Look, the past is the past. What we need to come to terms with is how do we work together and not spill each other's blood. We both had visits from the NYPD, and I'm sure they made it as clear to you as they did to us. If bloodshed continues they will come down on both of our operations with all they have. If need be they will bring the feds in as well. Neither of us can afford a disruption that will destroy us," Peter declared. Danny flashed Peter a look of anger for letting on their group wasn't as big and strong as he led people on the streets to believe.

"Your people took over the heroin business at a time when we were crippled by the law. That pizza connection fiasco put a lot of people away and the feds were brilliant. We had to let the 'smack' go and never asked for a piece or a tax back on that-ever. I'm sure here and there some of our people had their own action, but we never took the drug business back from you when we could have. Should we ask for it back now? The answer is best of luck with that business; we have no further interest in dealing with dope on a large scale. I just hope you are smarter than we were, and you learned from our mistakes. Just do your thing and we will do ours. You are to stay away from our core business, and we will work together to spread some union books where they are needed. It's as simple as that gentlemen," Gino stated.

"So we grow, how? With massage parlors and nail salons? With envelopes from our own store keepers and gambling rooms? Fuck that shit!"

Gino was taken aback by Cabbagehead's response, but he didn't let on. *Motherfucker*, he thought.

"Listen to me!" Cabbagehead continued. "We've been sucking the hind tit of yours for too long. It's far past the time the Hip Sing branch out into the more lucrative world of big business," Cabbagehead hollered. He stood again flailing his arms around like a mental patient for special effect.

Gino smiled again. This time he folded his arms in front of him.

"We're going nowhere with this cat and mouse game. I'm a lot older than all of you boys around this fucking table. I've been in more wars than I care to remember. Principle has put a lot of men in their graves in this city, and smarter guys than all of you have gone inside for the duration. If we can't settle our differences, get ready for total destruction of what we have right now," Mickey Roach preached.

Cabbagehead stared at Mickey for a long twenty seconds.

"Gentlemen…" Peter said.

"Shut your mouth," Cabbagehead rudely interrupted his second in command. Gino looked at Joey Clams with a blank face.

"This old man here is right. Ok, here's my best offer. We stay away from all union type jobs in the construction world. You grant us twenty union books a month in various trades we select. We forget about the hotel, you forget about your men, and we go forward.

"We can't do twenty. We can guarantee five a month and we work together on the selection of the trades," Joey said.

"Ten then. Ten union books a month." Cabbagehead insisted.

"Seven, and we have a deal," Gino added.

"Done. Plus, one more thing. We have your approval to open a Chinese owned sanitation company to handle only Chinatown garbage," Cabbagehead uttered.

"That is above my pay grade, Danny. I must be honest with you if we are to coexist; I am not in a position to offer you what I don't control. I can ask, but I can't promise what you're asking for."

"Your honesty shows me you are a man of respect. We can revisit that at another time," Cabbagehead offered.

"Good. We have a deal. Let's stick to it!" Gino announced.

CHAPTER 44

On the drive back to Manhattan Joey wanted to have a post mortem on the meeting with Cabbagehead.

"So? What do you two think of the meeting?" Joey asked.

Gino put his index finger to his lips for a second. "I have an idea. I could use a cigar and a drink right about now. Let's go to Club Macanudo and we can find a quiet corner table and discuss it then," Gino stated.

Thirty-five minutes later the two SUVs pulled up to the cigar lounge and restaurant. The bodyguards posted outside watching all those who entered the club closely. The two Sicilians went to the bar overlooking the corner table that Gino, his consigliere, and his best friend had occupied.

"I smell a rat. Maybe two, I don't know. That's why I didn't want to discuss anything in the car," Gino whispered.

"I agree. I was about to stop the conversation when you chimed in," Mickey uttered in a mere whisper also.

"What am I missing?" Joey said a little too loudly.

"Shhhh. I'll explain. Mickey jump, in if I miss something." All three men were huddled close around the table with their heads only inches from each other's so only they could hear. "First of all, this Cabbagehead is a pure maniac," Gino whispered. "His timeclock has to be stopped, once and for all. There is no way on this good earth we can trust him. He is totally out to prove he can bury us, and his greed is way over the top. He must go. The sooner the better. Listen to me though, I think I saw the weak link in his operation. The way he treated his man Peter was very telling," Gino stated.

"That kid hates that sfacime, Cabbagehead. You could see it written all over his face when he embarrassed the kid like that, telling him to shut up," Mickey added.

"Correct. We need to find a way to get to Peter and take his temperature. If he's smart, he will figure out he can work with us and the other families and set up a great situation for the Hip Sing," Gino stated.

"Yeah, but Gino, these people are very difficult to read. I can't tell what the hell they're thinking, forget about what they're saying. Is it just me?" Joey asked.

"You're partially right. Quiet, to themselves, pensive, call it whatever, but they make mistakes like anyone else. Let me bring up something else I caught. How do they know that we had a visit from the cops? Any guesses?" Gino asked.

"What are you talking about?" Joey asked.

Mickey sat back and smiled.

"Peter said both sides had a visit from the NYPD. How did he know we had a visit?" Gino pressed.

"Yeah...holy shit. Maybe the cops told them?" Joey supposed.

"Maybe, but I doubt that. How about the rat I smell in the NYPD as we speak?" Gino said rhetorically.

"My job is done!" Mickey blurted.

"What? What are you saying Mick?" Gino asked.

"You are finally thinking like a Don and I can retire back to Palermo," Mickey announced as a joke.

"You have a lot of work to do before you retire consigliere," Gino offered.

§§§§

Cabbagehead didn't wait until they returned to the city. He started up, right in the parking lot in Sparkill.

"You stupid fuck. All you do is talk, talk, talk! All that high-brow education and fancy logic and what did we get? We got shit. They shit in my mouth again, those scumbag, wop fucks!" Cabbagehead flipped out screaming.

"Danny, you can't afford to take these men lightly. They wrote the book on whacking people, they are..."

There you go again, Peter. What are you trying to do, scare me away from taking from the Italians what they took from the Irish and others years ago? Fuck you. If you don't have the balls for this ride just tell me, and you can go open a soup dumpling shop in a mall in Jersey," Cabbage-head yelled.

Cabbagehead held his crimson red, bald head in his hands for a few seconds before erupting again.

"Gino Ranno dies! That old man with him dies! And his friend Clams dies! That is my strategy... end of subject," Cabbagehead raged.

"Insulting me in front of them wasn't your most strategic move, Danny."

"Well, fuck you, and fuck them. The day for the quiet Chinese man is over. I am taking things over in this city right here, right now. Peter, you need to know your enemy better...like me. They actually fear us, you know? They are very afraid of the yellow race. Their bible says, 'blessed are the meek for they will inherit the earth.' I don't want the whole earth. I just want this city!" Cabbagehead raged.

CHAPTER 45

Inspector Mike Abbate called Matt Baker into his office at the O.C.C.B.

"Look at this, right off the Interpol daily intel report," Abbate said. He turned his desktop computer screen so Matt could read the information. Matt read with great interest before he responded.

"So some guy was killed in Hong Kong. Doesn't that happen almost regularly over there with the crazy drug trade that runs from that city? Why is this important to us?" Matt asked.

"Read the name of the victim," Abbate advised.

"Chung Leung. I guess I'm having a brain fart inspector."

"This guy was Suzie Ping's cousin and business partner in China. He was tortured before being executed. And an ax was left in his skull. This is the M.O. of the New York Tongs."

"So this homicide is tied back right to Cabbagehead and his crew."

"Right. The only question I have Matt, is why? Why would her partner be whacked when the Hip Sing is tied to Ping? There has to be a reason behind this," Abbate declared.

"Yeah...yeah. I see it. There is an internal conflict between Ping and Danny Chu. The plot thickens," Matt stated.

"Exactly! Maybe it's time we visited Ms. Ping. She's not going to open up but maybe we can read something through her bullshit."

"How about today?" Matt answered.

§§§§

"Are you free tonight?" Suzie asked. She called Gino for a date.

"Absolutely. How about dinner?"

"I was thinking we should just stay in and have a nice quiet evening together," Suzie offered.

"Sure. How about my place?"

"How about the Carlyle Hotel? I already booked a suite if that's okay with you?"

"Fine by me. I can't tell you how much I miss being with you, Sweetie," Gino admitted.

"I can be there at eight. I still have a lot to wrap up today. Oh, and plan to stay the night."

"I'll pack a bag," Gino laughed.

§§§§

At three o'clock that afternoon, Abbate and Matt Baker showed up at Suzie's office unannounced.

Alison went into Suzie's office looking a bit rattled.

"Miss Ping, there are two policemen here to see you. That detective from the Fifth precinct and an older man."

"Did you tell them I'm busy?" Suzie asked.

"Yes, of course. They said it would only take a minute. They were very insistent," Alison relayed.

"Tell them to wait. I'll be about twenty minutes."

Suzie could have easily seen them immediately but made them cool their heels for a while.

Matt and Abbate sat in the waiting area where Matt noticed the leather sofa was replaced by an inexpensive couch. He also noticed that the draperies were no longer on the windows, the sun glare from the street made the room uncomfortably warm and bright.

"This is a big difference from when I was here last week. This office was plush. Expensive furniture, draperies. It's like a shit box now. Maybe she's getting ready to move," Matt opined.

"Lots of moving parts going on," Abbate replied.

The time passed slowly for Matt and the inspector. Alison finally opened the reception door and escorted them to Suzie's office.

"Good afternoon, Miss Ping. Nice to see you again," Matt said.

"Hello, Detective. As you can imagine, I generally work by appointment, but I can see you as a courtesy," Suzie remarked. Her demeanor was less than friendly.

"Thank you. We won't take up too much of your time. This is Inspector Abbate," Matt introduced his boss.

"Nice to meet you, Inspector. What's on your mind?" Suzie asked. She did not stand from behind her desk and shake the men's hands as she normally would.

Matt began the conversation.

"It's come to our attention that your cousin, Mr. Chung Leung, was a victim of a homicide in Hong Kong. We were interested to know if you could shed any light on the case?" Matt asked.

"Yes, a terrible tragedy. I know nothing about why he was killed," Suzie blurted.

"Isn't he your partner?" Abbate questioned.

"Not nearly. Chung was a sales rep for me. He dealt with the money sources and marketing our services in the Far East. The money transfer business is quite competitive as you can imagine."

"Competitive enough so that he was tortured and had an ax buried in his skull?" Abbate was blunt.

"My God, please spare me the gory details inspector," Suzie replied.

"So if you had to guess, why was he killed in such a brutal way?" Matt inquired.

"Evidently, my cousin was involved in things that perhaps he should not have been. He was very headstrong and was in and out of drug rehab a few times. You can check on that fact, I'm sure."

"You think he was involved in the drug trade in Hong Kong?" Abbate queried.

"I tried many times to counsel him about using drugs and the life it brings. It's possible he was involved with the wrong people, but I would only be guessing," Suzie replied.

"We will be working with law enforcement over there as he also has a residence here in New York, right here in Chinatown," Abbate proffered.

"I see. Well, I hope you catch the people who did this terrible crime."

"And how about you, Miss Ping? What are your plans now that he is gone?" Matt asked.

"I guess I need to find another rep. Business needs to go on you know," Suzie replied coolly.

"Are you moving from here? I noticed some of your furnishings have changed since my last visit," Matt asked.

"Oh, no. I am just remodeling. I was getting tired of the old look. Change was needed. I have another two years on this lease and we are very comfortable here," Suzie lied.

"If you can shed any light on Chung's homicide, we would be very appreciative," Abbate stated.

"There is nothing that I can do to help you, Inspector. What happened to my cousin is nothing to do with me or my business affairs. After all, Hong Kong is over eight-thousand miles away and it's in another world as far as I'm concerned."

"Just curious…are you planning to fly over for services?" Matt asked.

"Oh, no. We were not that close even though he was a cousin. Besides, I hate that sixteen-hour flight. I'm a white-knuckle flyer," Suzie laughed nervously.

CHAPTER 46

Despite her hard, cool exterior, Suzie was fairly shaken up when Matt and Inspector Abbate left her office. She was sure she cloaked her feelings and didn't say anything to tie her to Cabbagehead and the heinous threats he'd made to her.

Suzie was still looking forward to seeing Gino later that evening in spite of her experience during the day. She planned to go to her apartment, shower, and dress for a romantic evening with her man. There were a few more things which needed to be finished before she left her office, but she didn't need Alison or Diana's services. She let them leave at four-thirty after telling them the visit by the police was nothing she or they needed to be concerned about.

Just after five, Suzie grabbed her bag, shut the office lights, and opened the door to leave the office.

"Well now, going home early tonight, I see," Cabbagehead announced. He, along with Peter and two of his Flying Dragons were waiting in front of her door. Suzie was understandably startled.

"I have an appointment I'm late for," Suzie proclaimed. She fumbled for her keys to lock the office door.

"You're going to be late, Baby Sister," Cabbagehead demanded.

He pushed open the door and forced Suzie back inside. The others followed.

"If you think are going to wreck my office again…"

Cabbagehead interrupted her.

"What? You were about to say something, Baby Ping. Are you going to call those two, mutt cops who where here earlier? I don't think so. I will do whatever the fuck I want to you, your office, or those two, nice young ladies who work for you. Get inside your office, now!" Cabbage-head ordered.

Peter and Cabbagehead went inside Suzie's office and shut the door. The Dragons waited in the lobby.

Cabbagehead sat behind Suzie's desk, commanding her to sit in one of the two chairs in front. Peter squatted in the other.

"I came to pay my condolences for your poor cousin. I just heard the bad news. What a shame, and so young," Cabbagehead pronounced.

Suzie glared at him. She showed no emotion.

"Anyway, life goes on. Business will suffer for a while but you are a smart lady who will figure things out. Now, about your new Italian boyfriend. This guy is our true enemy. When I say our, I mean the entire Chinese race, of which I believe you belong to. He is one of those white men who, like so many others in the history of our people in this great county, wants to keep us in our place. Like the Cooley workers who broke their backs, building their fucking railroads, and then the Chinese people were no longer welcome to share in this fabulous democracy, we were excluded. Excluded! Just like we are being excluded from growing right here in our adopted city. Just look at greasy, Little Italy here. It used to span dozens of blocks. Now, what? Two blocks and a stupid feast? Our people have taken over the streets where their grandmothers lived. So naturally they are upset with us. I say fuck them," Cabbagehead preached.

"What does all this have to do with me, Danny?" Suzie uttered.

"It has everything to do with you, Baby Ping. You are either one of us or you are just another Asian beauty opening her legs for the white man, and I'm afraid you might have become one of them. I certainly hope that's not the case with you. Remember blood is thicker than water. You have the blood of the Xia Dynasty dating back thousands of years, running through your veins, pretty lady and your business, which has made you wealthy, depends upon people like me."

"And so does the lives of my family in China, I suppose," Suzie blurted.

"Precisely. Dude, are you smart or what?" Cabbagehead offered.

"So, I'll stop seeing him," Suzie responded.

"No. That is exactly what you will not be doing. You will see him as often as we tell you to. And at the right moment, you will do what is necessary for us to defeat our white enemy."

"Are you serious? That's crazy!" Suzie yelled.

"Crazy like the fox, my dear, Baby Ping. Peter, explain our plan and how our lovely sister will help the Chinese race rise from the shit we have been subjected to." Peter put his feet up on Suzie's desk and smiled like he was watching a movie as Peter began to explain.

"We expect you to keep the romance with Ranno going for a short while. When the time is right, we will tell you what needs to be done with him," Peter said.

"What the hell does that mean? Shoot him in his sleep? I will not do it. I won't!" Suzie quivered.

"No. You will not shoot him, but you will poison him!" Danny took his feet down off the desk, stood up, and got right up into Suzie's face. "We will give you precise instructions, and he will, I repeat, will die the brutal, painful death he deserves," Cabbagehead ordered.

"You are totally insane," Suzie commented, staring right back into Danny's eyes.

Cabbagehead's skull reddened.

Peter stepped in. "It's either you do what we need you to do or that twenty- three-year-old cousin, Jing, who is soon going to medical school, will be carved up like a pig. Oh… and that precious niece of yours, Changying, what is she now, nine? She will be sucking cocks in Hong Kong. Such a tough life they live in that lovely, farming village of yours, Shengmei. There are so many of your relatives left there depending on you to do the right thing for your people," Peter exclaimed.

Suzie lowered her head trying hard not to cry. *They should both die a thousand deaths,* she thought.

Cabbagehead lifted her chin up, looked her squarely in the face and whispered, "Now that we understand each other? You go have fun with your white lover. You will have your orders in due time."

CHAPTER 47

"Jesus Christ, Joey, I can't walk three blocks by myself anymore?" Gino asked. His voice was raised to an annoying holler.

"Gino, don't you get it? These Chinamen will gun you down like a dog in the street. Mickey is already at the hotel checking things out with a few of his crew," Joey announced.

"I should have just not mentioned it and snuck the fuck out of here. It's just a date with my gal."

"Look buddy, you know how we feel about her...well not her actually, she seems very nice, at least she treats you great...it's what she represents. We just can't trust her while this craziness with these Chinks is in our face," Joey stated.

"So you think Suzie's a plant and she's going to cut my balls off and I'll bleed out? C'mon, will ya!"

"Just do what you need to do to protect yourself. I've read a lot of mob history, you know. I even read it when we were kids. After my Uncle Rocco went away, I was more interested in Albert Anastasia than I was in Davy Crockett and Superman. How many mob guys were gunned down when they didn't have a posse around them? Morrello, Ardizone, Maranzano, Masseria, Moretti, Giancana, Anastasia, Galente, Castellano. You want more? These times are as tough as they were back then, maybe worse because you can't trust anyone these days. Just be a good boy and listen to your friends," Joey preached.

"Do you really think she could be a set-up Joey?" Gino asked. He had a boyish, vulnerable look on his face.

"I hope not because you're going to fall hard with this one pal. I've never seen you so dreamy eyed. To answer your question, without hurting your feelings...she could be. It seems too much like a fairy tale to me. Smokin' hot, gangster, Chinese lady falls for aging mob Don who needs a Viagra drip to keep up with her," Joey laughed to break the tension.

"Not too far from wrong, pal-o-mine," Gino chuckled.

"If she is a plant, and we find out, you know she's gotta' go. If she's the real thing, tu salute, Don Gino," Joey added.

"Okay, let's get the cars and drive me three friggin' blocks," Gino ordered.

§§§§

Two SUVs pulled up to the regal Carlyle Hotel on East Seventy-Sixth Street where Mickey and one of his crew were waiting under the canopy. Gino opened the rear window of the vehicle and called out.

"Yo, Mick, how are the sausage and peppers in this joint?"

Mickey rolled his eyes and looked up to the clear evening sky. Joey leaned over Gino and pressed the button closing the window.

"Will you never grow up?" Joey asked.

"Hope not!"

Mickey ushered Gino into the lobby where two more Miceli soldiers were waiting. Joey was right behind him.

"She has you in suite twelve-eleven. The assistant manager is a friend of ours. No bugs, no nothing. C.C. and one of my crew will be staying in the hallway on your floor all night. Two of my guys will be down here in the lobby," Mickey announced.

"Thanks, Mick. Hey, I heard Kennedy used to bring his girlfriends here when he was president," Gino asked. His face was serious.

"And look what happened to that prick," Mickey blurted.

"Let's not get him started, Gino. He hates anyone who is an Irish politician," Joey added.

"No...I hate anyone who ever double-crossed us," Mickey whispered.

"Well, that's a story for another day. Can I go up?" Gino asked.

"Wait down here. She hasn't checked in just yet. Sit in that corner in the brown chair; this way you can see who comes in," Mickey ordered.

"Okay, just try to have your guys blend in with the all the rest of the chubby, mob looking guys without necks who come in and out of this joint," Gino joked.

A few minutes later Suzie showed up and saw Gino. She hurried over to him. She hugged Gino tightly and kissed him gently on his lips.

"It's not good when we are apart," Suzie said. Although it was early evening, Suzie still wore her Chanel shades. She wore a tapered green business suit, her hair pulled into a pony tail, accentuating her high cheekbones.

"Wait till you see the room I got for us...amazing view."

"I have a pretty good view right here in front of me. You look gorgeous," Gino stated.

"And I have a few surprises. Let's go check in." Suzie turned and walked to the mahogany surrounded reception desk. Gino watched in admiration as her ponytail bounced with every quick step she took.

With just a couple of small overnight bags, Suzie turned away a bellhop, taking the key herself.

Once inside the elevator, Gino pulled Suzie close to him, grabbing her butt with his right hand. He kissed her deeply. Suzie lost her breath for a second then quickly recovered, kissing her lover back. She lifted her sunglasses, propping them up onto to her head.

"Were you crying, Sweetie?" Gino asked, seeing her eyes were a bit puffy.

"Oh no, my love. Just my allergies. I took something in the cab on the way here. They will calm down in a minute," Suzie fibbed.

Gino didn't believe a word of her excuse.

The suite was nothing less than stunning. A small living room with a beige and gold divan and two orange club chairs with a fairly large, flat screen television was attached to the beige painted walls.In the next room, the king size bed did not overtake the large room. The walls, with maize colored wallpaper, blended beautifully with the padded, gold headboard and gold dust ruffle surrounding the base of the bed. Egyptian cotton sheets were pulled down awaiting the two lovers. Cotton slippers, and terrycloth robes were on either side of the bed. Original prints of yellow lilies adorned the wall behind the bed.

Gold and green carpeting ran throughout the suite from the door to the panoramic window. With pleated gold, yellow, and maize draperies, with a ruffled matching valance the window treatments framed a virtual painting of the city lights below.

"Isn't this so beautiful, my love?" Suzie gushed.

"Nice room. Is there a mini-bar? I can use a drink," Gino said.

"Ah…excuse me? Did you look on the desk in front of the window?"

"A bottle of Dom and chocolate covered strawberries. Well, that's a good start," Gino chuckled.

While Gino played with the cork on the DP, Suzie went into the bathroom. The sound of the cork popping was loud enough for C.C. and his sidekick to hear it in the hallway.

Gino poured two flutes of the bubbly, ignoring the fruit.

Suzie opened the bathroom door, clicking off the light behind her. She stood framed in the doorway with the soft light from a bedroom wall sconce accenting her stunning beauty.

"I would not wish any companion in the world but you," Gino quoted.

"Why thank you, my love. I see you quote Shakespeare as well as your other major talents.

I can quote the Bard as well, "I know a lady in Venice would have walked barefoot to Palestine for a touch of his nether lip," Suzie cooed.

She moved blithely toward Gino teasing him with the skimpy, red negligée and black stockings, complete with red garter belt and spikes. Her jet-black, delicious smelling hair, was now loose and flowing down her toned back.

Suzie slowly undressed her lover pulling him onto the bed on top of her. Gino kissed her hotly on her neck as he began to go down on her. Suzie entwined her fingers in Gino's salt and pepper hair, closing her eyes in anticipation of his tongue meeting its ambition.

"How could I ever hurt this man? How? I love him to my core," Suzie thought.

CHAPTER 48

"Good morning, Sweetie." Gino rolled over in bed. He put his arm gently around Suzie. The early morning light was peeking through the partially opened sheers.

"Good morning, my love."

"How did you sleep?"

"Not well. I was up most of the night," Suzie lamented.

"I would have thought you'd slept like I did. Dead to the world from all the great sex and the champagne. The second bottle did me in."

"I have a lot on my mind, I guess. Besides, I hate having to leave you this morning."

"I know there is something you're not telling me, Suzie. What's really bothering you?"

"Business problems, that's all."

"Nah… there's something else. I'll ask you again. Is it us? Are we moving too fast for you?"

"Is that how you are feeling, Gino? I'm a big girl, I can take it."

"Absolutely not. I'm prepared to spend the rest of my time on this earth with you."

"It's not you, my love. It's not us. You are the best man I could ever ask for. It's just that I'm under a lot of pressure."

"So tell me what's going on. I may be able to at least give you some advice, unless you don't trust me."

"Stop that. I trust you. I just don't want to burden you with any of my problems," Suzie's voice quivered.

Gino brought her closer to him. He felt his manhood quiver at her touch.

"Try me!" Gino exclaimed.

"My business has been put on hold. Not the money transfer business, the other thing."

"Why?"

"My key associate in China was murdered. He handled an important part of my business, and really without him, I have no supply source. Without him I am essentially shut down. And the plans to expand are no longer on the table."

"Murdered? By whom?"

"I honestly don't know. I have no way to prove what happened. All I know is he is dead, murdered in a cruel fashion. He was a cousin of mine on top of it," Suzie said.

"Was he killed due to your business? Again, I'm not judging but you have chosen a very tough business. Lots of bad people in that world."

"Yes, I understand that. If I am to continue I need to find a replacement, but it's not so easy to trust anyone. He was family and he did his job well."

"I can reach out for you and find out the story if you want."

"No…please don't. I need to decide if I will even remain doing this. In spite of what you may think, I still have a conscience. I know what I have done is not…"

Gino interrupted Suzie's thought by putting his finger to her lips. "Shhhh, my love. It's ok."

She sat up in bed. "No. No, it's not."

"Look, let's uncover the elephant in the room," Gino said. "Human trafficking. There, I've said the words. Trafficking human beings is not something even my people condone. It's a very dirty business which damages so many people. The suffering is endless." At that point Suzie started to cry. She knew the damage as she had experienced it first-hand herself. "Just like much of what I now do, it's not something to be proud of. The drug business, which also ruins lives, is something similar to what you do. In my world, I always have to say that, 'my world', the old timers would not permit dealing in that trade, yet it was done anyway for the big money. I sound like I'm preaching now so maybe I should just listen and shut my trap," Gino offered.

"But if I don't do it, don't you think someone else will?" Suzie asked.

"Of course, that someone else will make the money, but will also take the risks. I would hate to see you be taken down like your cousin, or wind up inside for a long time and die like your sister. After all, is money that important?"

"I will not go back to poverty. I did my time!"

"That is a cop-out, Sweetie. You are smart enough to find another business that is less hazardous. You can develop your legitimate enterprise and just walk away. Unless of course, you are afraid to, for some reason."

Suzie moved off the bed and draped herself in the bathrobe.

"So you're saying I should quit. Walk away… no, run away from the bad world I'm in. Should I ask you to do the same, Don Gino?" Suzie spouted. Her tone was sarcastic and angry.

"Hold on just a second. I'm just telling you how I see things for you. Yes, if we are to have a future together, I have a hard time with what you are doing, and…"

"And, what? Maybe I should just be your mistress and live in a big house somewhere and keep you happy? Maybe this nice, Chinese girl should open a restaurant, or a laundry?" Suzie yelled. Gino was stunned for a few seconds.

"That never dawned on me, Suzie, but being with someone who is so far over the line, so far into a business that is so sordid that you can wind up dead or in jail, is not something I'm enthusiastic about, if you want me to be honest," Gino replied.

"And, what about you? You can be killed like so many other mafia guys or thrown into prison because someone ratted you out or you said something the cops taped. Maybe you need to look at yourself in a mirror and not wag your finger and tell me I'm a bad woman. Maybe we need to back away from this...what should I call it now...love affair?... this...tryst?"

"What the hell has gotten into you? You tell me you are stressed out, how things are bad for you, and you have a conscience, and maybe you should walk away, then you attack me for the life I'm in? It will hurt me deeply, but if you want out, just say so. You said you were a big girl...well, I'm a big boy and you will not be the first woman who disappointed me," Gino stated.

Suzie fell onto the bed sobbing. She covered her face in both hands. Gino touched her back, letting her get the cry out. His suspicions were raging.

"I love you like no other in my life. I'm sorry, my love. I never want to hurt you in any way," Suzie said through her bawling.

Gino pulled Suzie to his chest. She buried her head into his upper body and kept crying. Trembling, she hugged Gino so tightly he could barely breathe.

"Don't cry, Sweetie; try to calm down. There is something you are holding back from me and I respect your privacy. Whatever it is, I'm here for you."

Suzie kept sobbing, and her tears ran down the hair on Gino's chest. She was inconsolable.

CHAPTER 49

"Hey Baker, what are you doing slummin' it back here at the Fifth?" Detective Kevin Wang asked. Matt Baker was back at the Fifth Precinct to review an old file, run it through the NYPD Domain Awareness System, and to look up a few, former Flying Dragon names and their prior arrests.

"Big Wang, my man, how are you? I miss this rat-hole," Matt answered and laughed.

"All good. I'm doing my turnaround tonight. Going to eat nice and sleep for a while. Wanna go to Hop Wong for some soup?"

"Thanks, but I can't do it. I can't get the reports on my stupid phone, and I was close by so I'm just looking up a few loose marbles in the neighborhood."

"Anyone I can help with?" Wang asked.

"Maybe you can. Speaking about Hop Wong, I ran into David Wong. I think he was carved up by a few of the Dragons. Cut his hand up pretty badly."

"Really, did he tell you by whom?" Kevin asked.

"Nope. You know, the old D & D. Deaf and dumb so they don't come back and cut his head off next time," Matt answered.

"That's my people for you. They prey on each other, been doing it for five thousand years and nobody sees shit."

"I'll catch you when I get back from my O.C.C.B. assignment," Matt offered.

"How's that going? Listening to wires all day?"

"Ha-ha, no, not at all. Although we did ask for a wire on Danny's place. Hopefully the judge will see it our way. I'll know in a little while. Maybe even tonight."

"Good luck with that. Are you still expecting fireworks between the mob and Danny? It's been very quiet."

"Like I told you last time we spoke, I met with both sides. Wanted them to know we will break their balls without mercy if they start things up. I've even been to the Puzzle Palace a few times on this thing. The brass is ready to lock things down."

"Look at you, rubbing elbows! So, did you meet Don Gino yet?

"Matter of fact, I did. Seems like a cool guy, but he lawyered up, and we just let him know we were watching. Usual bullshit. Hey, listen to this, though. I hear he's banging that Chinese broad, Suzie Ping," Matt announced.

"You're kidding? Get the fuck out of here!" Matt blurted.

"Yep. I'd like to go a few rounds with her myself," Wang offered. He made a crass gesture imitating a blow-job.

"I can't believe it! Isn't she involved with Danny Chu somehow? They're about to go guns blazing, and the Don is banging one of the enemy? You can't write this shit," Matt laughed.

"So which office are you bugging? Danny has a few you know."

"The Hip Sing office on Pell. He's spending a lot of time there lately. We've been tailing him for a few days now. If he slips up, you can watch him do the perp walk at the tombs. I'll be the guy with the frown standing next to him with my shield around my neck," Matt said.

"He's a pretty smart character. Just watch your ass, Baker. Don't get into the cross fire."

"Good seeing you, Wang. Let's go out one night if your wife lets you," Matt offered.

"You bet…I wear the pants in my family. I'm fourth on the list at home. There's the two kids, the mother-in-law, the dog, and then me.

Hey, by the way, I've been using your desk to do my reports. At least your window opens. I think mine has been stuck since eighteen-ninety-one. Hope you don't mind?" Wang asked.

"Be my guest. Just don't leave any crayon smears on the wood," Matt laughed.

§§§§

Matt went up to his desk on the second floor and checked a few things on the DAS. Nothing panned out for him on some notions he had on the Dragons. Out of force of habit he typed in Gino Ranno's name to check priors. No arrests, no warrants, nothing. Not one arrest. The head of a New York crime family and nothing. That's bullshit, Matt said to himself.

Before he left the Fifth, Matt called Inspector Abbate.

"I have some interesting, but unconfirmed gossip I though you would like to hear," Matt offered.

"Tell me the mayor is a faggot!"

"No, this is even better. I heard from a Chinese detective in the Fifth that Ranno is banging Suzie Ping."

"Lucky guy!" Abbate shot back.

"Can you imagine if it's true? If it is, the Don may find himself DOA one night, after she slits his throat," Matt declared.

"Let's keep our eyes open on this one. Oh, by the way, Baker, we got the okay on the wiretap for our friend on Pell," Abbate advised.

"Nice. Now, maybe we can find out what this maniac Danny Chu is planning."

CHAPTER 50

Gino headed back to his office the morning after his date with Suzie at the Carlyle Hotel, going back the three blocks in the SUVs with Mickey and C.C. who had pulled an all-nighter for the boss' security. Gino felt terrific, like he was thirty-five years old again physically, but the weight of his argument with Suzie made Gino emotionally feel his real age.

Gino whispered to Mickey once he got inside the vehicle.

"Mick, do me a favor, get Joey and come to my office as soon as we get back, okay?" Gino asked.

"Sure, Gino...problem?"

"I think so. I need to reach out to people a long way from here."

Within fifteen-minutes, Mickey and Joey were sitting in front of Gino's impressive mahogany desk. Gino sat back in his leather chair lighting a morning Cuban.

"If this desk could talk, Madonna mio. I have to tell you both something. I don't know how Carmine, Sr. did it. All those years, decades as the boss of this family with all the pressure, all the risk, the peril if he made the wrong move. Cops, feds, wise guys, all looking for a piece of his ass in a life where you're always looking over your shoulder. Gambling every day with your life and the lives of the people around you. If you say the wrong thing, or even the right thing, you could get clipped, and maybe by your best friend. It's a tough gig guys, but I'm starting to enjoy it. I must be crazy, but I wake up ready for the challenges of this thing of ours every day," Gino articulated.

"And you learn something every day...no?" Mickey asked.

"I learn something every day, yes," Gino replied.

Gino continued. "I've learned to listen not only to what people say, but how they say it, and what choice of words they use, and more importantly, what they don't say. That's why I wanted to see you. I have a job for you both. I'm not nearly ready to let you two guys say I told you so, and Joey you have said those words to me a thousand times since we were ten, but my sixth sense is raging,"

"About the girl?" Joey asked.

"Yes, about the girl. She tells me her business is basically shut down because her cousin, the guy who lined up the kids she traffics to get them here, was killed. I don't know where, but I do know it wasn't pleasant, and it was recent. I think she has another headache also she is not willing to share. She lied to me, and I'm pretty sure she knows who put her out of business and I want to know who that is."

"Gino, why is this at our doorsteps? What is her business to us? This reminds me of a thing my father used to say in Sicily, "Di guerra, caccia e amuri, pri un gustu milli duluri," Mickey preached.

"Sorry, I don't get it," Gino stated.

"In war, hunting, and love you suffer a thousand pains for one pleasure," Mickey translated.

"Okay, I still don't get it," Gino repeated. He looked at Joey for support. His oldest friend just shrugged his shoulders.

"It's simple; this isn't worth it, Gino. There is too much pain, and not enough gain with this thing," Mickey advised.

"Just do what I ask, please. I have my eyes wide open because of you two, and now I want to see if she is the real thing or not. If she is… well…" Gino pleaded.

"Of course, Don Gino. Tell us what you need done," Mickey asked.

"Mickey find out from our people in Palermo if their Chinese contacts know of any recent murder of a man. I don't know exactly where. China, Vietnam, Hong Kong somewhere in Asia. Find out who he was, what he did, why he was clipped, and who did it. I just don't want anyone to know we are the ones who are asking. I think I know who did it and why, but I want to confirm my suspicions," Gino offered.

"Who do you think whacked him?" Joey asked.

"I have a Sicilian saying as well, 'a megghiu parola e chidda ca nun si rici,' the best word is that which is not said. I'm holding that card close to my vest," Gino announced.

"It may take a day or two but I'll reach out now. It's still early over there," Mickey stated.

"And Joey, I want you to find out all you can about Suzie Ping's legitimate business dealings. Everything you can get your hands on. I don't even know her real name for Christ's sake. I mean her real Chinese name. I want to know about her old boyfriends, driving record, last PAP smear, every fucking thing you can find out about her," Gino ordered.

"I'll start with my old friend at the I.R.S. I'll have to throw her the long high hard one again but I can take it for the team. The rest is easy," Joe said.

"Let's go, Valentino. Let's go do what we gotta do," Mickey replied.

CHAPTER 51

The morning after Gino gave instructions to Mickey and Joey Clams to find out all they could about Suzie and her murdered cousin, there was a meeting taking place at the Hip Sing Association on Pell Street.

"Danny, this is our new…" Peter started to make an introduction to a new face when Cabbagehead put his finger up to his mouth indicating the need for silence.

"Let's go 'round to the park and get some exercise with the old people. They will show us their moves to keep the body limber," Cabbagehead proclaimed. He pointed to his ear and the ceiling, telling the two men with his signs, they were being listen to.

Once outside, Cabbagehead lit a cigarette, mixing the tobacco with the fresh morning air as he inhaled it deeply.

"Excuse me for a minute," Cabbagehead uttered. He took Peter by the arm and walked down Pell, leaving the stranger standing with three Flying Dragon bodyguards.

"Our guy in the Fifth tells me we are about to be wiretapped. Could even be done already so I want to take no chances. The only meetings we have upstairs is to feed the cops some bullshit. That motherfucker Baker is like a worm. He's crawling around putting his nose where it doesn't belong. I'll deal with that when the timing is right. Now, who is this nerd you brought to me?" Cabbagehead inquired.

"You asked me to find out about poisons. This is the guy who has all the answers. He's a genius, molecular biologist from Beijing. He's all checked out. One of our Dragon's cousin. All he wants is money, and a passport for his wife and son to come here," Peter informed.

Cabbagehead walked back toward the man with a broad, welcoming smile and his arms outstretched for a man hug.

"My apologies. I am Danny Chu."

"I am Manchu Hing. My friends and associates here call me Manny," Hing sprouted.

"Danny, this guy is one of the smartest guys from the homeland. He has a PhD in things I can't even spell, and he is an expert on what we are looking for," Peter exposed.

Hing spoke in Chinese; "Peter tells me you are looking for a toxin like the CIA was trying to use on Castro. I can obtain it for you and fully explain how to administer it. Peter understands my fee structure and I guarantee excellent results.

Cabbagehead sized up the diminutive Manny Hing. Manny was wearing a white, button down shirt, baggy black pants, black and white sneakers, and black-rimmed eyeglasses with thick lenses. Manny may have weighed ninety-five pounds soaking wet and had a distracting facial tick that involved his upper lip and nose that resembled Cornelius in the Planet of the Apes movie.

"Tell me, please, as we walk around the park my new friend," Cabbage-head requested.

"Certainly. The product is called Black Leaf 40. Believe me, if the CIA had been able to administer Black Leaf 40 to Castro, he would have been dead for fifty-years already, so first let me give the details in technical terms. Black Leaf 40 is a nicotine alkaloid and nicotine sulfate. It is known as an alkaloid insecticide. Understand that little or no nicotine is produced in the U.S. and a very small amount is imported from India. Two basic types of nicotine products have been sold on the market; the alkaloid and the sulfate. Nicotine alkaloid is relatively volatile and acts both by contact and by fumigant action.

The sulfate is usually marketed as an aqueous solution containing forty percent nicotine equivalent. When added to alkaline water or to a soap solution the alkaloid is liberated, being then more active than the sulfate.

Cabbagehead interrupted; "Slow down, Manny! You lost me with the fumigant action and liberated talk. I never got out of high school. Just tell me how it works on people."

Manny twitched in a series of three convulsive facial tics.

"Black Leaf 40 is a colorless liquid which darkens slowly and become viscous on exposure to air so the product must be ingested fairly quickly. Now this may get somewhat technical again but listen closely, please. Nicotine preparations, especially those using the free alkaloid like Black Leaf 40 are well absorbed across the gut wall, lung, and skin. Poisoning symptoms from excessive doses appear promptly. They are due to transient stimulation, then prolonged depression, of the central nervous system, autonomic ganglia, and motor end-plates of skeletal muscle. Central nervous system injury manifests itself as headache, dizziness, uncoordination, tremors, then convulsions leading to tonic-extensor convulsions which are often fatal. In some instances, convulsive activity is minimal, and death by respiratory arrest occurs within just a few minutes. Effects on autonomic ganglia give rise to sweating, salivation, nausea, abdominal pain, diarrhea, and hypertension. The heart slows down, and often becomes arrhythmic. This toxin blocks skeletal muscle motor end-plates, causes profound weakness, then paralysis. Death may occur from respiratory depression or from shock. Bottom line? Black Leaf 40 is the real-deal toxin and it works without any doubt, and is not a pleasant way to die," Manny lectured.

"If it's good enough for the CIA boys it's good enough for me! How do we get it into the dude?" Cabbagehead asked.

"There are multiple forms of administration.. First, there is transdermally, which means through the skin, and orally. Of the two, I prefer the oral method for rapid absorption, but there is also injection which would also do the trick. A pill, though, in food or a drink, would be the fastest way, but it cannot be in warm drinks as Black Leaf 40 tends to smell a bit fishy at eighty degrees Fahrenheit," Manny replied. He pushed his glasses back onto the bridge of his nose with his finger and did a double twitch.

"When can I get some of this stuff?" Cabbagehead asked,

"I can have enough to do an adequate job for you within seventy-two hours. Whoever is administering must work with me to learn how to handle this toxic product to be certain they themselves are not contaminated," Manny added.

"Interesting. What if we want the person giving it to croak as well?" Cabbagehead asked.

"Hmmm, I suppose my instructions can be inaccurate," Manny blurted.

"Manny, you did a great job so far. We will have your fee ready, plus a nice bonus, and the passport for your wife and daughter when the Black Leaf 40 does the job you say it will. Three days is perfect timing, my new friend," Cabbagehead declared.

"You will very pleased with the results Mr. Chu…very pleased."

CHAPTER 52

The next day, Gino was in his office when he called Suzie to make a date for dinner.

"Hi, gorgeous. I'm missing your face."

"Hi! I was just going to call you. I'm missing you, too," Suzie purred.

"How about dinner tonight? Nice Italian place."

"Love it! What time and where?

"Let's do eight. My guys will pick you up at seven forty-five, tell me where." Gino said.

"My apartment. Can't wait to see you, my love."

At noon, Mickey and Joey came to the office for a meeting with the Don.

"You guys look like you have something important to say. What's up?" Gino asked.

"We have most of the information you were asking for," Joey stated.

"Great; who wants to go first?"

Mickey worked by memory. He never wrote things down.

"I contacted our friends in Palermo; they send their respects to you. Gino, we should make a visit soon to keep the relationships fresh. Some new names are moving up. Anyway, the murdered guy was Chung Leung, a cousin of your lady. They hit him in Hong Kong. The guy was a freak with very young girls and lots of drugs around him. He spread money all around town, big player at the tables where our people gave him good credit. He was always good with covering his markers. He drove around China like a big shot in mostly small towns, sending girls and boys, from nine to twenty for the flesh game, mostly here. Took special orders for some middle-eastern countries too, and for big money. As far as the hit, it looks like a Triad in Hong Kong, with ties to the Hip Sing Association here did the piece of work. They left a hatchet in his head, just like our guys on Doyers Street got. Your lady has a pretty good reputation in her country as a ruthless snakehead who has plenty of protection here and over there."

"Snakehead?" Gino asked.

"Yeah… Chinese word is snakehead. That's what people who trade in the flesh business are called. They make millions but there is a tie to the Hip Sing. They provide security and buy the kids, too. If she is paying for protection to Hip Sing, it's in cash and the green circulates with no backup," Mickey added.

"Joey, what did you find?"

Joey read from notes he took in a black and white Composition book.

"The dead guy, Chung, would wire some funds through the Bank of China on at least a monthly basis, mostly at 42 East Broadway in Chinatown and some up at 410 Madison, but the bulk of the cash is made here in New York and other cities. The accounts are assigned to Asian Rim-America LLC, owned by Shuchun Ping. That's her real name. The money transfer business is designated as import and export of novelty items, rugs, glassware, things like that. They paid very little tax here. Not a lot of profit shown on the money transfer business. Last year they showed a loss of eighty-six thousand. Year before, a small profit. Ping has a line of credit for a half mil, they pull from it in regular installments but always made good by the close of every month. It looks as if the money transfer thing is a front for the real big money. It's all cash so impossible to trace," Joey reported.

"No obvious tie to the Hip Sing Association?"

"Just fifteen-thousand in a check last year as a donation to an education and training fund," Joey replied.

"And her personal life?" Gino inquired.

"Other than she was never married in this country, she lives under the radar. Nobody knows sto gatz about her. Nothing! I didn't want to ask around too much not to wave any red flags, like you asked," Joey added.

"Not too much help. I was hoping for a direct tie to Cabbagehead on the transfer business," Gino muttered.

"No way could I cut through the maze, Gino," Joey replied.

"And if I pushed our friends back in the old country too hard, it would raise too many eyebrows. She works with the Hip Sing but not exclusively," Mickey offered.

"Whatever she is, she is one, smart fortune-cookie," Joey added.

"Thanks, guys. Mickey, have the boys bring her over to Sam's Place on Lex by eight o'clock from her apartment. Send a chase car and make sure she isn't followed," Gino ordered.

"Does she know you're taking her to Sam's?" Mickey asked.

"Absolutely not!" Gino blurted.

"Good," Joey and Mickey replied together.

§§§§

Gino arrived at Sam's Place with his security detail at twenty-minutes before eight. He hadn't seen Massimo, the owner in quite some time. He enjoyed the restaurant owner's animated stories about everything from politics to women.

"Look who is here!" Massimo approached Gino with outstretched arms. "Oh, my God, I am the luckiest man in town tonight!" Massimo announced. He hugged Gino and kissed him on both cheeks under the watchful eye of the two Sicilian bodyguards.

Sam's Place is a small, street level, walk in restaurant on East 39th Street with eight tables on the first level and three or four tables on the second floor where the restrooms are snuggled in one corner. The Italian fare is nothing less than amazing, and Massimo insists on keeping his eye on every dish going to each table.

"I thought you were too big of a shot to come see your old friend Massimo. What a great moment it is to see you, my friend."

"And I've missed you, my dear friend. But…you never change! The same as always: thin, handsome, always happy and smiling," Gino stated.

"How is your family? I mean…you know what I mean Gino, not the big family but your own family."

"Tutta posta…all good, thank you. And yours? How is that gorgeous wife of yours and your son?"

"I think my son may one day listen to a word of advice that I give him. At least I hope to live long enough. My wife, she hasn't killed me yet so I will say she is good."

"Max, I have a special young lady coming in tonight. Is my usual table free?" Gino asked.

"What kind of question do you ask?" If she is anything like the last one you had here I may go home and beat my wife with a stick," Massimo laughed.

"You be the judge; she will arrive soon. For now, just a bottle of your best red," Gino ordered.

"Subito, Gino. How happy I am to see you. And I have the baby clams tonight and the branzino if you are in the mood."

Suzie arrived. One of the bodyguards held the front door open for her. She tripped slightly on the high, stone step leading into the restaurant and burst out laughing. Massimo moved quickly to the door.

"I am so sorry, Signora. One day I will take a pick and shovel to that step. Are you okay?"

"What a way to make a cool entrance, don't you think?" Suzie was still laughing. "Oh, I'm sorry, I am meeting Mr. Ranno," Suzie announced.

"That, signora, is impossible at this moment. Mr. Ranno is inside saying his prayers that a woman like you would even look twice at him," Massimo whispered as he took Suzie's hand and kissed it. "Right this way, bellissima," Massimo flirted.

"Ah, there you are!" Gino said as he stood to meet his lady. Suzie greeted him with a kiss on the lips and a long hug. Massimo could barely contain himself.

"Massimo, this is my girlfriend, Suzie…Suzie say hello to my dear friend, Max."

"Oh, yes, we already met at the door," she said to Gino." She quickly looked around and then said, "What a quaint place you have here, Max."

"I have no words, Gino. She is the most gorgeous woman who has ever entered this place. I must go in the kitchen and cry that she is with you…and not me!" Massimo joked. He turned and left the table.

"You Italians really know how to pour on the compliments," Suzie exclaimed.

"What does he know about Italian? He's one hundred percent Albanian, born in Tirana. But he is smooth, isn't he?"

"Gino, thank you for tonight. I really had to see you," Suzie stated.

"Why? What's wrong?"

"Wrong? What makes you always think something is wrong? I had to see you because I love you, silly man," Suzie whispered. She reached her hand across the table and touched Gino's.

"You make me so happy, Sweetie. A drink or some red wine?"

"The wine is fine, my love."

Suddenly car wheels screeched on Thirty-Ninth Street disturbing the normally quiet, peaceful neighborhood. The sound of gunshots popping alerted Gino to trouble. He pulled Suzie onto the floor of the restaurant, spilling the wine all over the two of them. Other diners stayed in their seats, oblivious to any danger. Massimo ran from the kitchen and peered out of the window facing Thirty-Ninth Street.

Three of Gino's men saw a van coming up Thirty Ninth Street at rapid speed, swerving erratically past two double parked cars. The van came to a screeching halt just before the corner at Lexington Avenue. The side panel door swung open loudly, exposing three men with automatic weapons. Gino's men were ready and sprayed the shooters with precise automatic fire. The would-be assassins got a few errant shots off, hitting the brick on an adjacent apartment house but no other damage. One of the Sicilians calmly walked up to the three dead or dying men, shooting them all with rapid fire from his AR-15 assault rifle, splattering their heads apart like melons on the asphalt pavement.

"Signori Ranno, andiamo, we must now go!" the other Sicilian demanded inside Sam's Place. Suzie stood up looking angry, but not at all worried.

"Gino, go…go and be safe my friend," Massimo advised.

"I'm so sorry Max. So very sorry," Gino uttered.

Gino took Suzie by the hand and led her out the door. The two Sicilians sandwiched the couple between them as they walked as one to the open door of one of the SUVs.

"Please stay down, Mr. Ranno. We had to take out that van over there. These guys came loaded for bear. We got three of them. The fourth, the driver, ran down toward Second Avenue, so please stay down," one of the bodyguards said.

"Jesus Christ! Any of our guys get hit?"

"No, sir, we got lucky."

"Okay, let's get far away from here," Gino ordered.

The sounds of police sirens were getting closer by the second. The three-vehicle caravan, in close formation, made a left on Lexington Avenue, pulling away from the curb at Sam's Place without screeching tires and revving engines.

As they made the left turn, Gino looked up through the rear passenger window. There on the corner of Lex and Thirty-Ninth, next to an all-night grocery store he saw his failed assassins, all bloody and quite dead.

Three young Asian men were on the street, their lifeless bodies outside of a bullet-ridden, cream-colored van. The same van that was used in the hit outside of Enzo's restaurant in the Bronx.

CHAPTER 53

Thirty-Ninth and Lexington Avenue became the convergence of a small platoon of NYPD's finest.

Patrol officers arrived from four directions, two of them going down one-way streets at a high rate of speed. The patrol supervisor, a sergeant, notified her operations unit when she got to the scene. She called for a level one mobilization. A patrol duty Captain was dispatched from Manhattan South Precinct and arrived a short time later with lights and sirens, as did the Manhattan South duty inspector. Surveying the carnage, two of the top cops on the scene huddled together.

"I think we need to raise this up to a level two, captain," the duty captain advised the patrol supervisor.

"I agree, let's do it! This is a big one," the captain blurted. He nodded to the lady sergeant.

The sergeant clicked on her remote radio. "Central, I'm eighty-four at Lex and Three-Nine. Need to bump up to a level two. Copy?" Eighty-four is code for on the scene in NYPD lingo.

The cavalry was called. A citywide, duty chief was expected on the scene, and men from the deputy commissioner for public information were en route. Detectives from the Chief of Department's office, the Chief of Patrol's office, and the Chief of Manhattan Detectives arrived almost simultaneously. A crime scene unit pulled up just as an NBC news truck and a Channel 5 news team made it to the scene. Independent photographers, hearing the chatter on their police radios, were there well before the major media arrived.

The three bodies weren't yet covered as the yellow crime scene tape was being rolled out around the scene. This was sure to be a headline story, gory dead bodies and all, in the morning tabloids.

Matt Baker called his boss, Inspector Mike Abbate.

"I got a call from the one-seven. There was a shooting at Thirty-Ninth and Lex less than an hour ago. Three DOAs in the street, all Chinese. From the tattoos, it looks like Flying Dragons. I'm eighty-four right now. Things are being pieced together," Matt advised.

"On my way. Any sign of the Micelis?" Abbate asked.

"Our guys from the one-seven are canvassing the area for witnesses and videos. So far no information to go on.

Matt went into Sam's Place where uniformed officers and detectives were interviewing patrons, wait staff, and Massimo who were all now detained for their eyewitness testimony. Matt listened to the detectives who were questioning the shaken customers and staff.

"I heard a lot of what sounded like firecrackers. Didn't really sound like gunshots, but I never heard live gunshots in my life anyway," a diner remarked to a uniformed sergeant.

"Did you see anything from the window?" the cop asked.

"It all happened so fast. No, I didn't."

Closer to the kitchen was heard, "Yes, I am the owner. Your captain knows me. I am Max." Massimo said to the officer.

"You heard the shots?"

"No, I was inside the kitchen, too noisy to hear anything," Max lied.

"Do you have any video cameras of the street we can view?"

"Sorry, I don't believe in them."

"Was there anyone in here tonight who could have been involved with this shooting?"

"In here? Of course not! We have a nice, small, local clientele, all fancy people. No trouble makers in here, never!" Max exclaimed.

The police department did their extensive canvassing, photography, fingerprinting, and tagging and bagging until the wee small hours of the morning.

Matt and Abbate worked side by side with the crime scene investigators trying to make a tie-in with the organized crime angle. There supposition was straight forward. Three Dragons were not killed that evening in midtown Manhattan without cause. The young detective and the organized crime veteran inspector both wanted to find the real reason why these three, young, Chinese men, with automatic assault rifles and shotguns were splattered on the fancy pavement of East Thirty-Ninth Street.

Forty blocks away, Gino and Suzie were in the Miceli headquarters on East Seventy-Ninth Street. Gino was surprised his lady was not unnerved by the shooting. They sat in the study, each with a Johnny Walker Black on the rocks in their hands.

"You don't seem so shaken, Sweetie. Are you really okay?" Gino whispered.

"Gino, there is so much about me you need to learn. I lived in a bad world back in China. As a child, there was death always around us. Mostly sickness, but violence too. People do desperate things when they see their children practically starving. My own parents were willing to sell me into a life that would have turned me into...who knows? Who knows how long I would have survived? And here in New York, I can't count the funerals I have gone to for young people who have died on the streets of Chinatown. Death is a part of life, and I have been fearless for a long time, my love, but perhaps now that I've met you, I may soon understand how precious time is, and I will be afraid of everything," Suzie replied.

"That is sweet of you to say. My people have prepared for you to stay here tonight. Things may be a little tense out there so it's best if you stay put and out of harm's way. Here you will be safe. Besides, I have an extra toothbrush," Gino winked.

"Can I wear your new, silk smoking jacket?" Suzie teased.

"Mmmm. You will look better in it than I ever will. I have to meet with a few of my men now. Relax here, or go up to the suite. I'll find you," Gino whispered. He kissed Suzie softly on her lips.

In the living room, which was not used since Carmine Miceli, Sr. passed away, Gino met with Joey and Mickey. The bodyguards were outside the townhouse making themselves inconspicuous by remaining in several sedans. The Miceli's SUVs were taken to a safe place in College Point, Queens by C.C. and his crew, where they would be garaged for a while.

The two Sicilians and five other bodyguards, with automatic weapons strapped to their chests, sat quietly in various parts of the townhouse.

"Gino, we got word from Cabbagehead. He swears on all his ancestors he didn't give the order to hit you. He wants to talk again, face-to-face, and tell you himself. He said these were rogue Dragons looking to make a mark and gain favor with him," Mickey said.

"What did you say?" Gino asked.

"I told him nothing. I said we would be in touch."

"I want you to get me the best there is. From Sicily, Naples, Calabria, the North fucking Pole. I want the best team as soon as you can get them here to take care of this situation. Enough is enough," Gino demanded.

"Yes, Don Gino," Mickey said.

"Gino, one thing." Joey interrupted. "I don't like that she was with you when this happened. How did they know where you would be? She had to have told them. I'm sorry but she is bigger trouble than you bargained for."

"Joey, she had no way of knowing where we were going for dinner unless she has a bug in her bra. I made sure of that. My guys picked her up, drove with a backup car and everything. I never mentioned Sam's Place to anyone and I haven't been there in over a year," Gino indicated.

Joey's phone rang. It was C.C.

"Excuse me, Gino. Yo, Charlie! Yeah…yeah…you're fucking kiddin' me? All three trucks? Okay, thanks."

Joey looked at Gino and then at Mickey with lost puppy eyes.

"All three SUVs had bugs attached to their undercarriage."

Gino folded his hands on his lap. He examined his fingernails for a second and smiled at Joey. Gino looked at his consigliere, his smile turning into a cold, bitter stare.

"Why are you sitting here, Mick?" Gino growled.

CHAPTER 54

The next morning, the news of the shooting was all over the media. To save time, Inspector Mike Abbate called Saul Atkins for an interview with Gino Ranno regarding the homicides on East Thirty-Ninth Street the evening before. The police wanted to speak with Gino immediately. Abbate insisted the meeting take place at the one seven precinct, not at Saul's office or Gino's office. Atkins cajoled him into meeting at his law office on East Fifty-Sixth Street just off Madison Avenue. He promised his client would be there at three in the afternoon.

Manuel Carcano, the homicide detective assigned to the case, conducted the interview in the presence of Detective Matt Baker, Inspector Mike Abbate, Atkins' partner, Lewis Sunshine, and a cute stenographer hired by Ranno's lawyers.

After all the preliminary questions, such as, state and spell your name, place of residence, and the rest, Carcano dove right into his query.

"Mr. Ranno, last evening were you in the vicinity of Lexington Avenue and East Thirty-Ninth Street at approximately eight twenty in the evening?" Carcano asked.

"Yes, I was," Gino answered truthfully. Atkins and Sunshine spent hours preparing Gino for the line of questioning he would likely be facing.

"May I ask what were you doing there?"

"Having drinks," Gino responded.

"And where, sir, were you having drinks?"

"A small restaurant. I believe it's called Sam's Place, something like that?"

"Have you been there before?" Carcano pressed.

"Yes, I think so. But not for quite a long time."

"Mr. Ranno, who were you having drinks with?" Carcano probed.

"Detective, my client was with a lady. And that is all my client is prepared to say on that matter. Her identity will remain confidential," Atkins interrupted.

"If she was a witness to a crime, at some point we will require an interview with her," Carcano stated.

"Please proceed with your questioning of Mr. Ranno," Atkins said, his voice going up a few octaves.

"Mr. Ranno, did you hear the sound of gunfire outside of Sam's Place?"

"I heard something which sounded like firecrackers, to be honest with you."

And how did you react to the sound?" Carcano asked.

"I really had no reaction at all. I didn't really think of gunshots quite frankly."

"Do you remember falling to the floor of the restaurant and shielding your companion, Mr. Ranno?" Carcano pressed.

Gino paused and looked at Detective Carcano with a small smile on his lips.

"I really don't recall that, Detective," Gino retorted.

"I'm sure by now you are aware that three men were gunned down outside of the restaurant where you were having cocktails," Carcano stated.

"Is that a question or a statement detective?" Atkins asked.

"I will put it as a question. Do you know that..."

"I do. I read it in today's Post," Gino interrupted with a reply.

"Mr. Ranno, are you aware the dead men were all Chinese and members of the Flying Dragons Chinatown gang?"

"I read that but with all due respect Detective Carcano, what does that have to do with me?"

"Mr. Ranno, we believe that you were the target of an assassination attempt by these gang members, and that this action was part of a bigger problem you are having with the Hip Sing Association," Carcano articulated.

"Detective, my client has no knowledge of any street gangs and denies his business operations have any involvement with any such association about which you are talking. Perhaps you need to do some homework on my client's business interests," Atkins scolded. Carcano ignored the attorney's rebuke and his tone.

"Mr. Ranno, do you have a security team?"

"Define the word security and define the word team detective," Atkins bellowed. Carcano didn't flinch.

"Mr. Ranno do you have people who watch for your safety, who protect you when you are out and about?" Carcano rephrased.

"Yes, I do."

"And of the person or persons who protect you, are you aware if they thought your security was in question last night, or that your life was in danger?" Carcano asked.

"No, not at all," Gino blurted.

"So your men didn't tell you if they shot the three men who were found dead in the street?"

"Asked and answered, Detective. My client said he was unaware his safety was an issue last evening. I think you need to interview some witnesses on the streets," Atkins said. His tone was sarcastic, almost comedic.

"We have done that counselor and we are still piecing this crime scene together."

"So look at the video cameras from the streets. I'm sure you will not see my client shooting anyone detective. If anything, you may see him leaving the scene in a vehicle but in no way, was he involved with this unfortunate situation," Atkins preached.

"That was my next question counselor, Mr. Ranno. Did you leave before having your drinks?"

"Yes, I did."

"Why did you leave, sir?"

"Diarrhea. I suffer from a bad stomach and I just wanted to get home and take some medicine and go to bed," Gino answered.

"So you didn't leave as a result of having three men shot to death less than one hundred feet from you and at the urging of your security team?" Carcano pressed.

"Asked and answered already, Detective! Come on, now. My client has a serious stomach ailment. He had to have his gall bladder removed not too long ago. I can get his doctors to attest to his embarrassing, chronic diarrhea if you want," Atkins yelled.

"That won't be necessary, counselor. I can see I'm not going to find out more that we already know. I appreciate your time Mr. Ranno, counselors," Carcano stated.

"Can we go off the record for a minute?" Abbate asked.

"Inspector, every word my client utters is on the record. Feel free to say what you have on your mind," Atkins answered.

"If this shooting last night is the sign of an escalation of the problems we spoke about recently, rest assured those above me are ready to make life miserable for these pain-in-the-ass gangsters who are shooting and blowing things up in our city. I'm sure you all join the good citizens of New York City who are looking for peace and tranquility in their daily lives. Good day, gentlemen," Abbate lectured. His voice was dripping with sarcasm and filled with warning,

CHAPTER 55

Suzie went back to her office the next day after another passionate night with Gino. The excitement of the shooting seemed to have turned her on, while Gino's mind was racing like a Ferrari around a test track.

§§§§

Days went by without any NYPD interference in any of the Hip Sing or Miceli operations, but everyone in the underworld was on high alert, waiting to be pounced upon.

Cabbagehead learned, to his dismay from his man inside the Fifth precinct, there was no clear video showing that the Miceli crew killed his three Dragons. His explosive anger erupted like Mount St. Helen's. He lost his best hit squad and even worse, Cabbagehead lost his face among the Hip Sing Association for no gain.

The time for him to make his move had arrived.

§§§§

Mickey Roach had put together Gino's request for assassins from Mickey's friends in Palermo. Four specialists came from Marineo and Lercara Friddi, in the Province of Palermo, Sicily, the latter being the Miceli and Gino's family home town, and were set up in an old, one-family house, tucked away in the Clason Point section of the Bronx, far away from Gino and the Manhattan operation of the Miceli clan. The crew came from Palermo through Canada under falsified, Corsican passports.

The veteran of the four was Gaspare Alia, known throughout the Sicilian Mafia as la Pietra, the stone, for the cold, ruthless way in which he handled his duties. Word was that in 1992 the young la Pietra worked with the Corleonesi mafia killer Giovanni Brusca, in the assassination of Italian Judge Giovanni Falcone at a culvert on the A29 motorway, near the town of Capaci, between the Palermo Airport and the city of Palermo. Falcone, his wife, and three, police bodyguards were blown apart by a half-ton of explosives. Falcone was a tough judge who would not be bought by the mafia. He paid for his patriotism with his life.

At the celebration after the assassination party thrown by Salvatore Riina, the mafia chieftain, who was called Toto 'u Curtu, Gaspare Alia was considered a guest of honor. Riina was called Curtu not because he was short in stature, as the name implies in Sicilian. An idiomatic dialect translation connotes bloodthirsty, ruthless, arrogant, and ambitious as definitions.

"La Pietra could use a bomb or a shoelace to dispatch his targets with equal efficiency.

The other three killers, none over the age of twenty-eight, had learned at the elbow of la Pietra. They were his go-to hit men for any special piece of work they were ordered to complete. Their orders came from the highest command of the Sicilian Mafia in Palermo, out of respect for the Miceli family in New York. None of this crew's targets has ever survived their special expertise.

Mickey knew Gaspare Alia's family well, and trusted him without reservation. All Mickey had to do was formulate a plan to send Cabbage-head to whatever type of hell Buddhists believed in.

CHAPTER 56

Cabbagehead and Peter, along with three, tough-looking Flying Dragons showed up at Suzie's office. The two leaders of the Dragons wore fitted, Canali suits, white shirts, and sincere silk ties, a first for Cabbagehead.

"Here, you two ladies go and spend a few bucks on yourselves," Cabbagehead announced when he barged into the office. He handed Diana two, crisp, hundred dollar bills.

Diana looked at Alison and neither young woman rose from their desks. Cabbagehead laughed at their scared faces.

"This is not a suggestion ladies. Go…now!" Peter yelled. The frightened ladies made quickly for the door. Both of their butts were grabbed by a Dragon on their way out.

Suzie heard the commotion and went into the front of the office.

"What the hell are you doing?" Suzie asked.

"We just need some quiet time with you, that's all. Your girls just got a few bucks, and they didn't have to even blow anyone," Cabbagehead replied. The other men laughed loudly.

"Not funny! They have work to do Danny," Suzie exclaimed.

"They'll be back. How do you like my new business look? Very sharp, don't you think? I'm here to do business with you, so I thought I would dress the part…like the Italians do. Smell me, I even have cologne on like the wops use."

"Spare me!" Suzie blurted.

Cabbagehead and Peter walked into Suzie's office. She reluctantly followed. Cabbagehead once again sat in her seat, pointing to the chair

261

at the front of the desk for her to sit.

"Have you found a replacement for your dear cousin, Chung?" Cabbagehead inquired.

"No, not yet."

"Good. We have a guy for you. Lots of experience. He's coming to New York in a few days to meet with you. I'm absolutely sure you will just love him."

"I'll find my own employees, but thank you for your concern," Suzie said.

"I don't think you understand. He is already hired and he has arranged for ten young women to come here, two by plane, eight on the water. All high-quality flesh," Cabbagehead insisted.

"I don't want any partners, Danny," Suzie exploded. Her voice was dripping with bitterness.

"And I don't want my partner to be upset, so I won't take too much of a percentage."

"This is not going to happen. I don't want any part of this."

"You don't have a choice, my sexy sister. But this is not our only reason for coming to see you. We have other business to discuss, and my dear Peter will explain what you will need to do for us," Cabbagehead retorted.

"We have a very simple task for you. You will be given a vile of a substance which will take our enemy into a long sleep. It's up to you to administer the liquid at an intimate moment. You will have an option of injecting your friend with a syringe while he sleeps, or dropping some of it in a cold drink. The result will be the same. He will become very ill, very quickly. His boys will take him to the hospital where they will have no idea how to save him. You will not be blamed for his sudden illness, and your rewards will be plentiful," Peter offered.

"Are you both crazy? I will do no such thing! First of all, I love this man. Besides, his people are not stupid. I will be killed if not that night, the next. I'm not going to forfeit my life for your greed," Suzie blurted.

"Hmmm. We thought this would be your response. Do you not remember what we said about your family? I think you need to call your dear auntie back home. That's if they even have a telephone. Did you know your niece and your cousin have been missing for a couple of days now?" Suzie let out an audible gasp. "Relax, you bitch. For the moment, they are unharmed. They both will be returned to the safety of their homes and be allowed to get on with their lives. That is, only if you do what you are told. If not, well, you already know what we have in store for these two, innocent kids. And they will only be just the beginning of the tragedies which will befall your family," Peter articulated.

"Why don't you just fucking kill me right now?" Susie screamed.

"What a silly thing to say, Miss Ping. We wish you no harm. Especially now because you are a partner. Besides, you are Chinese, and you will soon see the fruits of your work. With Ranno gone, our Chinese people will no longer be excluded from the millions which can be made in this great country we now live in. Our growth on the streets will be exponential, and you, little Miss Suzie Ping, will also reap the benefits beyond your wildest dreams! You think you've made a lot of money now with your businesses? Think about it! With your love buddy, Ranno out of the way, all of Chinatown, the Bronx, and more will be ours. Or, if you like, you can sink back down into the life you were lucky enough to escape when you left China. Or you can die in prison. No, you are going to do this. You are going to kill Gino Ranno, head of the Miceli crime family and our troubles will be gone once and for all. This time is a long time coming for our people. I know you haven't forgotten what life was like. Danny heard you telling your new lover all about it the other night!"

Suzie shot Danny a glance. How does he always know where and what we're doing? Suzie asked herself.

"And you haven't worked to get to where you are, to lose the life you have built for some Italian gangster now, have you?" Peter asked.

"Does your evil have no boundaries?" Susie blurted.

"My dear, Baby Ping, you will get over this affair in no time. Before you know it, you will see that your choice to support your heritage and the great Chinese people was your best solution. Now listen carefully to Peter as he tells you how to handle Black Leaf 40," Cabbagehead advised.

CHAPTER 57

Matt Baker stopped by at the Hip Sing Association office on Pell Street. Knowing Peter was the second in command, Matt asked for a casual meeting with Danny Chu to discuss the shooting on Thirty-Ninth Street. It was agreed they would meet the next morning for Dim Sum at Jing Fong restaurant, on Elizabeth Street, directly across the street from the fifth precinct.

Jing Fong's entrance brings the visitor to a long escalator which empties upstairs into an enormous dining room that seats eight-hundred people. At the top of the moving staircase is a massive, three-tiered crystal chandelier with gold trimming. The walls have muted, gold panels around the colossal ceilings with ivory colored panels from the ceiling down to the first floor. Once inside the dining room, the patron's senses are awakened by a sea of red and white tables and chairs. There are square tables for four and large, round tables which can seat ten, maybe twelve diners. Each table has bright, white table cloths, surrounded by deep red chairs. In the middle of Jing Fong, a gigantic, round, recessed lighting fixture with red designs and a two-tone blue metal rim around the circumference seems to dwarf the diner. The modern fixture illuminates the center of the restaurant, with the help of strategically placed recessed, high-hat lamps and huge, modern, rectangular fixtures. In the rear of the eating place, there is a stage with two steps which leads to more tables and a thirty-foot-high, red textured wall. Two, magnificent, multi-colored, ornate, ceramic dragons face each other from about sixty feet apart as if they were ready to do battle. Between them, in white Chinese characters, "welcome wedding guests," for a marriage planned that evening.

The Cantonese style cuisine is a magnet for thousands of diners every day, with dozens of buffet stations and moving carts which serve incredible selections of authentic, Chinese food.

Jing Fong opens at ten o'clock in the morning, and wouldn't be an ideal place for Cabbagehead to be seen with detectives from NYPD.

Peter saw to it that Jing Fong opened at eight thirty that morning just for one table of diners. Breakfast Dim Sum was served by two waiters and four rolling carts.

Cabbagehead arrived with Peter and an entourage of six Flying Dragons for security. Matt and Inspector Abbate were waiting at the front door. One of the restaurant's managers opened the doors and locked them behind the group.

"This place is incredible. I've never seen a room this big," Matt stated.

"Not every Chinese restaurant is a small storefront. You have a lot to learn about our culture detective," Cabbagehead smiled.

"Let's sit here. The food will come to us. I hope you like Chinese food, Inspector," Peter asked.

"My favorite, along with Italian," Abbate replied.

"We are very much like the Italians, gentlemen. Food is a very important part of Chinese culture. But our wine is not so good as yours," Cabbagehead laughed.

"My family is from Mulberry Street, Mr. Chu. My grandparents came from Italy and lived here all their lives. We have always had incredible respect for Chinese people and lived next to them in this neighborhood since 1905," Abbate boasted.

"Yet, by exclusion your government didn't want us here Inspector, but we can save that discussion for another time," Cabbagehead stated.

Three carts were pushed to the large, round table.

"Gentlemen, please select what you would like. You will see that we eat much differently than you do at breakfast time," Peter offered.

Matt took a creamy, rice soup. Abbate chose steamed pork buns. Peter and Cabbagehead took what looked like placenta.

"So, gentlemen, what can I do for you?" Cabbagehead began.

"Mr. Chu…" Matt said and was interrupted.

"Please, call me Danny. Mr. Chu is way too formal for me," Cabbage-head smiled.

"Thank you. Danny, I'm sure you're aware of the three, Chinese men who were killed on Thirty-Ninth and Lexington Avenue," Matt said, tossing out the reason he and Abbate had asked for the meeting.

"Of course, I am. These boys are from this community. This is my neighborhood. If a bird farts in a tree here, I know about it. Now, unfortunately, Mulberry Street will be busy with their funerals for the next few days."

"From what we can gather, from their ink and their look, they were Dragons," Matt posed.

"Yes, they all were part of the youth organization. Very good basketball players too, I might add."

"They were found with automatic and semi-automatic weapons. That sounds like a pretty rough youth organization to me," Matt pressed.

"You know, detective, like in any community, some kids go bad. Evidently these boys went down the wrong path in life. I like to call them rogues. Looking for the fast buck instead of getting themselves jobs and working hard to make a living. Some kids just want the easy way out. It's a real shame, don't you agree?" Cabbagehead preached.

"All of them have priors. Some worse than others," Matt responded.

"That's why we have our youth counseling sessions. However, sometimes we just can't rehabilitate them."

"So these boys as you call them were not part of a hit-team that you were aware of?" Matt asked.

"Come on, Detective. Danny is here of his own free will. He is not here with his fancy lawyer like Mr. Ranno was when you spoke with him. Please don't infer any criminal activity," Peter imparted.

"Detective, Inspector, I think you need to understand the word tong a bit. A tong is a meeting place. So many Americans think tong means gang, or something bad. They are sadly mistaken. The Hip Sing Tong, the organization for which I work, is nothing more than a meeting place for business people in our community whose function is to help our fellow Chinese merchants and business men. Now we call it Hip Sing Association. Do you understand now?" Cabbagehead asked.

"Sort of like the On Leong Chinese Merchants Association I guess?" Matt asked. He pretended to be naïve but Cabbagehead saw the subtle sarcasm in Matt bringing up a rival gang. Cabbagehead's bald dome started to become noticeably red. Matt noticed Cabbagehead had grown tense at his comment, and he had all he could do not to crack a little smile.

"Yes, they very similar indeed," Peter responded.

"It's interesting to us down at the station, that right where these boys were gunned down, Gino Ranno happened to be in the restaurant across the street. And these Dragons fit the description of shooters who rubbed out three, Miceli wise guys up in the Bronx not long ago. This sounds to me like a you hit us, we hit you, kind of thing. Am I right, Danny?" Matt asked.

"I don't know anything about that. Like I said, there are some bad kids who fall through the cracks, Detective. Evidently, these three boys went off the rails. Have you considered perhaps this was a drug deal gone bad? We hear so much of that nowadays!" Cabbagehead claimed.

"We will find out sooner or later. In the meantime, we hope this kind of thing doesn't get too far out of hand," Matt offered.

"May I interject?" Abbate asked. "Your merchants' association, I assume, is looking, like any store or restaurant would want, for its members to do well. I can assure you both, the community you serve will be turned upside down if there's any new flurry of violent activity. The streets around here will be empty of shoppers and restaurant goers when they see what's going down. These DOAs, I'm sorry, these dead Dragons were dispatched to kill a known mobster. We are all aware that the Miceli family and the Tong or the Association, or whatever we want to call it, are at odds. My advice? And it's strictly off the record after being at the NYPD for a long time, is not to fuck with us," Abbate warned. Cabbagehead's cranium was as red as the chair he was sitting in.

"Gentlemen, try the fried bean curd with this sauce. I think you will enjoy it," Peter advised.

CHAPTER 58

"We have an internal leak inspector," Matt declared as he and Abbate were on the escalator leaving Jing Fong.

"You caught that, too? Yes, how else would they know about us meeting with Ranno and his attorney?" Abbate queried.

"Exactly! I didn't tell anyone in the precinct, and I'm shit sure Ranno didn't, and unless you told someone at PP1 who is on the Hip Sing payroll, it leaves someone in the Fifth Precinct who's a bad cop."

"So how did this rat get the information?"

"ECMS has all of my reports. Could it have been hacked?" Matt was alluding to the NYPD Enterprise Case Management System detectives use to make their reports.

"Matt, anything can be done with a computer if you know what you're doing," Abbate advised.

"Now I'm starting to wonder if I was careless with my lap top. You know, leaving the program open on my desk," Matt lamented.

"That would be considered negligence. You know you should always log out, right?"

"Of course, but maybe I was just stupid."

"Inexperienced or careless would be better terms. We all make mistakes. However, if you were hacked, there isn't much you could have done to protect your reports."

"So, now what?"

"Very simple. You know what disinformation is? We set up whoever the corrupt fuck is and we take him down," Abbate advised.

"Should I go to my friend at I. A. B?"

"Listen to me, and remember this throughout your career. You never have a friend at the Internal Affairs Bureau. You report this and somehow you will come out on the shitty end of the stick. Let's think about something you can report that we want Cabbagehead to know. If it comes out, then at least we'll know our theory isn't just a bunch of bullshit," Abbate formulated.

"I'll come up with something and let you know. I'm really pissed off," Matt admitted.

"Is there anyone at the Fifth you think of who would be dirty like this? On Cabbagehead's payroll? Anyone who asks too many questions?"

"Come to think of it, yeah! One guy in particular. He happens to be a Chinese first grader in the Fifth."

"Let's keep it simple. When he asks you questions, feed him what we want and avoid using the ECMS altogether. Keep things nice and clean on your end," Abbate advised.

"There's no substitution for experience, Inspector," Mike added.

"You're learning fast, Matt. If you learn from a mistake, turn it to your advantage, and keep your nose clean, you can be Chief of Detectives one day."

"That's if I pass the sergeant's test," Matt stated.

"Take that word IF out of your vocabulary, will you?"

CHAPTER 59

Gino called Suzie several times during the day, getting her voice mail each time. He left a message offering a rain check for their spoiled dinner at Sam's Place. He knew of another romantic place in Tribeca. Suzie heard the message but didn't reply.

Gino finally sent her a text message, asking if she was okay. Thirty minutes later Suzie responded she had a headache, was tired, and not able to make dinner. There was no I love you or heart emojis attached as she would normally add.

Gino read tone into her reply and decided to see for himself if his girl was truly not feeling well or simply blowing him off for another reason.

Gino took the two Sicilians and C.C. in his sedan and quietly left the Miceli headquarters for Suzie's Chinatown apartment. Mickey was busy with the Sicilian hit squad up in the Bronx while Joey went to see his granddaughter in a school play.

The doorman recognized Gino from the newspapers and stood at attention behind the desk in the building's lobby. Gino asked which apartment Miss Ping lived and slipped the star-struck doorman a fifty, asking him not to be announced. Both Sicilians remained in the lobby while C.C. took the elevator ride with Gino to the twentieth floor to the penthouse apartment.

"Gino, not for nothing, but maybe she's with another guy. Then what?" C.C. asked.

"Tell you the truth, that did cross my mind. Then what? I say good-night and goodbye and all you guys will be thrilled," Gino replied.

"Sorry, boss, but I just had to ask in case you...."

"I appreciate your concern, Charlie. Let's just see what happens," Gino interrupted.

Gino brushed his hand through his hair, inhaled deeply, and rang the door-bell.

Suzie looked through the door's peephole and gasped. She wiped her eyes with a tissue and opened the door.

"This is a surprise! Come in, please." Suzie offered. She gave Gino a peck on his cheek and quickly moved into the apartment.

"Just wanted to see if you were okay," Gino stated.

"Are you checking up on me Gino? Go ahead and look under the bed, check the closets. You'll find I'm alone." Suzie wasn't happy with the intrusion.

"I was thinking maybe you had second thoughts about us. Your text was a bit cool to say the least."

"Are you that insecure? Did I seem cool to you the other night?"

"The opposite," Gino blurted.

Suzie just stared at her man.

"Real nice place you have here, Sweetie."

Her apartment was a study in feng shui design. Very simple, yet elegant. A red, microfiber sofa stood in front of a black marble low burning fireplace. A white, alpaca rug and another red, microfiber sofa stood below a Steuben chandelier. An original oil painting of cherry blossoms on a sky-blue background adorned the living room wall. A red, leather, chaise lounge, in front of her double terrace windows gave view to the captivating lights of the Manhattan Bridge. In the distance, the new, tall, glass buildings of Brooklyn cast an eerie reflection upon the quickly moving water of the East River.

Suzie's dining room featured a thick, round, glass table with a curved steel pedestal base. A black-framed, pewter, rectangular mirror loomed over a black, lacquer Chinese buffet.

Suzie mumbled something Gino didn't ask her to repeat.

"You've been crying. And don't tell me it's allergies this time," Gino stated.

"Yes, I've been crying. I have a lot on my plate at the moment and I just need some space. It's just…"

"Anything I can help with?"

"Why must you insist on rescuing me, Gino? I'm a big girl and I will figure things out. I've been handling my shit my whole life."

"Figure things out with or without me?"

"Would you stop? Please! How about just kissing me good night and leave me to my misery?" Suzie asked.

"Okay. How about you call me when you get out of this funk. Maybe we can do Montauk again," Gino said.

Suzie thought for a moment, *Montauk would be perfect for what I have to do.*

She looked sadly into Gino's eyes.

"That would be nice," Suzie cooed.

CHAPTER 60

Matt made it his business to spend more time around the Fifth Precinct house and the local eateries the detectives frequented. He needed to see the first grader he suspected as being on Cabbagehead's payroll and play with him just a little. A part of Matt told him the guy was straight, the other part of him was sure Kevin Wang was a dirty cop. There was just something about Kevin that always bothered Matt, yet he could never put his finger on it.

Matt ran into Luis Figueroa, his boss at the Fifth, who was sitting with Kevin Wang at Forlini's Restaurant.

"Look who just walked into Part F! The up and comer, Detective Matt Baker!" Figueroa applauded. The lieutenant was very proud of his detective on loan.

Matt shook both their hands and sat in the red booth next to Wang.

"What's part F, Fig?"

"Part F? Oh yeah, that's right! You haven't been at the Fifth too long. You know when you go to the courthouse down the block and they call the criminal court, Part A, and the juvenile court, Part C? Well, there are so many judges and lawyers eating at Forlini's everyday they call this place Part F now," Figueroa stated.

"There are more plea deals made around these tables than in the courthouse," Kevin added.

"Well, all I can say is the food at Part F is amazing," Matt said.

Matt continued. "Wang, how are you? Haven't seen you too much since I'm over at O.C.C.B.," Matt asked.

"I'm great. My daughter just got into NYU for nursing. Big deal at the Wang household," Kevin said.

"Congratulations. Isn't your wife a nurse?" Matt asked.

"Yeah, and I told her she needs to work O.T. so I can have help paying the tuition. That, plus my son in now at Xaverian High School. That place sets me back fourteen large plus a year," Kevin moaned.

"So are you gonna have another kid?" Fig asked, jokingly.

"Fuck, no. She can have one but it won't be by me," Kevin laughed.

"You're a maniac!" Matt chuckled.

"So what's up in the underworld?" Kevin asked.

"My head is spinning. We're just waiting for the next shoe to drop. So far there are eight DOAs, two at the Tea Parlor, three in the Bronx, and three on Thirty-Ninth. And I was looked at with the hairy eyeball when I predicted a bloody war at 1 PP. I think the Puzzle Palace is starting to agree with me," Matt bloviated.

"What's the next step?" Kevin inquired.

"We start cracking down, making collars, breaking balls, usual stuff," Matt offered. He took a sip of water, then continued. "Hey, I'm starved. Did you guys order yet?"

"Nope. We just sat down. The service at Part F is brutal today," Fig said. He waived for a waiter.

"So, cracking down on both sides?" Kevin pressed.

"Of course. I think the plan is to hit the Hip Sing hard right now," Matt added.

"I suppose we'll close down a few gambling rooms and a couple massage joints," Kevin said.

"Yeah, tonight that big joint on Mott near Canal; you know the one. Downstairs from the Buddhist temple. And they plan to make a move on the Happy Family joint on Baxter. Word is that Danny Chu owns that place."

"I haven't heard anything about any raids. Where's this coming from?"

Fig asked.

"The Commish started a task force just for this Miceli-Tong thing. Looks like he pulled guys from the boroughs. Gang units mostly. They should have let you know, Fig," Matt offered.

"Hey, whatever they want to do is fine with me. I'll probably get the call a half-hour before it goes down," Fig guessed.

"So, NYU? That's a big number! David Wong told me his daughter is going there, too. Maybe that's why he raised his food prices," Matt declared.

"I haven't been there in a while," Kevin mumbled.

"He's having a tough time with that bandage on his hand. Whatever happened, he got cut right to the bone. Poor guy," Fig said.

"We'll never know what happened there," Matt added.

Kevin looked at the menu.

The three policemen ordered hot sandwiches and Cokes. They chatted about politics, NYPD promotions, demotions, resignations, and gossip. Forty minutes later they each went their separate ways. Figueroa walked back to the second floor of the Fifth Precinct, and Matt joined Fig as he headed for his unmarked Ford which was parked in front of the Fifth. Kevin Wang walked eight or nine blocks to the Baby Panda 99 Cent variety store on Henry Street. Fig asked Matt if he had an extra minute to talk.

"I need to say something to you, Baker, and I need to say it as bluntly as I know how."

"Sure, boss, shoot!" Matt offered.

"In the position you have at O.C.C.B., you really shouldn't be discussing what action is about to take place. I've always used the old World War II slogan, 'loose lips, sink ships.' You don't want to be that guy who spills his guts all over the department and loses any and all confidence of command. You said a bit more than you should have at Part F," Fig declared. Figueroa laid the cards on the table.

"Boss, I need to come up stairs with you. I have something to tell you I should have shared with you already.

§§§§

Wang walked into the Baby Panda and motioned for the proprietor to meet in the rear of the store, behind the overstocked shelves where the monitors who watched for shoplifters from the ceiling cameras sat. No one in the semi-crowded store spoke nor understood a word of English.

Cabbagehead would have the information he needed within minutes.

CHAPTER 61

Mickey drove from the Bronx to Lower Manhattan with the four Sicilian buttons. It was their first time in New York, however there were no oooh's and ahh's or questions about the big city coming from Mickey's passengers. Once during the ride, Mickey pointed out the United Nations building on the east side of Manhattan. Their obvious indifference to the sites embarrassed Mickey who quickly ended his tour guide duties. The four killers were as cold as ice, just here to do a job, get paid, and get back to their towns and their families in the mountains of western Sicily.

Mickey spoke in Sicilian dialect so there could be no confusion with the limited English the men understood.

He passed around a recent photograph of Danny Chu.

"This man, Danny Chu who they call Cabbagehead, has a distinctive look. His bald head becomes red when he is agitated. He is famous for his bad temper. There are several well-armed men with him always. Practically on a daily basis he works out at a public gymnasium, gets a massage, and has sex with a different young girl, mostly two at a time, in various stores, most that he owns," Mickey instructed.

Mickey's Cadillac sedan zipped from Soundview Avenue down the Bruckner Expressway from the Bronx toward Manhattan. Taking the FDR drive, they arrived in Chinatown in twenty-five minutes. It was one of those rare occasions that the FDR wasn't bumper-to-bumper.

"Aspanu, I will take you and your boys around in the car. It would not be good for us to walk around the streets of Little Italy and Chinatown together. I would be recognized and with you four, we may raise suspicions," Mickey cautioned. He called Gaspare "la Pietra" Alia his childhood nickname, Aspanu. Back when they were boys Mickey and la Pietra would hunt together for the family tables in Lercara Friddi. They were both the men of the house at an early age. La Vendetta took both of their fathers on the same June evening, during the Festa di S. Antonio. The feast of St. Anthony of Padua. Their lives as ruthless killers were forged at a very young age.

"And where does this Cabbagehead live?" La Pietra asked.

"Very simple apartment. He is not one for too many creature comforts, but makes a big show with fancy clothes and shoes. No wife, no children living with him. Generally, he is alone in his home but spends most of his time at two offices."

Mickey drove the car slowly down Pell Street.

"Now, here is the Hip Sing Association office. Look, you can see the skinny guards outside milling around. Don't let their stupid looks fool you. These are Flying Dragons who would kill their own sisters for Cabbagehead. They use automatic weapons, but they are notoriously poor shots. One time they shot up an entire restaurant only to wound their target and a bystander. They place was sprayed like a child using a coloring book for the first time," Mickey continued.

Mickey drove around for some time so the men would get the feel for the streets. He handed out maps of Chinatown, highlighting Cabbage-head's haunts in red and the easy access and exits from the tightly situated neighborhood.

They were driving down Mott Street when one of the men in the back seat opened the window for fresh air.

"Que puzza!" The killer who sat in the middle moaned.

"Yes, it's smelly down here. So many people in a small place," Mickey advised.

"And the second office?" La Pietra asked.

"Right here. This is Doyers Street. Below this street are offices and some stores. Cabbagehead is well protected down below and there is no safe and easy escape for our men. I don't recommend it. Look, this is the restaurant where our men were slaughtered. Bastards!" Mickey exclaimed.

All four visiting murderers made the sign of the cross and kissed their hand as a sign of respect for their fallen comrades.

"Maybe me and Carlo go down there and see what goes on. I like tight places, especially for a bomb. This Cabbagehead can die from a thousand nails just as easily as with one bullet, am I right Michele?" La Pietra insisted. He called Mickey by his given Italian first name.

"Aspanu, you are the boss of this job. I'm just your servant. Whatever makes you happy, makes me happy," Mickey replied.

La Pietra and his cold-eyed protégé Carlo got out of the car and strolled around like tourists taking in the sights and smells of the streets of Chinatown. Twice, Carlo nearly tossed his cookies from the various smells which came from the restaurants, fish stores, and sewers. The blend of the three aromas was enough to bring tears to the first-time visitor's eyes.

Mickey drove around with the other two hit men for about twenty minutes until they would meet up again with La Pietra on Mott Street. The only thing which peaked their interest were two Caucasian women in black spandex leggings and tight tank tops, walking hand-in hand down Canal Street. When one of the girls leaned over and kissed her partner while they waited on the corner for a traffic light, one of the two killers made a low and long whistling sound.

"I a love-a New York," the other one said.

La Pietra and Carlo returned. Carlo stated he needed a bath from the stink. His boss shot him a hard look. Carlo should have realized the old-timers did not tolerate whining.

"This place is perfect for a backup. We can wire a nice bomb in minutes which can cut him to pieces, just in case he gets lucky and hides down there. I prefer the gymnasium or the massage house as our first choice," La Pietra stated.

"Good. Let's go back up to the Bronx and have some nice lunch and good espresso. Carlo can have his bath tonight," Mickey joked. No one laughed.

CHAPTER 62

Suzie barely slept. The smell of Gino's cologne seemed to linger in her apartment and her sinuses.

I love him so much…but how can I let my family, my own blood be slaughtered? Suzie thought. Maybe I can just walk in and shoot that fuck Danny and end this whole drama, she imagined.

Back and forth the entire night, Suzie's thought process seemed to leave her no choice but to do Cabbagehead's bidding. After all, Gino is a mobster, and in that life, the danger of death is always around him, she reasoned. Besides, their love affair has not been for too long, and at least she has the memory of what true love truly feels like.

She called Gino in the morning to thank him for his concern. She told him Montauk would be a perfect getaway for them, and would help get her out of the depression she had fallen into.

Suzie did her homework. The medical care in remote Montauk is virtually non-existent. On the eastern end of Long Island the nearest hospital is in Southampton, nearly an hour's drive from Lake Montauk. If a helicopter were available, it would be minutes, but in the early morning hours that would not be a viable option. Helicopters ran by schedule and weren't waiting around Montauk airport like taxis. Aside from that, Peter had informed her even a hospital would likely not be able to diagnose and treat a victim of the super toxic, Black Leaf 40.

Gino got to the office mid-morning. He called Joey Clams to come in for a meeting.

"I'm going back to Montauk to make an offer on that house. Can you help set it up?"

"Of course. When?"

"Tomorrow."

Joey just looked at Gino with the knowing eyes of an old friend.

"What? What's that look for buddy?" Gino asked.

"Another romp with that girl? Don't you think you're pushing the envelope on your safety? Mickey is tied up with that crew in the Bronx, getting ready to make the move! You should be cooling your heels. Your place is here, Gino," Joey advised.

"Nah, it's better if I'm not around anyway. After all, I can be back in no time if I'm needed."

"Did you run this past Mickey?"

"What am I reporting to him now? I run this family and I need to get away. That's that! Please make the arrangements. Bring the two Sicilians and a few other guys. I'll charter the helicopter so there will be no pain-in-the ass passengers on board. Just us," Gino ordered.

"And I will have to hear the old man screaming at me, I guess," Joey lamented.

"I'll handle it with him. Let's try to leave around two in the afternoon tomorrow. I'll call my friend who owns the house and get the chef out there. You can bring someone if you want," Gino offered.

"Thanks, anyway. I'll be working."

§§§§

Cabbagehead's people were ready for a siege from the NYPD. The big gambling room under the Buddhist temple on Mott Street was nearly empty. The high rollers were told to stay away, or go to the other gambling places on East Broadway and Canal Street. The massage parlors had only one girl in each place and they were forbidden to do any more than a real massage. No happy endings, no sex, nothing. Green lantern trainees manned the doors of the rub and tug places Cabbagehead owned. No one of rank would be affected by an arrest. Business was effectively shut-down, lawyers were at the ready, and Cabbagehead was doing a slow burn.

"By ten-o'clock that evening, not one raid had occurred. Cabbage-head's knot was as red as the flag of The People's Republic of China.

"Call that fucking Kevin Wang! Find out where he is, and get him to the 99-cent store. I don't care what the fuck he's doing, I want his ass in front of me, now!" Cabbagehead screamed. Peter made the call.

A minute later, Peter had made the arrangements.

"Danny, Wang is on the four to twelve shift. He's at the Fifth. He's heading over to the 99-cent store right now," Peter informed.

"Good. Let's go. I can't wait to see that little prick," Cabbagehead seethed.

Within six minutes, Cabbagehead and his entourage of four Dragons and Peter were inside the Henry Street store. The Dragons scared all the shoppers away, and dismantled the backroom camera monitors. Kevin Wang arrived moments later. He walked to the back of the twenty-four-hour store. The look on Cabbagehead's face and the scarlet hue of his bald pate made Wang's stomach flip.

"You fucking cocksucker! Do you have any idea what you cost me tonight? Any clue at all?" Cabbagehead hollered.

"What are you talking about, Danny? What the fuck?" Wang asked.

"I basically shut down operations because of your bad information, you asshole fuck."

"I swear, I was told the raids were going down tonight. How was I supposed to know if they called it off? It doesn't involve my house. The commander of the Fifth wasn't even aware of the move on you," Wang uttered.

"That's because there was no raid planned, you stupid motherfucker! How much do I pay you Wang? Fifteen hundred a week, something like that? Plus, holiday money and free pussy!"

"C'mon Danny. So, it didn't go down as I was told. What the fuck? Shit happens sometimes," Wang argued.

"Yes…shit does happen. And shit may happen to you! I could end your shitty-ass career with a little information to that fucking, young detective. What's his name? Baker? Oh, yeah. He plays it straight. That nice, clean cop can get a promotion with all the information on you we can feed him, you stupid asshole."

"So now you own me, is that what you think?" Kevin swallowed hard.

"Fuck you, cop. I owned you the day you took your first envelope from me. Get out of here before you get shot dead in a 99-cent store robbery," Cabbagehead bellowed.

CHAPTER 63

It wasn't a good beach day in Montauk. When Gino and the entourage arrived at the house on Lake Montauk, the air was salty and damp, the sky was gray and overcast, and the house looked a bit weather beaten and old. For some reason, that happens in Montauk when the sun isn't bright in the sky.

Suzie seemed a bit quiet, if not sullen on the helicopter ride from Manhattan and Gino was lost in his own thoughts.

My mother was right. I could be in Boca right now with the newlywed and the nearly dead, being chased by widows and cemetery plot salesmen, Gino thought.

"The lake is a bit agitated. All those white caps from the wind mean a storm is coming," Gino stated.

Suzie was pensive, staring out at the bubbling lake. Her hair was pulled back in a messy bun, her sunglasses were in her bag, and the borrowed Miceli Realty blue windbreaker she was wearing was two sizes too big for her petite frame.

"It's so beautiful and the air is so fresh. Can't we just stay out here forever and forget all that shit we have to deal with back home?" Suzie asked.

"How come you never had children, Suzie?" Gino asked. His question came out of left field.

"Talk about spoiling a moment. Where did you come up with this one, my love?" Suzie countered.

"Just wanted to know. You were contemplating living out here, like this instead of the rat-race we're in, and I saw you with a couple of kids, in my mind's eye at least," Gino answered.

"If you want the truth, I will share it with you. I lost a child when I was sixteen. Well, I didn't lose it, I had an abortion. From time to time, when my family was flat-broke and we had a poor crop, I had to do what I had to do to survive. I don't like to even think about it, but I decided to end the pregnancy. I've always regretted that moment and that I didn't have children. When I see kids at different ages running around, laughing, crying, going to school, getting married, and having their own children, a wave of 'what ifs' crash down on me. I wonder how my child would have done in this world. Maybe…now I'm…" Suzie placed her hand on her mouth to stop her quivering lips.

"Sore subject. I'm sorry I brought up something so personal. I feel like a jerk now," Gino uttered.

Suzie composed herself and continued, "So after that I put up what I call, The Great Wall of Ping. I never let anyone get in a position to get me pregnant again. Sure, there were men in my life, but none I wanted to have kids with. Well, at least until now, and look at me. Forty-five, with old eggs," Suzie lamented.

"And I'm sixty-six, and I have no idea if I'll see my next birthday," Gino retorted.

"And here is where one of us says, and if we had a child, it wouldn't be fair… and older mom and an even older dad."

"Right. It really wouldn't be right for the child," Gino imparted.

"And what is right? Two people in love who can give life, even if they can only share it for just a short while? It's far better than the loneliness and what ifs I've lived with," Suzie bemoaned.

"This conversation is freaking me out," Gino declared.

"You were the one that opened the door, my love. Now you know another of my hidden secrets and I don't know one of yours."

"Patience, Sweetie. I'll tell you all the gory details of my not-so-sordid life. First, let's have a drink and a snack. You hungry?"

"Let's just go up to the room and make love, Gino. Maybe I'll get lucky and you can give me your baby," Suzie said in all seriousness.

Gino stared at her for a moment and brought her close to him. A seagull flew closely above them and made a cry like a small child. *That's all I need at this point, a friggin' baby!* Gino thought.

"Suzie, you are the love of my life. That is so sweet of you to say, but how much time do I have left? God only knows. I can drop dead tonight, maybe next week, get shot in a barber's chair next year, and that's it," Gino contemplated.

"At least I would have something to remember you by."

CHAPTER 64

Up in the Bronx, at the Clason Point safe house, Mickey, his childhood friend and renowned killer, La Pietra, and the three young Sicilian button men sat around the kitchen table going over a step-by-step plan to murder Cabbagehead. Mickey poured black coffee from a dented, jumbo, old-fashioned Neapolitan maganette coffee pot. A bowl of sugar and a bottle of Marie Brizzard anisette were the only things on the table aside from the maps of Chinatown and the cups.

Mickey had heard from Joey about Gino's taking off to Montauk, but his focus was on the hit. Mickey was not one to go into a piece of work like this without a detailed blueprint of the upcoming action. He also wanted the final order to clip Cabbagehead to come directly from Gino.

"So there are no mistakes, everyone has to know what their job is, second-by-second. Let's all hear the plan one more time," La Pietra ordered. "Mickey, let's hear it again."

"Ok. Carlo will be ready to wire the explosive once we get the order. This will be only if we miss the target and Cabbagehead flees to his office underneath Doyers Street. The device is small and will be placed under the big chair behind the desk. It's an easy break-in. No alarms, no cameras that we could see in that office. If the office is occupied, that will create a problem, and then our backup plan will not be used. Aspanu will be dressed like one of our homeless people, pulling a cart with bottles and cans. I have it all ready and the dirty and torn clothes Aspanu will be wearing. Everyone will have their earpieces and I will direct our movements. Depending on where the target will be, the gymnasium or the massage parlor, Carlo will return to meet us. He and Pietro here will both be walking along the street when Cabbagehead leaves his location. Pietro will have a camera hung around his neck and Carlo will have a map in his hands. You will both look like tourists. Carlo and Pietro will take out the bald one's bodyguards. All head shots. There are usually three, maybe four, no matter. They will be surprised when two tourists blast them. Be quick boys. Paulo you will back up Carlo and Pietro in case they go down, God forbid. Aspanu, you will approach Cabbagehead mumbling to yourself like you're a crazy man. You will make the hit. Paulo you will also back up Aspanu. Everyone drops their metal into the street when it's over. I will be in the car to make our escape across the bridge into Brooklyn. The car will be there after the hit. Any questions?" Mickey asked.

"And if the police are there before the hit, we abort and retreat. If the cops are there suddenly after the work is done, they have to go," La Pietra stated.

"I will bring you to Brooklyn to a safe apartment we keep. The next day to New Jersey where a private jet will take you to Amsterdam. Our friend there will return you to Catania. Our driver will take you home," Mickey advised.

La Pietra put his hands together, his fingers pointing to the ceiling as in a prayer. "Michele, and when?" he asked.

"Soon as I get the word from Don Gino, we go. We must be ready at any moment," Mickey replied.

§§§§

Detective Kevin Wang sat quietly on the second floor of the Fifth Squad. All he had on his desk was a large cup of Starbuck's coffee. He gazed out of the window onto Elizabeth Street in a daydream like trance.

"Wang, tough night?" Figueroa asked.

"Geez, ahh yeah. Man, I need to lay off this coffee. Makes me jumpy," Wang blurted.

"I'm waiting for Baker to come up. He's on four to twelve, too. Maybe we can grab some Dim Sum across the street," Fig suggested.

"I'm gonna pass, boss. Wait, Ya know, on second thought, yeah, I'll join you," Wang said. He quickly thought he might be able to find out why there were no raids in Chinatown as Matt had said were going to happen.

Matt showed up and the three cops went across the street to Jing Fong.

"The last time I was here I met with Danny Chu and Abbate," Matt said. He purposely floated a trial balloon.

"Must have been fun," Fig stated.

"What kind of guy is he, Baker?" Wang asked.

"He starts off really nice and ends up really bad. In my opinion, and I'm no doctor, he is a certified psychopath. I don't know how he's been around so long," Matt answered.

"Smart, I guess," Wang answered.

"Ever see him in the neighborhood Wang? He's one, scary looking dude," Fig asked.

"Yeah, couple of times in passing," Wang responded.

"I'm starved," Matt blurted.

"You skinny prick! You're always starved. If I ate like you I would have diabetes and liver problems," Fig laughed.

"I'm a growing boy; what can I tell you?"

"Hey, Matt, did we do that bust last night like you said. I didn't hear anything about it on the street," Wang asked. His face showed more anxiety than it should.

"Nah, the Puzzle Palace called it off last minute. Looks like they have a bigger game plan in mind," Matt responded.

"Like what? Close down all the restaurants this time?" Wang chuckled nervously.

"No. I heard they will be looking to do a big drug bust and kid trafficking thing. I'm not privy to any of that. I wish I was back in narcotics for a week," Matt added.

"What the hell is that?" Matt asked. He looked down at a Dim-Sum cart to one of the four, rounded, metal, steam cups.

"Chicken feet. Really good!" Wang said.

"All kidding aside and with all due respect, Wang. Your people will eat anything that walked, right?" Matt asked.

"Pretty much. In China, they eat dog, cat, intestines, everything," Wang replied.

"Jesus, how about *rat*?" Fig asked. He gave a quick glance to Matt.

"I guess so," Wang answered.

CHAPTER 65

Gino couldn't believe how long he and Suzie had made love that afternoon. He never admitted he used a male enhancement drug but he had from their first date. He did it for his own pleasure and of course his ego. Suzie just thought he was a superstar in bed, so Gino kept it as his secret. After all, there was over a twenty-year difference in their ages, and Gino was reliving his youth, probably for the last time.

The chef prepared a zuppa di pesce using all the great, fresh seafood available at Gosman's fish market and from a few of his fisherman buddies at the pier in Montauk Harbor.

Joey, the two Sicilian bodyguards, and the other men had already eaten in shifts and were walking the property, doing their jobs. The fear of being attacked by a hit squad of Flying Dragons was palpable. Joey decided to call in for a few more Miceli soldiers who were from the middle of Long Island. Help would be there shortly, but Joey could hear his pulse beating into his ears. "If they found out Gino was at Sam's Place for dinner, what makes us think they can't find out we are out here tonight?" Joey stated. His warning to the bodyguards put Gino's security to another level.

It was a little damp and chilly for Gino and Suzie to have their dinner outside by the lake. They were both famished from their afternoon activities and Gino was developing a headache from the hunger.

The two lovers had their dinner on the long, oak dining room table in the dining room. A view of the lake wasn't so spectacular this evening as fog was beginning to set in from the ocean. Gino and Suzie could feel the warmth from the cracking fireplace in the adjoining living room. Gino kept the romantic day going by dimming the interior lights and lighting candles around the first-floor rooms. A chilled bottle of Fiano di Avellino, Gino's favorite Italian white wine went perfectly with the zuppa. Candlelight bounced off the wine glasses, twinkled on the teardrop crystals which hung from the elegant drum chandelier above the table, and reflected a blue hue off the beveled wall mirror.

Gino could not believe how beautiful Suzie looked in the candlelight. Suzie smiled for a moment at how handsome Gino was. Her smile quickly turned to a pensive, removed look, down into her wine glass.

"This is the best meal I've ever had. And this wine is making me enjoy it even more," Suzie announced.

"I wish I had a loaf of Terranova's bread from the Bronx to soak up all this soup," Gino wished.

"This bread was good Gino, although just a small slice is really enough."

"Look, do I tell you about rice? Leave the Italian bread to me, will ya?" Gino joked. They both chuckled at his Robert De NIro impersonation.

"Did you ever notice that De Niro does the same character in almost all of his movies?" Suzie asked.

"He's a good actor. Except his last good movie was with Pacino in Heat. Since then, fuggetaboutit!" Gino mimicked a thicker, New York accent.

"And that was like 1995. You're right, not much since, unless you like those silly Focker movies," Suzie replied. Her animated smile returned for a second.

"Are you okay, Sweetie? Suddenly, you seem a bit down again. I thought coming out here would do the trick for you, but the weather isn't cooperating all that much," Gino asked.

"It's great out here even with the damp air and the fog. I'll be fine. Let's just enjoy the time we have together, okay?"

Gino held his wine glass up to Suzie's and they clinked glasses, sipping the cool wine while gazing into each other's eyes.

"Were you this romantic with all your ladies, you Italian stud, you?" Suzie quipped.

"There was never a lady in my life like you, Suzie. I never dated an Asian, never dated a more beautiful woman, and never dated a gangster lady. I hit the trifecta with you," Gino joked.

"You say that to all the pretty, Asian, gangster chicks you've met, I'm sure."

"Excuse me, Sweetie. I need to go to the restroom and then get another bottle of cold Fiano. Be right back." Gino kissed her on the lips and went about his business.

Suzie opened her black, Louis Vuitton gold chain shoulder bag and fumbled for the Black Leaf 40 liquid vile that Peter had given her. Gino's wine glass was empty so Suzie became momentarily flustered. She put the vile back into her bag, next to the hypodermic syringe with the fatal pre-measured dosage already in the tube.

"Well, Miss Ping, how about a little Frank Sinatra music and some more of these delicious mashed grapes?" Gino said when he returned.

"That depends. Sinatra's Capitol or Reprise years?" Suzie asked.

"I'm surprised a woman your age even knows the difference."

"Are you kidding? There is no comparison. The Reprise years were fun, but Capitol was by far his best work," Suzie said.

Suzie started to sing in a sultry voice;

"All of me, why not take all of me?

Can't you see, I'm no good without you.

Take my lips, I want to lose them...."

"Here's one of my favorites from the Capitol years. Gino gently took Susie from her seat to dance as the CD brought Frank to life;

How little we know,
How much to discover,
What chemical forces flow
From lover to lover

How little we understand - what touches of that tingle
That sudden explosion - when two tingles intermingle

Who cares to define?
What chemistry this is?
Who cares with your lips on mine?
How ignorant bliss is

So long as you kiss me - and the world around us shatters
How little it matters - how little we know,
How little we know, how little we know..

Gino twirled Suzie around a few times, each time pulling her back close to him and kissing her gently.

A few more dances, the rest of the bottle of Fiano, and it was time for bed.

Joey and the crew, plus the reinforcements, were outside smoking cigars and cigarettes and drinking espresso to stay alert. One of the Sicilians sat in the kitchen, ignoring the two lovers.

Suzie placed her shoulder bag on the night table next to her side of the bed and went into the bathroom. Gino was mostly smashed from the wine, undressed down to his boxer shorts and got under the sheets.

Suzie took a quick shower, got into the silk smoking jacket she bought for Gino and went to the bed.

Her Italian stud was sound asleep and snoring. Suzie's hands began to tremble. Her heart was beating so fast and so hard that she started to become lightheaded. She inhaled deeply and exhaled slowly to try and calm down and control her heart rate.

Gino was lying on his side, his arms over the pillow under his head. The only light came from the bathroom where Suzie had left the door open a quarter of an inch.

Suzie opened the shoulder bag slowly and looked at the syringe. Peter had told her the needle was ultrafine and Gino would likely not even feel the pinch.

Her quivering hands could barely take the plastic cover off the thin needle. The throbbing in her ears began to overpower her senses.

Suzie pulled the sheet gently away from Gino's body, exposing his bare back and black trunks. She put the syringe's plunger between her fingers and prepared to use her thumb to inject the deadly Black Leaf 40 into Gino's exposed fatty love handle.

She squeezed her eyes shut as hard as she could, the pounding in her ears again nearly overcoming her consciousness. Suzie opened her eyes and saw spots and softly closed them. She saw the faces of her cousins, held captive by Cabbagehead's butchers in China. The faces of her sobbing aunts and uncles as they would be led into the rice field to be slaughtered.

Suzie, opened her eyes, took a firm grip of the syringe and brought it to Gino's flesh.

I can't do it! I can't kill the man I love! Not for anyone, not for anything on this earth!

Suzie let out a murderous scream and flung the Black Leaf 40 loaded syringe across the room.

Gino jumped out of his semi-drunk slumber and grabbed Suzie by her quaking shoulders. Gino heard the pounding of multiple footsteps approaching the bedroom door.

"Gino! Gino, are you all right?" It was Joey Clams behind the door. Joey tried the locked doorknob. He and one of the Sicilians, both with weapons in their hands crashed in the door with their beefy shoulders.

Gino was hugging Suzie, her legs exposed up to her crotch, the silk smoking jacket barley covering her privates. Gino took the bedsheet quickly covering Suzie. Gino was still in a mild stupor.

"Miss Ping, what's wrong? Why did you scream?" Joey asked.

"They wanted me to kill him! They wanted me to poison him with that shit over there!" Gino jumped out of bed, wide-eyed, staring at Suzie, not believing what his own ears were hearing. Suzie continued, "It's a deadly toxin; don't touch it or it can kill you! There is more in my bag. They wanted me to assassinate you, baby and they have my cousins held captive in China, and if you're not dead, they will... that bastard Cabbagehead will kill my whole family one-by-one like they are chickens! But, I just could not harm you; I thought about it, but I could never do such a thing," Suzie pleaded. "I love you more than myself, baby. Now my family will all die. I'm so sorry, Gino to bring this into your life," Suzie sobbed.

Gino looked at Joey. The Sicilian walked over to survey the smashed syringe on the floor, standing down his AR-15.

"Get Mickey on the phone," Gino ordered.

CHAPTER 66

Mickey spoke with Gino very briefly on the telephone. Having seen so many men in the life succumb to the wiretap, Mickey was not one to use many understandable words in any phone conversation. He often used a Sicilian form of pig-Latin which was not discernible to anyone outside the close-knit family unit.

It was decided Gino would not wait and would take a helicopter back to the city. If Cabbagehead knew where he and Suzie were, shit could still go down Suzie didn't even know about. There were just too many eyes and too much risk for the convenience. The boys would take him and his 'braciola' by car and Mickey and Gino would meet at the office. With the added muscle, Joey and Mickey were confident in Gino's safety.

Two and a half hours later, at three o'clock in the morning Gino was at the Seventy-Ninth Street headquarters, still seething from the events of the prior evening. He and Suzie slept restlessly in the car ride back from Montauk, and would not likely be sleeping for a while.

Suzie went into the study while Gino met in his office with his inner circle, Mickey, Joey, and C.C.

"I want to move today. I want that fucker dead and done with," Gino said.

"Don Gino you will be making a tactical error if you move too quickly. First of all, we are ready to do that other piece of work you need done. Just listen for a moment and think things through. Like in a game of chess, you need to think several moves ahead to win. I suggest we somehow get to this Peter Fong. With Cabbagehead gone he can choose to take over the Hip Sing Association or die. Remember when Cabbagehead made an absolute fool of his second in command? I saw contempt along with embarrassment in Fong's face. I believe Peter would prefer to live and be boss than to be dead and gone. Make our bed with Peter now, take out

Cabbagehead, and life will be good all around. Trust me on this, please," Mickey stated.

Joey and C.C. showed no emotion as Gino looked to them for an approval.

"Any more news about Suzie's family in China? Her two cousins have already been kidnapped and one of them will be summarily executed. Her little girl cousin can be sent to a whore house in Hong Kong for Christ's sake. Then the rest of her family is in peril. I want to take him out before he gets the chance," Gino offered.

"Listen to me. They may have met their fate already for all we know. Their only hope is that Cabbagehead is still holding them hostage for leverage. If we can get to Peter, and there is no guarantee he will flip, her family has a chance. If it doesn't work out…that's the way it is. Your job is to protect this family, not her family," Mickey advised.

"You have no heart, Mick. Look, she saved my life. Isn't that worth my loyalty?" Gino asked.

"Saved your life? She almost took you out! Ok, you asked my opinion and now I am free to speak. The time for her to have come to you was when they gave her that poison, not to wait until the last minute and crap out. She could have put that needle into you and we would be picking your replacement today," Mickey said.

"But she didn't!" Gino hollered.

Joey stood up from his chair.

"If someone had come to me, or C.C., or Mickey over here, and asked us to whack you, do you think for a second we would have needed time to think about it? The answer is no. No, we would have either died on the spot or told you immediately, not wait until our fingers were in the trigger, Gino," Joey argued.

"And if they had Joey Jr. or your mother by the throat, you're trying to tell me you wouldn't have thought twice? You guys don't understand. Suzie and I love each other. Is it because I'm an old fuck and she is a gorgeous younger woman? Is it so impossible for us to love each other?"

"Our oath is to you. As the head of our family… "

Gino interrupted Mickey. "Fuck that shit! How many guys do you know who have flipped, gone state's evidence, became cheese eaters, and put guys away for life? Loyalty? She showed absolute loyalty above the lives of her own family or I would be on a slab with rigor mortis by now!" Gino argued.

"Just give me the order, Don Gino. I act on your command," Mickey said.

"Charlie, you've been like Humulus the Mute. Do you have an opinion?" Gino asked.

"You're not gonna like what I have to say, buddy. We go back a long way as kids, and I always looked up to you like a big brother. I still do," C.C. replied.

"Try me," Gino uttered, his voice more calm.

"I say you listen to Mickey on this. If her family goes, it was their fate. At the end of the day you must act like the Don of this family and not like a love-sick teenager," C.C. swallowed hard.

Gino stared at his old friend with unblinking eyes.

"Okay. Okay," Gino sighed. "Mick, what's your plan?"

CHAPTER 67

Kevin Wang decided not to report the information Matt had given him on a possible drug raid in Chinatown. If he told Cabbagehead about an attack by the NYPD and again nothing happened, he could find himself in the East River. If he said nothing, and the intelligence that Matt leaked came to fruition, he would be blamed for not warning the Hip Sing Association. Wang felt trapped by his position of stoolie in a damned if you do, damned if you don't, no win situation.

What Wang didn't know is that Figueroa was having him tailed from the day Matt opened up to him about the Chinese cop being dirty. Fig had what he needed with the surveillance on Wang, twice seen entering the 99-cent store, one of those meetings being with Danny Chu. The undercover details and Matt's testimony would finish Wang's career.

Wang's world was soon to come crashing down on him in the worst way possible. Official misconduct charges, a visit to the NYPD trial room, civil charges for a felony action, loss of his job, loss of his pension, and a probable jail sentence faced him. His wife would likely file for divorce, his daughter would have to leave NYU and her dream of becoming a nurse would be shattered. His son would have to leave his parochial high school and his prospects of going to a good college would be erased.

Most cops in that position would swallow their gun rather than lose everything and disgrace their family, all for a weekly cash envelope.

§§§§

The day Suzie and Gino returned to New York City from Montauk, and Suzie was holed up in the Miceli headquarters, Cabbagehead and three of his Flying Dragons showed up at Suzie's office at nine-thirty in the morning.

"Where the fuck is she?" Cabbagehead demanded. Cabbagehead's surveillance equipment had been destroyed by some of the Miceli crew.

Alison and Diana, petrified with fear and without knowing Suzie's whereabouts could not tell the maniac anything.

"Maybe she will be in later. She doesn't tell us where she goes and when she is coming in," Alison stated.

"Is she with her Italian boyfriend?"

"We don't know about her private life. It's none of our business," Diana uttered.

Cabbagehead went to the office door and locked it. The Dragons moved around and stood behind the two girls' chairs.

"Please, we have nothing to tell you. I can try to call her. Please do not hurt us," Alison pleaded.

"So I guess we need to leave her a message to call us again?" Cabbagehead bellowed.

Diana began to cry. Alison attempted a scream but was slapped hard across her face by a muscle-bound dragon. Duct tape was wrapped around both girls' mouths. One of them pulled Alison by her hair into Suzie's office and threw her hard onto the large desk. The other two forced Diana onto the sofa in the waiting room where they ripped off her clothes and began to rape her. Her muffled screams were useless and unheard. One Dragon held Diana's arms behind her head while the other forced himself inside her. They would trade places a few times.

Alison got the worst of it. Cabbagehead and the muscleman beat her until she was unconscious, smashing her head onto the wood desk several times. Blood ran from her nose and right ear. The Dragon cut Alison's clothes off with a switchblade knife and sodomized her as Cabbagehead burned the girl on her smooth face and back with his lit cigarette. The smell of burning flesh permeated the office. Her muffled screams were making Diana sob.

"Tell her if I don't hear from her tonight, she will be hearing the sobs all the way from China," Cabbagehead stated to the naked, cowering Diana who was on the floor next to the sofa, before he kicked her square in her face. He laughed as he and the Dragons left the office.

CHAPTER 68

Peter Fong wasn't interested in sitting down with Mickey. Not now anyway. Peter had already made his deal with the devil.

Mickey asked for another meeting of the inner circle that same day. He told Gino, Joey, and C.C. he had no success in obtaining a sit-down with Peter.

"I say we make our move tonight. This Peter snubbed his nose at us so I say we clip him, too," Joey stated.

"Hold on, Joey. We know Peter is a bright guy. Maybe he's just cautious, doesn't trust us, who knows? But we know him a little. He's American born, not a lunatic like Cabbagehead, and we could probably make a deal with him on the construction end if he's smart. I agree with you on one thing, Joey...we move now, but don't touch Peter. We have no idea who's behind him, and for all we know, whoever that is in the Hip Sing pecking order can make Cabbagehead look like an Eagle Scout," Gino advised.

"I was just about to say the same thing. Don Gino, you are learning the finer points of the game of chess," Mickey uttered.

"Joey, C.C., you agree?" Gino asked.

Both men nodded their heads in the affirmative.

"All hands on deck, Mick. Let's do this thing," Gino commanded.

Mickey responded, "We will all be in position tonight at seven o'clock. We got information from a friend of ours on Mulberry who plays ball at the Y in Chinatown all the time. I asked him to tell me when the Dragons shut the court down. Cabbagehead has a basketball court scheduled for six o'clock. They usually play for two hours. Afterward, they have a few beers, smoke a few blunts. We'll be waiting."

§§§§

Suzie couldn't reach her office by phone. She thought the worst and hoped for the best. Never an alarmist, Suzie imagined that the phones were down or the girls were both sick, but this time, in her gut, she knew there was a problem.

Finally, Suzie's cell phone rang and the Chinese characters on her phone told her it was Diana.

"Are you okay?" Suzie asked.

"No…no!" Diana cried.

"Okay, take a deep breath. Try to calm yourself."

"I'm at Bellevue Hospital. Ali is in the critical care unit, and my jaw is fractured," Diana sobbed.

"Danny?"

"Yes. They came to the office and…and…Ali's head is fractured. I called 911 and the fire department's EMS came. I told them she fell down the flight of stairs but the police knew I was lying. Suzie…that animal burned her all over the place! They raped us both and laughed," Diana seethed.

Suzie tried to swallow the lump in her throat. She could barely breathe, never mind talk.

"I'm so sorry. I promise you…your lives will be better than this from here on. I will get there when I can, Diana," Suzie said.

"I never imagined people could be so cruel, so mean," Diana cried.

"I wish I had words to comfort you. I just don't."

Suzie knocked on Gino's office door, opened it, and ran behind his desk and into his arms.

"That fucking animal put my girls in the hospital! Alison could die! They raped both of my girls in my office. I want them dead...all of them...dead!"

Gino looked blankly at C.C. and Joey. Mickey had already left to mobilize the crew up in Clason Point.

"That's horrible, Sweetie. Just calm down. C.C., send some people over to the hospital and make sure those girls have everything they need. Get me as much information as possible," Gino ordered.

"This is all my fault. All of it. I brought these two young girls from China and I thought I was sparing them from a life of prostitution and drugs. Brought them into my office and look what's happened to them. All my fault! I have to go to the hospital right now," Suzie sobbed into Gino's shirt.

"Not right now, Suzie. That's exactly what Cabbagehead wants you to do. Instead of going there, call him on the phone now. Tell him you're with me, tell him in a few hours you will give the poison to me and he can release your family. Tell him if you fail, you will come to his office tonight and he can do whatever he wants to you," Gino advised.

"What if he doesn't believe me? What if he sees through my lie?"

"Come on, Sweetie. You love the old black and whites as much as I do. Think of Ingrid Bergman, Olivia deHavilland, Ida Lupino, Joan Crawford, Betty Davis. All you need to do is act. He must believe you Suzie or people you love will die. That's your motivation!"

A half hour later, Suzie was drinking a soothing tea. She had calmed herself down. She spoke to Cabbagehead just as her Gino advised.

She could have won an Oscar.

CHAPTER 69

Like clockwork, Cabbagehead arrived at 273 Bowery for a basketball match with his Flying Dragon Players. He and five of his players stretched, warmed up, and took layups and outside shots before choosing up sides for the first game.

Cabbagehead was trying to perfect a skyhook from the foul line. Peter begged out because he wasn't feeling well; some sort of stomach virus kept him close to his toilet.

Three Dragons were situated outside the gymnasium doors and two more were on the street, smoking cigarettes, making sordid remarks to the girls who passed them.

The first team to get to twenty-two points wins the game and one hundred dollars per man. They would choose up again or the winning team would claim double or nothing for the second game.

Carlo made his break-in at the Doyers Street office without any difficulty. All the stores and offices beneath the Nom Wah Tea Parlor were closed by this time, and the surveillance equipment was already destroyed the night before, so Carlo went unseen. The bomb was taped underneath Cabbagehead's fake, leather chair and armed for the remote device. He locked the door behind him and made his way back to street level to join the others.

Cabbagehead's team lost the first match twenty-two to eighteen, and only one Dragon on the opposing team got a bloody lip from a flagrant hack Cabbagehead had laid on him. They stayed with the same teams and decided to do two out of three games for the money and bragging rights.

La Pietra, walked up Bowery pushing his Whole Foods shopping cart, with black and clear plastic bags filled with empty soda cans and used water bottles for recycling refunds. In an old rug on the inside of the cart was a sawed-off Beretta shot-gun and a Glock .45 automatic handgun. La Pietra was wearing a torn and dirty, dark blue sweatshirt, filthy cargo shorts, low-top, black Converse sneakers too big for his feet, and a black, knit skull-cap pulled down to his eyebrows.

The second game went to Cabbagehead's team by a big score of twenty-two to twelve. His team was pumped up for the rubber game. The money was no longer important in the face of man-pride.

Carmine took his position at a bus stop on the other side of the street. With a plastic cup of coffee in his hand, he kept checking his watch, pretended to be looking for a bus.

A raucous third game finished in overtime with Cabbagehead winning with a skyhook with his right hand and an offensive foul into the head of the defending Dragon with his left. No one on the losing team had the balls to call the foul and Cabbagehead erupted with howls, fist pumps, and high-fives all around.

Carlo and Pietro walked slowly down Bowery nearing the YMCA building. Pietro took a few photos with the camera hanging from around his neck. Carlo referred to his unfolded map of Chinatown, looking like a confused tourist.

A couple of beers were downed and a couple of joints were passed around as the players listened to Cabbagehead brag about his winning shot.

"Let's go to my place on Baxter and take showers and enjoy the girls. Keep your money, that victory was way too sweet," Cabbagehead bellowed.

The players and the bodyguards made their way to the front door of the YMCA. Detective and turncoat Kevin Wang stood by the door, waiting patiently to speak with Cabbagehead.

"What the fuck do you want, cop?" Cabbagehead queried.

"Listen Danny, I know things got fucked up, but I think this time they are coming at you big time," Kevin stated.

"Sure, and I should shut down for how long? A week? A month?"

"Look, they are planning a bust. Narcotics bust I was told. I figured if I didn't tell you, you would be more pissed than last time."

"When and where?" Cabbagehead asked.

"That I can't tell you. I don't know. I can nose around a bit and maybe get some details."

"You do that, cop. Until then, whatever you do for me is cash and carry. No more weekly Uncle Danny payments, you got that?" Cabbagehead said.

"I got it!" Kevin answered.

"You wait in here until we are gone. I don't want to be seen with a rat fuck like you," Cabbagehead seethed.

The automatic doors of the Y swung open and Danny, the ball playing Dragons, and the bodyguards walked out into the not-so-fresh smelling air of Bowery Street.

From behind them, from inside the Y, three figures appeared in the doorway of the building, all brandishing automatic weapons. Andy Phan, his cousins Nguyen van Hoang, and Will Phan, the New Orleans Vietnamese, were hiding in the men's room of the Y and opened fire on the crowd of Dragons. Cabbagehead and his crew were caught off guard, and four of the Dragons hit the ground, severely wounded or dead. The Vietnamese made their way onto the sidewalk, their weapons bursting with dozens of shots.

Carlo and Pietro, also caught flatfooted but with ice in their veins, began shooting at whoever was left standing. Cabbagehead ran down Bowery right into the old street-guy's shopping cart. La Pietra and Danny Chu made eye contact. La Pietra took the top of Cabbagehead's cranium off with the sawed-off from two feet away, with a large splash of blood, bone, and gray matter covering the concrete sidewalk.

Detective Kevin Wang, out of instinct, came onto the street with his service weapon in his hand, his last mistake as a policeman. Carmine had come from across the street to back up his crew as planned. All he saw was a Chinese guy with a gun in his hand. The Sicilian sprayed Kevin with ten, nine millimeter shells from his hidden UZI Pro Pistol UPP9SB. The officer died where he stood.

The Vietnamese Van Hoang's thin chest exploded from the cross fire of Carlo and Pietro. He was dead before he hit the sidewalk. Andy and Will fled down Bowery toward a waiting car Peter Fong had provided.

Mickey rolled up to the scene, picked up La Pietra and the three other Sicilians, and made his way toward the Manhattan Bridge.

"Aspanu, what shall I do with this?" Carlo asked. The young killer showed his boss the remote control for the bomb he placed in Cabbage-head's office under Doyers Street.

La Pietra looked toward Mickey for advice, shrugging his shoulders and gesturing with his face and hands in the typically, Sicilian manner.

"Fuck them all…light it up," Mickey ordered.

The explosion could be heard and felt by the hit squad as Mickey's car got onto the entrance of the bridge toward Brooklyn.

CHAPTER 70

Inspector Mike Abbate was at PP1 with Matt Baker. They were both ordered to see the brass and met outside of Police Commissioner Boyle's office. Matt was a bit apprehensive. Abbate wasn't helping.

"Holy crap! Now the shit's gonna hit the fan!" Abbate claimed.

"Looks bad, right?" Matt asked.

"For Christ's sake, just think about it, will you? A bunch of dead bodies all over Bowery. And a dead cop to boot!"

"Honestly, with what we had on him, they did him a favor. At least for his family anyway," Matt said.

"Yeah, I get that, but it's the visual. Chinese cop killed with a bunch of Flying Dragon gangsters and an out of town Vietnamese gang maniac. All of them shot up like it was a war. And then a friggin' bomb to boot. Eleven innocent bystanders at Bellevue waiting for a reason to blame the NYPD. Yes…it's bad Matt, very bad," Abbate preached.

"Come in, gentlemen," Commissioner Boyle's assistant announced somberly.

"Sit, gentlemen. Coffee, anyone?" Boyle asked.

"No, sir," Matt nervously responded.

"Light and sweet for you, Mike?" Boyle asked Abbate.

"Yes, sir, like the old days," Abbate chuckled. The commish and Abbate were partners in the old days when they were first coming up. Matt had no idea and gave the inspector a side glance.

"Okay, so here is what we have as I see it. A hero cop. A Chinese, hero cop who infiltrated the treacherous Hip Sing Tong slash Flying Dragon

319

gang slash Vietnamese gang out of New Orleans. Preparations for an inspector's funeral, bagpipes, a thousand men, the whole nine. Tomorrow's Daily News will say HERO COP as their headline instead of calling it Bowery Massacre. The Post will say New York's Finest with a photo of Wang and Chinese lettering underneath instead of Carnage in Chinatown. The bombing will be part of the whole drug thing we are closing in on. Thank God there were no fatalities. The New York Times will bury this whole story on page twelve and come up with some liberal, bullshit exposé of underpaid restaurant workers in Chinatown for their magazine on Sunday. We have full control of the situation and everyone goes home happy," Boyle articulated.

"You called it, Detective Baker. You were in my office and said that there could be a bloody war. I brushed it off at first thinking maybe you were over reacting. When we put you with Inspector Abbate you did some great work on the O.C.C.B. We should thank you, Lieutenant Figueroa for being a team player and lending out your star detective. That's team work. And, of course John Esposito never says no when we need him," First Dep. Frank Byrne announced.

"What's your call now, detective, or are we piling on the pressure?" The commish chuckled.

"No, commissioner, not at all. I think the potential for a gang war is diminished. Danny Chu was a thorn in our side and a pariah in Chinatown. Chu being out of the picture brings up his second in command, Peter Fong. An ABC, who is a lot less greedy than Cabbagehead was. He's smart and, unless I'm mistaken, and I'll be guided by Inspector Abbate's experience on this, I believe the Miceli family will stand down and play nicely in the sandbox," Matt stated. He exhaled slowly through almost closed lips.

"I agree, Commissioner. The worst is over. We can drop by and see Gino Ranno and just check in, and close the loop on this thing," Abbate stated.

"Do that, Mike. I can't tell you how awkward it is for me to see Mr. Ranno at all these charity events. I want to throw him over a table and cuff the prick," Boyle said. Everyone laughed.

"May I have the honors, Commissioner?" Chief of Detectives Esposito asked.

"Go right ahead, John," Boyle smiled.

"Detective, tonight at the press conference on the events in Chinatown, you will be standing with the mayor and Commissioner Boyle. You will be asked to speak, so be cautious with your words, son. We have people in the crowd who will throw you some softball questions like, 'you look too young to be a Detective First Grade', and 'how was it working with Detective Kevin Wang in the Fifth Squad', stuff like that, okay?"

"Sir, I'm a Third Grade not a Detective First Grade."

"Not anymore, Baker. You were just promoted. You will be assigned to intel in the Police Commissioner's detail. Your lieutenant and John Esposito signed off on that already."

Fig was beaming, Esposito was difficult to read.

"Thank you, sir, I mean sirs, just thank you, everyone," Matt stammered. His boyish charm had worked well for him so far.

"One more thing, Baker, get your dress uniform ready. You will be with me and the mayor up front at the funeral on this one," Boyle ordered.

§§§§

Going down in the elevator, Matt looked puzzled and tried to say something to Abbate.

The veteran cop put his hand on Matt's arm and signaled him to be quiet as if the elevator had ears.

Once outside of the Puzzle Palace Matt opened-up.

"I'm blown away. I'm promoted? Kevin Wang is a hero cop? Going back to speak to the press in an hour? Tell me what I've missed, Inspector,"

Matt asked.

"Remember, as in any large organization, it's all about who you know first, the level of compliance and cooperation second, and the job you do, third. You've already met the requisites. Now it's all up to you not to fuck it up," Abbate offered.

"Am I allowed at least a dumb question?"

"Sure, just one!"

"We had the goods on Wang. Had him dead to rights?"

"We take care of our own, Matt. The wife and kids will be taken care of, there is no report that exists saying anything other than Wang went to his grave a hero. Got it? Good!" Abbate didn't wait for an answer.

CHAPTER 71

"Suzie, are you okay?" Gino asked. She was sitting in the study, looking out the window of the townhouse.

"Not even a sparrow lives on this street," Suzie said into the air.

"I'm sure we can find at least one sparrow, Sweetie."

"Looked for almost an hour. I saw a couple of pigeons, but they don't live on this block. They live in the park."

"Now, if I were a sparrow I would live in the trees in Central Park and eat from the hands of children and old people, not here with all these rich people who don't care about little birds," Gino whispered as he walked up behind his lady.

"Maybe I don't belong here, Gino."

"You belong wherever I am, Suzie Ping. And that's final," Gino teased.

"I wish we could move somewhere else. Somewhere I can be happy and not be in this awful business. I'm a fucking, human trafficker. And look where that got me? Look where it got my sister? Oh, I'm Baby Ping, the white slaver. Not Dr. Ping or Professor Ping or even waitress Ping! I've ruined so many lives, Gino…so many," Suzie lamented.

"I have some news for you, my love. Want to hear it?"

"Good news, I hope. If it's good news, yes I do!"

"Good or bad are relative terms. For you, the news will be good. For Danny Chu's mother…not so good," Gino teased.

"What? Danny Chu's mother?"

"He's dead. Killed by a pissed off person who took a large portion of his head off with a big gun."

"When? Where? Who killed him?"

"Just a little while ago, down in Chinatown. I have no idea who killed him. There were so many people who wanted him dead. He was gunned down in the street with some other guys, and guess what? No one saw anything. Lots of people walking around Chinatown who are blind when it comes to anything bad that goes on," Gino shared.

"Oh, my God! What about my family in China? How do I find out if they are alright?"

"We're working on that, Sweetie. I can't promise anything at this point but we are making all the necessary moves we can. Just hang in there for a little while," Gino advised.

"I love you so much, Gino Ranno. You are such a kind man," Suzie whispered.

"I love you too, Suzie, but I'm a little concerned about a couple of things. Why didn't you have the courage to tell me Danny was black-mailing you to kill me? The fact you brought the poison to Montauk tells me you were planning to kill me. I would never have thought of killing you Suzie…never."

"I was in a trance. My family is my blood, and I wanted to save them. My auntie and uncle were better than my own parents to me. They hid me from men who would have made me just another bitch in a brothel. They fed me, clothed me, and when I got sick, they helped me to recover. I didn't want to see them sad, or suffer in any way. I've done a lot in my life I'm ashamed of, Gino, but helping my family with money, and lots of it, had made me proud of myself. But I learned my love for you comes even before my own blood. In the short amount of time we've been together you have become more than my blood; you've become my soul. The fact you are standing here has proven my love for you, doesn't it? Unless there are Sicilian rules that I will never understand."

"There are no Sicilian rules that control me, Sweetie. And if I'm being totally honest with you, if you had turned out to be a Danny Chu spy or worse, you would have been killed at my order. This is a terrible world, Suzie, and the very thought of you being hurt makes me physically ill. I want you to be with me for the rest of my life, and if I can die looking at your face, I would be content with my life."

Suzie jumped into Gino's arms, nearly knocking him to the floor. Gino caught his balance and laughed.

"If we're going to stay together I'd better get a personal trainer!" Gino laughed.

"Just one more thing, my love," Suzie offered.

"And what would that be?"

"You said there were a couple of things on your mind and you only mentioned one."

"Ah, yes there is another thing that's troubling," Gino hinted.

"I'm done with it. It's over," Suzie said.

"Are you sure you can walk away from the big money?" Gino asked.

"I don't want blood money anymore. I just don't know how my conscience will deal with what I've done," Suzie quivered.

"So what will you do with yourself?"

"Even the money transfer business has a scummy feeling to it. I don't want to be around those pig bankers and scratch for a quarter of a point more. I need to reinvent myself, I really, really do. And I will! Any ideas, my love?" Suzie asked.

"Don't let's ask for the moon. We have the stars," Gino answered.

"Awww, that is so sweet…wait a minute, mister, that was Betty Davis in Now Voyager!

"Yes, but the timing was perfect!"

Made in the USA
Middletown, DE
20 May 2018